The Sinner's Love Song

Book TEN in the HOBBY RUN Variety Praise Band Series

Arlene James

Sillypa LLC

Contents

Preface

He was not the man for her.

Looking past him into the distance, Mary Sofia paused then slowly said, "Allie as good as told me, um, that the two of you are...involved. I mean, there were other hints." Her gaze finally met his. "Was I wrong?"

He shook his head, unable to hold her gaze. "You weren't wrong. I'm just sorry she mixed you up in our private business."

"It did seem somewhat, um, calculated."

"It was. It's all about her jealousy of you."

"She's jealous of me?" Mary Sofia chuckled dryly. "That makes no sense."

"Oh, but it does," he told her, realizing the truth as he spoke the words. "She knows you're beautiful in a wholesome, endearing way that she can never be. Your inner beauty outshines even your outer beauty." Clearing his throat, he told himself to get a grip. The last thing he should do was come off as flirtatious. He wasn't the right man for her. Her brothers would never approve. And he couldn't blame them.

Prologue

The bride looked like a fairy princess in a softly flowing gown of white gossamer and sparkling beads. Her short, blond hair hugged her head in a gleaming cap of delicate curls, calling attention to her heart-shaped face and enormous, moss green eyes. The long veil floated from a ringlet of tiny red rosebuds, interspersed with miniscule white daisies and violets.

Although Valentine's Day had already passed, the red seemed appropriate for a February wedding, and white signified purity, but the purple gave a nod to the bride's signature color, as evidenced by the antique amethyst hat pin piercing her right ear diagonally and the dress worn by the obviously pregnant Matron of Honor, the groom's stepsister. A pair of flower girls wore a paler shade of purple. The bridal bouquet sprouted with fully blown red roses, big white Gerber daisies, and a profusion of violets. They trailed, entwined with ivy, almost to the floor. Somehow, the color combination worked beautifully.

The blazing red hair of the eleven-year-old who escorted the bride down the aisle clashed wildly with the red of his boutonniere, but he could not be faulted for his solemnity or the cut of his white, tailed tuxedo. Ninety percent of the packed sanctuary could be heard sniffing back tears before the bride and her young escort made it halfway down the aisle. That might have had something to do with the eager groom beaming an enthusiastic smile of unbridled delight as he waited at the altar for her to draw near.

Once a runaway hiding with his sister and their friend, the redheaded youngster now known as Rafe, completed his journey down the aisle with the bride and stood proudly with her as the minister instructed the onlookers to retake their seats. After the general rustle of bodies being lowered to pews ceased, the tattooed minister, brother-in-law to the groom, addressed the business at hand.

"We are gathered here today to witness the joining in marriage of Ronan Don Younger-Camstock and Tessa Mae Jae Empire." He looked straight at Rafe and asked, "Who gives this woman in marriage?"

Rafe immediately and loudly proclaimed, "I do, your honor," eliciting smothered chuckles from the congregation.

As attorneys, the groom and his indulgent stepfather—now standing at Ronan's elbow as best man—dealt with courts and judges. To the amusement of those in the congregation, the legal nomenclature had made an impression on young Rafe, who had been adopted into the family along with his sister, Ilona, one of the flower girls.

Both the groom, Ronan, and his stepfather/best man, Drew Camstock, played with the locally popular HOBBY RUN Variety Praise Band, so no one watching from the packed pews could have been surprised when, after the vows, Drew handed Ronan his acoustic guitar. At the same time, Anabeth Camstock Pacarel, the matron of honor and Ronan's stepsister, passed a cordless microphone to Tessa. No doubt, Ronan had insisted that his bride sing on their wedding day. She did have a glorious voice, and Charlie Biggs, perhaps the most talented member of the band, had exercised his influence as a successful songwriter, producer, and musician to launch her into a career as a Christian vocalist. Her first cut already played incessantly on the local Christian radio stations.

Tessa sang to her new husband, her eyes glowing as her pure mezzo-soprano effortlessly slid over the notes and words of the song. When Tessa sang, she appeared transported, and the effect raised goose flesh on her rapt listeners. Tears rolled freely down faces all around the room, accompanied by sighs of envy and delight. When the song concluded, Ronan and Tessa quickly unburdened themselves of guitar and microphone, coming together in an ardent embrace.

The minister chuckled and quipped, "You may kiss the bride," as if Ronan had needed to be told and they were not already engaged in that very activity.

The congregation surged to their feet, applauding and sniffing and laughing as the minister loudly exclaimed, "Ladies and gentlemen, I give you Mr. and Mrs. Ronan Younger-Camstock."

Charlie Biggs and his partner, Matt Polo, began playing the recessional, Charlie on the harp and Matt on the cello. Despite the lilting, stately music, the newly married couple rushed down the aisle, laughing and clasping hands. The groom's mother quickly followed, escorted by her husband, Drew, who carried their youngest son, three-year-old Ryan. The pastor, George Pacarel, stepped in to escort his wife, Anabeth. Rafe offered an arm to each of the giggling flower girls, his sister, Ilona, and their fellow former runaway, Selene. People surged into the aisles after them, eager to set out for the reception and what would surely be a delightful celebration.

One among the happy crowd, however, wanted nothing so much as to go home and pull the covers over his head.

Chapter One

Stuart Champion, known by most of his acquaintances as Champ, stood uncertainly beside the closed concession stand in the noisy foyer of The Milking Barn. The converted barn just over the Missouri border belonged to Maggs Ogilvie, manager of the HOBBY RUN band and the wife of the band's elder statesman, Wyatt. She had offered the venue, where the band played to sold out crowds every other Friday evening, for Ronan and Tessa's wedding reception. From sheer habit, Stuart had entered via the musician's entrance at the back of the building. Now he couldn't help feeling a bit disoriented, however.

The milling crowd dressed in wedding finery rather than the usual denim and casual shirts, milled about a lavish buffet, complete with elaborate ice sculptures and a chocolate fountain, much to the delight of the numerous children present. One of the Polo youngsters had his finger stuck in the flow of chocolate at that very moment. His mother, Joanna, appeared at his shoulder, bent over to speak to him, and retrieved a napkin from a stack on the table to wipe his hand after he stuck his finger in his mouth to taste the chocolate.

Stuart knew well that Joanna had always wanted children, and now she had five, including the daughter she'd finally conceived after she and her husband, Matt, had adopted three brothers and their baby sister from an orphanage in Honduras. The marriage had been rocky before that. In fact, Stuart had secretly nurtured hopes of a relationship with the beautiful artist until she and Matt had returned from Honduras. Stuart wished them the best and counted them both as friends, but a harsh stab of an old, familiar envy kept him from drawing closer.

Just then, a helpful uniformed server approached with a tray of tall glasses filled with a variety of beverages. She informed Stuart that tables and chairs had been set up in the performance area, with the table for the wedding party erected on the stage itself. The buffet would open and the guests could take their seats as soon as the wedding party arrived. Meanwhile, he could help himself to the appetizers. With recorded music playing in the background, the band members were as free as everyone else to mingle and enjoy the evening. If only he could do so.

The last of the original ten members of the HOBBY RUN band to remain single and the one who had most wanted to marry for the longest time, Stuart had felt an increasing burden of loneliness as each of his closest friends had found and claimed his or her life's partner. The weight of his disappointment had become so heavy that he no longer felt able even to pray about it.

That's what he told himself, anyway.

He chose a glass of unsweetened iced tea and had just enough time to tilt back his blond head and swallow a gulp of the cold liquid before the Carter horde descended on him. His bandmate JoJo Lansing Carter had the lead, one of her triplet toddlers on her hip. Where JoJo went, her Marine husband, Hugo, followed, shepherding his brood of siblings and progeny. The oldest and loveliest Carter sister, Mary Sofia, brought up the rear, her small hand firmly gripping the even smaller hand of JoJo and Hugo's young son. Despite his melancholy, Stuart could not suppress a grin. The Camstocks, Polos, and Carters seemed to be vying for the title of Largest HOBBY RUN Family.

Stuart couldn't help envying the lot of them. As an adopted only child of two only children, both of whom had died before his nineteenth birthday, Stuart knew well the value of family. So did Hugo Carter, obviously.

Mexican on his mother's side and apparently enormous on his Caucasian father's, Hugo's dusky skin and black hair and eyes belied his paternity of the triplets. The twin girls, Lizbet and Caro, had identical blonde curls, pink skin, blue eyes, and cherubic faces, while their brother, Marc Everett, stood both taller and thinner, his pale skin and orange-red hair a neon-sign testament to his complete lack of Mexican blood. Even JoJo, though purely Caucasian, had dark hair and brown eyes, but she made no claim to biological maternity, having adopted Hugo's acknowledged babies with another woman straight out of the hospital. Whoever their biological father actually was, he looked nothing like Hugo, not that Stuart doubted Hugo's ability to love, nurture, and instill the proper values in either his own children or his siblings.

Being adopted himself, Stuart knew well how loving and nurturing adoptive parents could be. He still missed his parents. After their deaths, he'd started a search for his birth parents, which had brought him together with the rest of the Young Rockers, the four young men who accounted for the Y and R in the HOBBY RUN acronym. They'd all had an interest in locating their birth parents, with varying degrees of success, or in his case, failure. His biological mother had succumbed to breast cancer before he'd discovered her identity, leaving no clue to his biological father's name or location. Because her own parents and two sisters, both childless, had pre-deceased her, his search had come to a stark, ignominious end.

One of the Carter's little girls—Stuart could not tell them apart—suddenly set up a wail, setting off the twin on JoJo's hip. Solemn little Marc Everett grabbed hold of Mary Sofia's knee-length skirt, as if to steady himself, while the twin in JoJo's grasp reached for her father. JoJo handed off her squealer to Hugo, whose expression of utter contentment never changed, and picked up the other twin. The demanding wails shut off like a faucet. Seventeen-year-old Gabrielle, Hugo's next younger sister, quickly grabbed the hand of the youngest, Ana, thirteen, and made for the appetizer table, while Mary Sofia lifted the boy into her arms.

Patting her cheek, he crooned adoringly, "Sofi," before laying his head on her shoulder. Stuart thought the boy was too big for petite Mary Sofia to hold, but the way she smiled and nipped the boy's fingers playfully with her straight, white teeth told him that she doted on the child. Hugo, meanwhile, ignored his daughter's attempt to pry the bars off his uniform jacket and reached out a hand for Stuart to shake. Dressed in full military uniform for the occasion, he looked every inch the Marine he was. Technically, he served in the Reserves, but that in no way diminished his military bearing.

"Champ, how are you?"

"Not as well as you, I suspect. I'm no expert on military markings, but I believe you've been promoted."

"You may call me Captain Carter, thank you very much," the big man acknowledged proudly.

"They made him a commissioned officer as soon as he finished that last college course," JoJo informed Stuart. "He made Second Lieutenant within six months. I don't doubt he'll make major soon."

Hugo chuckled complacently. "Nah. My commanding officer is retiring. The new guy won't be so generous with the promotions. But that's okay. With my income from the Reserves and the furniture business, we've got no worries."

A skilled carpenter, Hugo's uniquely designed, handmade furniture had proved quite popular nationwide.

"Going well, then, is it, the business?" Stuart asked idly, attempting to ignore Mary Sofia's byplay with the boy. He'd had a lot of experience ignoring Mary Sofia over the girls, watching at a respectful distance as she'd grown from promising teen to enchanting adult.

"Very well," JoJo reported, unaware, as usual, of his awareness of her sister-in-law. "We've had to hire half a dozen skilled workers to keep up with the demand."

"I largely design and just build the prototypes now," Hugo chimed in. "With foreign supply chain woes what they are, American-made products are selling well."

"Glad to hear it," Stuart told them, sipping

his tea. "Merchandising complains constantly about the supply chain, and it gives us guys in Marketing plenty of headaches, too. We will no longer launch campaigns unless the product is actually stateside, and still getting them onto shelves can be iffy, even for the world's largest retailer."

"Marketing," interjected Mary Sofia. "I didn't realize that's what you do."

He smiled, guiltily glad to have a reason to address her personally. Someone should have advised her to wear something warmer than the strapless, royal blue cocktail dress with its flowing knee-length skirt, however. February always seemed to be the coldest month in northwest Arkansas. She might have worn closed-toe shoes, too, rather than silver, high-heeled sandals. Then again, the shoes perfectly matched the wide silver belt at her narrow waist and contrasted beautifully with the blue. She looked innocently glamorous, a ripe berry ready to be plucked and savored. He only wished he could be the one to do it, but that was never going to happen. Even if he'd felt able to approach her, Hugo would gut him first.

Dragging his gaze to her lovely face, he took in the tilt of her slender brows over those fathomless dark eyes. Her nose might be a trifle short, but her plump lips would draw men like bees to flower petals. He bludgeoned his mind back to the subject at hand.

"I thought everyone knew that marketing is my stock in trade."

"I found the marketing aspect of my business courses fascinating," Mary Sofia told him. A frown brought a barely discernible crease to her smooth forehead. "Maybe I should've gone that way instead of taking a general business degree."

"We're having a little trouble finding full-time employment," Hugo divulged, leaning closer to Stuart.

"Oh, that's too bad."

Frowning, Stuart assessed the situation. Over the years, he'd watched her grow from an impish, impulsive teenager to a beautiful, self-possessed young woman. Her protective older brothers, Hugo and Rey Carter, must be proud of her. The problem had to be that Mary Sofia didn't look her age. She had to be over twenty-one—probably a couple of years older, now that he thought about it—because she held a college degree from the University of Arkansas. Nevertheless, she must look like a teenager to anyone who didn't know her well. A shapely, very lovely teenager.

She shifted the boy in her arms, and the thick, artful knot of brown-black hair at the nape of her slender neck shifted slightly, giving the impression that it might tumble down at any moment. Stuart almost hoped it would. He'd always admired her long, dark hair.

"I've told her she can always come to work for me in the furniture business," Hugo went on, "but she's not having any of it."

"You're all up in *my* business as it is," Mary Sofia told him teasingly. "The last thing I need is you looking over my shoulder at work, too."

She shifted the boy onto her hip. He immediately latched onto the straight neckline of her strapless dress with his little fingers. Stuart quickly looked away, fixing his attention on Hugo, who gusted out a huge sigh, but the twinkle in his eye belied any true frustration. Stuart ducked his head, hiding a smile, only to see the boy tugging at Mary Sofia's neckline in an effort to hoist himself higher on her hip.

Quickly switching his gaze back to Mary Sofia's sweet face, he said, "Maybe we can sit down together at a computer and go over the openings in my company."

To his surprise, Mary Sofia hesitated. "That's very nice of you, Champ, but I've already applied for several positions there and nothing has come of it. Besides, I wouldn't want to put you to any trouble."

He should leave it at that, he knew, but instead he put on his most congenial smile. "Don't be silly. It's no bother, and a reference from me could help. I think we might find something that would fit. I'll even bring my laptop over so we'll have easy access to the company database." There. That should tell everyone that he had no ulterior motives, such as luring her alone to his house. It occurred to him that she'd never seen his home, and he suddenly regretted that she wouldn't.

"That's a very generous offer," JoJo said, repositioning the toddler to one arm.

Keeping his smile in place, Stuart reached into his coat pocket for his phone. "Let me get your number so we can set up something."

"Oh, um..." Again she hesitated, hefting the boy a little higher onto her hip. "It's four-seven-nine..."

She didn't allow him time to open his contacts and set up the thing properly, so he typed it into the keypad of his phone and hit the call button. A moment later, the tiny handbag hanging from a narrow chain from her shoulder started ringing. He ended the call. "There. Now you've got my number, too."

"That should do it," JoJo said, smiling and glancing from one to the other of them. "If not, I have both of your numbers."

"I think all the band members have each other's numbers," Hugo rumbled, sounding as if he didn't quite approve.

Stuart chose to ignore that and addressed Mary Sofia directly. "Call me in a day or two, and we'll set something up."

Mary Sofia nodded. "Thank you."

"My pleasure." He widened his smile, already regretting the offer and at the same time looking forward to it.

Perhaps he regretted it because he looked forward to it. Good grief, what was wrong with him? Deciding to make a hasty departure, he spread his smile around the group.

"Now, if you'll excuse me, I think I'll check out the appetizers."

***

As Champ walked away, Mary Sofia hugged Marc Everett to her side. She loved this little boy and his sisters. She considered them good practice for when she had children of her own, a day to which she looked forward. In truth, she felt drawn more to marriage and motherhood than a career in business or anything else. For that reason, she'd made more than one mistake in choosing boyfriends, but not for a long time now. Those were mistakes she didn't want to repeat, and Stuart Champion tempted her fall right back into her foolish, dreamy ways.

The most handsome, sophisticated, kind, and enigmatic of the HOBBY RUN set, he had to be seven or eight years older than her twenty-three years, which was no doubt why he'd always been unfailingly polite but rather aloof. He'd never be romantically interested in an ordinary someone like her, so she'd kept her distance, focusing her attention on his younger bandmates and her college friends, instead. Still, she'd always found his rusty, soft-spoken voice as equally mesmerizing as the contrast between his deeply set, brown eyes and pale blond hair. Her heart always pounded when he was near, and he didn't even have to speak to her to make her pulse race.

Sadly, she knew herself to be too much like her mother, a romantic fool. Sylvia Ruiz Carter had cared only about the man in her life. Her compulsive adoration and jealousy had driven away her husband, Mary Sofia's father, a long haul trucker. He'd taken every opportunity to hit the road with his tractor-trailer rig. When he'd died in a traffic accident, Sylvia had completely fallen apart. She'd burned herself alive by setting the house afire as soon as the four youngest of her six children—Mary Sofia, Gabrielle, Ana, and Tomas—had left for school. If the oldest brother, Rey, hadn't come home from the military to whisk them off to Arkansas, Mary Sofia shuddered to think what might have become of them. Hugo, second oldest, had taken over the care of the younger siblings when Rey had moved away to pursue a solo career in music. After Hugo and JoJo's triplets had come along, Tomas had elected to join Rey and his growing family in Tennessee.

Mary Sofia had vowed never to start building castles in the air around some male again. Instead, she'd promised herself that she would allow God to choose the right man for her. By throwing her into close proximity with her secret crush, was God telling her that Champ was the one? Or was that her foolish wishful thinking again?

Hugo, meanwhile, in big brother form, had been pondering. "That was a generous offer Champ made," he concluded with a frown.

Mary Sofia rolled her eyes, knowing what came next.

"Well, that's Champ for you," her sister-in-law claimed blithely, winking at Mary Sofia.

True to form, Hugo bit his lip, frowning as he considered all the possible ramifications of Mary Sofia spending time with the man. "Do you think it's all right?"

Here it came, the overprotective big brother bit. Not that she could blame him. Both he and Rey had pulled her out of questionable situations in the past.

"What do you mean?" JoJo asked innocently, producing a clean tissue to wipe Lizbet's face. Lizbet, as usual, protested, twisting her head away from her mother's hand, but JoJo doggedly persisted. "He said he'd bring his laptop over to our house. What's wrong with that?"

"Well, he's a single man," Hugo mused while JoJo struggled with their headstrong daughter. "And there was that thing with Matt's wife," he went on, lowering his voice.

Now JoJo rolled her eyes. "There was never anything serious between him and Joanna Polo. They're just friends, the three of them, Champ, Matt, and Joanna. Really, Hugo, where did you hear such gossip?"

He shrugged and followed Champ with his gaze. "I overheard Allie Justus discussing it with her brother. Bart seemed concerned that she was getting too friendly with Champ."

"That's just what the world needs," Mary Sofia muttered, "another overprotective brother."

JoJo chuckled. "Bart doesn't strike me as the overprotective type."

"Everyone says he's changed a lot since he became a Christian," Hugo argued.

"That doesn't mean he's trying to run his sister's life," Mary Sofia pointed out. "Besides, she's older than him."

"So what?" Hugo rumbled. "And no one said anything about running anybody's life."

"No one has to," Mary Sofia shot back, smiling sweetly. "In this family, it's a given."

JoJo sighed and addressed her daughter. "See what you have to look forward to, darling? Daddy's going to be breathing down the neck of every boy who even glances at you or your sister, starting with kindergarten."

"What makes you think he'll wait 'til then?" Mary Sofia asked dryly.

Laughing, JoJo said, "Good point. Let's get something to eat." She started for the appetizer table with Lizbet.

"Make fun," Hugo called after them, "but it's my responsibility to take care of y'all."

"And you do a stellar job of it, sweetheart," JoJo assured him, never slowing down.

Hugo put his nose to Caro's. "You don't mind if Daddy protects you, do you, punkin? You know it's 'cause he loves you so much."

Caro pursed her bow lips and kissed him on the chin. The big, bad Marine melted like butter in a hot oven. Lizbet might be the scrappy one, but Mary Sofia had an inkling that, in a few years' time, calmly sweet Caro would be the one to lead her doting daddy on a merry chase.

He set off after JoJo and Lizbet, still crooning to Caro. Mary Sofia shifted Marc Everett higher on her hip again and followed. He immediately began playing idly with a lock of hair that had escaped the loose chignon at her nape. She derailed his hand, but then she caught sight of Champ standing near the buffet tables with a small plate as he chatted with none other than the aforementioned Allie Justus.

Sophisticated and beautiful, Allie ran the real estate development company inherited from her parents. Mary Sofia watched Allie casually pick an appetizer from Champ's plate with her manicured fingertips and take a bite of it. Champ said something to her, and she delivered the remaining tidbit to his mouth. A look passed between them before Champ stepped back, casually glancing around as he chewed and swallowed. Allie turned away, smiling like the cat that caught the canary. Mary Sofia's heart dropped to her knees. The two were definitely involved. So much for Champ being the guy for her.

She'd never had a chance with Champ and never would. He and Allie Justus made sense. Tall, blonde Allie would attract any man, especially one as sophisticated as she. They looked exactly right together. Both were single. Why shouldn't they get together?

Mary Sofia told herself that she was happy for them. Champ had always seemed a bit introverted and very much alone. Mary Sofia couldn't count the times she'd wanted to comfort him for reasons she couldn't even explain, but of course she'd dared not do so. A man like him would never welcome the overtures of someone like her. She should be glad that Champ finally had found someone. That, sadly, did nothing to explain the yawning hole growing in the pit of her stomach.

In a bid to reclaim her attention, Marc Everett tugged on her hair again, and pins fell to the floor as the mass of it tumbled down onto her shoulders in a messy clump. Setting Marc Everett on his feet, she crouched to pick up the fallen pins. Embarrassment heated her face.

"Sofi," he whispered, patting her back consolingly.

Mary Sofia flashed him a quick smile before walking him to his mother and escaping to the ladies room with her hair pins. Her hair gathered in her hands, she walked into the mirrored antechamber, and there stood none other than Allie Justus.

The tall, seductive blonde leaned over the narrow console table, refreshing her lip gloss. She glanced at Mary Sofia's reflection and smirked before putting her back to the mirror. Her dress, a champagne colored knit, boasted long sleeves that puddled around her wrists, in deference to the cold, no doubt, although Mary Sofia couldn't see what difference they made, given the way the bodice of her dress plunged both in back and front and how the slit in her long, narrow skirt revealed her leg right to the top of her thigh.

"The dreaded hair catastrophe, I see."

Hoping the heat rising to her cheeks did not show, Mary Sofia returned a lame smile and began plucking the remaining pins from the drooping mass on the back of her head.

"Little fingers. My nephew pulled it down."

"That's why I avoid both," Allie said dryly. Turning back to the mirror, she began neatening the lip gloss with the tip of her pinky finger.

"Both?"

"Children and long hair."

"Oh. But Marc Everett's a darling, and I wouldn't want to cut my hair."

"All children are darlings so long as they get what they want," Allie said in a bored voice. She flashed a grin, adding, "But then the same can be said for most adults. As for the hair..." Glancing at Mary Sofia, she turned back to the mirror and examined her own appearance carefully, her slender, tapered fingers smoothing the already perfect ends of her chin-length bob. "Long hair has to be too severely contained in a business setting. I prefer the ease and convenience of shorter hair. It goes from bed to business meeting in a blink." Her reflection caught Mary Sofia's, a Cheshire Cat grin curling her lips. "And back to bed, if you get my meaning."

Allie's meaning shot through Mary Sofia like a jolt from a live electric wire. Allie implied that she and Champ were more than a couple. At the very least, she wanted Mary Sofia to believe they were having an affair. Why else would she speak in that sultry, throaty tone? Mary Sofia didn't want to believe it, but the hole in her middle swelled into her chest, crowding the air out of her lungs.

Allie picked up her tiny, expensive handbag from the top of the console table, dropped the lip gloss inside, turned, and strode from the room, hips swaying, but that grin stayed on to taunt Mary Sofia as she struggled to fix her hair. She tried to tell herself that what went on between Champ and Allie was none of her business, but a dark, heavy disappointment soured her stomach. She knew Champ to be a Christian man like her brothers, so he must intend to marry Allie.

In any event, Mary Sofia told herself, it wasn't her place to judge. Still, she felt a bone deep dismay at this latest disillusionment.

It doesn't matter, she silently told her reflection. He was never going to be hers, anyway, and she didn't want to be like her mother, so enamored of a man she had no time or focus for anything or anyone else. Her crush on Champ felt too much like obsession. She thought of him much too often.

She should be relieved. This was for the best. God at work.

Nodding to herself, she went back to the reception.

Chapter Two

S tuart watched that Allie leave the reception moments after the wedding party arrived. Then he scolded himself for watching her. What if someone noticed?

She'd have been amused at his chagrin, but she just didn't understand why he felt uncomfortable about making their affair public. Relieved that she had departed the reception already and at the same time swamped with guilt because of his relief, he told himself for perhaps the thousand time that this couldn't go on. Obviously, the only satisfactory way to end the affair was with marriage, but Allie refused even to discuss it.

The whole thing frustrated Stuart to the point of madness. How could he justify their relationship if they didn't marry? Surely that was what God expected. Allie, unfortunately, didn't believe in "all that mumbo jumbo," as she put it. Watching Ronan and Tessa move about the building, scattering joy in their wake, Stuart wanted to pray for God to change Allie's heart and mind, but as usual, the words fled him as soon as he tried to gather them into a coherent plea.

Clearly, God did not want to hear from him. At least not until he rectified this situation with Allie.

Depressed, Stuart forced a smile into place. When the newlyweds appeared in front of him, he dutifully kissed the bride's cheek and clapped Ronan on the back in a brotherly hug, as their friendship and good manners required. After a few seconds, they moved off to greet other guests, leaving Stuart feeling alone and abandoned. He thought about following Allie's example and simply leaving, but the etiquette instilled in him almost from birth would not let him ignore all the trouble and expense to which his friends had gone in order to include him in the celebration of their nuptials. He started looking for his place card among the dining tables, only to find himself seated next to Allie's brother, Bart Justus. Allie also had a card at the table, but Bart made her excuses.

"Some sort of business appointment." He shook his head. "Though what it could be on a Saturday evening, I can't imagine."

"Some sort of international call perhaps," Stuart offered in as offhand a manner as he could manage. It was common knowledge that Allie had taken the company international a few months ago.

Bart shrugged. "I never know where she gets

off to. She sure doesn't spend much time at home. She practically lives in that penthouse at the office."

Knowing where she spent quite a few of her evenings, though rarely the entire night, Stuart said nothing.

"Home" for Allie was a six-thousand-square-foot French-style chateau that stood behind ten-foot-high stone walls and monitored electronic gates. Stuart never visited her there, even though she'd given him the codes to both the back gate and the kitchen door. Allie and her now ex-husband had begun building the place even before they'd married, but the construction had outlived the marriage, so Allie had moved into the mansion alone. Soon after, Bart had sold the forty-year-old, four-thousand-square-foot house where he and Allie had been raised and moved in with her.

Stuart told himself he was protecting Bart by never visiting Allie at her house or the office, but he couldn't deny that he feared what Bart and the rest of the HOBBY RUN band would think about his relationship with Allie. That Allie had kept their affair to herself thus far both surprised and confused him. She complained about his unwillingness to go public with their affair, which to him meant that she cared about him beyond his bed. If so, then why wouldn't she marry him? It couldn't be because of Bart.

Once Bart had been selfish, entitled, and

abusive. With his very successful adoptive parents deceased and his older sister firmly in charge of the family business, he'd determined to make himself a Rock superstar, with all the attendant excesses. When the other three members of the Young Rockers, all Christians, had joined the HOBBY RUN conglomerate, Bart had set out on a solo career, which hadn't worked out as he'd hoped. Thankfully, Bart didn't seem resentful or even bummed by his failure to make himself into a great Rock 'n Roll star. This Stuart chalked up to the influence of Bart's birth parents, Wyatt and Maggs Ogilvie. Under their guidance, Bart had eventually found Christ and matured into the good man Maggs had prayed for during the twenty-five years of separation from her husband and her long search for the son she'd given away shortly after his birth.

Everyone had been astonished to find that angry, insolent Bart was the son of gentle Wyatt and flashy Maggs. Once the truth came out, however, the resemblance between Wyatt and Bart had instantly become obvious. Stuart hadn't liked Bart much when they'd played together as part of the Young Rockers, and he'd been terribly envious when it had been discovered that Bart could claim Wyatt and Maggs as his dad and mom. Since replacing Rey Carter as HOBBY RUN's lead singer, however, Bart had proved himself a caring, reliable friend to everyone in the band. Apparently, he'd found a level of serenity and peace and now seemed content to teach music and perform with HOBBY RUN as the replacement for Rey Carter, who had been their main vocalist.

Allie didn't understand that. As a hard-driving businesswoman who had recently expanded the family company into international markets, she simply did not countenance failure. No amount of success seemed to quell her ambition, either. Champ felt equally parts proud of her and troubled by her acquisitive nature. If only she would claim the same faith that her adopted brother had found, Champ thought, but then he asked himself what he, the greatest of hypocrites, had done to help her truly understand her need for Christ. Taking her to bed—or, to be more precise, letting her take him to bed—went against everything he believed. Why should she want to follow his God after that?

Sometimes he thought the guilt would eat him alive.

Over these past months, ignoring guilt had become a habit with Champ, so he now simply thrust it away and pretended to a lightheartedness he did not feel. He chatted with those around the table, ate his meal and his allotment of wedding cake with apparent gusto, and circulated among the other wedding guests. He danced with a pair of polite but disinterested secretaries from a local law firm, one of them at least fifteen years his senior. Next, he danced with Sam Cody's mother, a pastor's wife. He even danced with young Gabi Carter, who couldn't wait to leave high school behind at the end of the semester and get on to college, where she intended to study early childhood education.

He did not dance with Gabi's older sister, although he might have if she hadn't remained at a distance the whole evening. Every time he started in Mary Sofia's direction, she seemed to dart off somewhere else. That bothered him, perhaps more than it should, but he was in no mood to analyze the situation.

Tired, his duty to his good friend Ronan more than done, he collected the suit jacket he'd shed earlier and his outerwear then took himself off home. For once, he didn't mind being alone. He'd play with the dog for a bit and go to bed with a book. Sunday had become a day of loose ends for him. He decided he'd take the dog for a lengthy run early tomorrow morning, along one of the area's many scenic trails, provided the weather cooperated and the path remained free of ice. He could cope with the cold so long as precipitation did not accompany it, and Trooper wouldn't complain. The dog loved an easy jog, and at one-hundred-and-thirty pounds, the great Cane Corso, a breed of Italian Mastiff, could use the exercise.

Champ drove his granite gray Jeep pickup truck from The Milking Barn to Bentonville, where he found the downtown square predictably deserted and silent on this chilly February night. On the other hand, with closing time still an hour or more away and despite the sharp plunge of the temperature after dark, the lighted windows of the restaurants he passed showed many customers lingering over their dinners. He made the requisite turns onto vacant streets, before pulling in to his customary bay in the large carport behind his large, empty dwelling.

Attached to the historic Greek Revival house only by a covered walkway, the carport had been an addition built by his late father. When Champ had begun driving, the carport had been enlarged to cover all three of the family vehicles. Now, two of the roomy bays remained permanently empty and had for over a decade.

He got out of the truck and went to the back door, his fingers automatically finding the right key as he climbed the brick steps. Once again he thought of installing a lock with a key pad. It would mean much easier access for the handyman and various contractors who so often came and went. A historical home of this size required almost constant maintenance, but he couldn't think of living anywhere else. As soon as he swung open the door, he knew he was not alone in the house, after all, because the dog did not silently wait for him on the other side. Still, he called in case the big lummox had fallen asleep.

"Trooper, I'm home."

"Trooper has already gone to bed," said a familiar, sultry voice. "Come in and do the same."

Champ sighed inwardly even as his body responded to what, who, he knew he would find in the comfortable back parlor. Allie couldn't understand why anyone bothered with pets, and she hated that Trooper drooled when hungry or excited, so she habitually locked him in the laundry room when his devoted master wasn't looking. Champ walked across the mudroom and let out the dog. The huge black dog gave Champ his usual snuffling greeting, falling into step beside him, the very epitome of stoic patience as they moved through the short hallway to the room Allie insisted on calling "the den." As soon as they entered the dim parlor, the dog padded over to his bed beside the fireplace and flopped down. Champ paused to look at Allie, who sprawled across one corner of the corduroy sofa, wearing nothing more than his second best white dress shirt.

"What took you so long?" she purred, one expertly manicured hand going to her pale hair. The fire she'd built in the fireplace, one of many in the rambling old house, cast a golden glow over the scene.

"I had a wedding reception to attend," he said, shrugging out of his overcoat and tossing it onto the overstuffed chair. He sent his yellow-gold scarf after it, yanked at his cuffs, and took a seat on the edge of the sofa cushion farthest from Allie. "It wouldn't have killed you to stay."

"I wasn't in the mood for a crowd. I would think you'd realize that."

"And I would think you'd realize that I couldn't be seen leaving too soon after you."

She put her head back and groaned. His unwillingness to flaunt their affair irritated her greatly, but tonight she didn't launch into argument as so often happened. Instead, her long, slender legs bare beneath the hem of his shirt, she stood and held out her hand. "Come to bed."

He pulled in a deep breath, gathered what little resolve he could muster, and stared into the flames flickering around the logs in the fireplace. She constantly urged him to install a gas insert, but she'd become quite adept at building a fire when she wanted one.

"I don't think so, Allie, not tonight."

She kept insisting that this "thing" between them didn't have to be about romance, so if she wanted romance from him, she'd have to earn it.

"All right," she said, undeterred. Ignoring the shake of his head, she began freeing the top buttons of the shirt.

"Allie, don't," he pleaded, his tone a mixture of rebuke and resignation as she let the shirt fall to the floor.

"Who needs a bed anyway?"

***

He always felt so close to her, so hopeful, after sex, but then she inevitably grew distant and cool. Tonight, as she dressed, she abruptly said, "You seemed to be having quite a conversation with the little Carter girl at the reception."

Shocked at the edge of jealousy in her tone, he scrambled for a safe reply. "Which one?"

"Don't play dumb. Mary Sofia, of course."

Ridiculously pleased by this show of possessiveness, he couldn't quite capture his smile before it slipped across his face. "We were discussing her job search. She's having trouble finding work in her field since her graduation."

"Oh?"

"I think it's because she looks so young."

"How old is she?" Allie had asked.

"Twenty-two, I think, or maybe twenty-three. She's had to work her way through college, so she could be older, but she looks about seventeen. Don't you think?"

Allie didn't answer that. Instead, she asked, "What is her field?"

"General business. I told her I'd check around at work, see if we had any openings there."

Allie's cellphone dinged, indicating that her Uber had arrived. She dropped the subject as abruptly as she'd introduced it, tugging on her pale, expensive, faux fur. "Gotta run."

Without another word or so much as a kiss

on his cheek, she snatched up her small handbag and headed for the back door. Disappointment crashed through Stuart as he followed her. He wanted to believe that she demanded his body because she truly loved him but just wouldn't admit it. Bart often said her ex had ruined her for love and marriage, but Stuart wanted to believe he could win her heart and trust. He followed her to the door in his bare feet, wearing nothing more than slacks and his wrinkled dress shirt. Despite the cold, he stood on the walkway, watching her hurry pass the carport, her heels clicking on the frozen pavestone, and climb into the Uber waiting at the curb. At least she'd been thoughtful enough not to park her luxury vehicle next to his for all the world to see, the part of it that might be out and about in downtown Bentonville on a cold February night that was.

Numbed by the cold, he trudged back into the parlor to close the doors on the glass fireplace insert, but beneath the insensate surface lurked the twin tortures of guilt and disappointment. He stood for a moment, watching the dying flames flicker behind the thick glass, and pondered the situation. He'd been deeply flattered and thrilled when Allie had first expressed interest in him.

As if.

She hadn't expressed interest. She'd simply showed up at his door one evening, pressed up against him, wrapped her arms around him, and demanded, "Take me to bed."

To his shame, he hadn't argued. What was the point when he'd already indulged in the forbidden fruit of sex many times? Not lately, however. Not in years. Since becoming part of the HOBBY RUN band, his thinking on the matter had shifted. As a younger man, he'd reasoned that what happened between two consenting adults was no one's business but their own. The HOBBY RUN band members were all dedicated Christians, however, and they all tacitly agreed that God meant what the Bible said about sex being reserved for marriage. Those he admired most—Wyatt, Drew, even Matt —made no bones about their past mistakes or their determination to do better, to live deeper into their personal relationships with Jesus, even, perhaps especially, when it came to sex. Their determination to live lives pleasing to God shamed Stuart. A nominal Christian to that point, he'd privately decided to follow their examples, and despite his loneliness, he'd pretty well steered clear of temptation. Until Allie.

Early on, he'd convinced himself they'd embarked on a great romance that would inevitably culminate in marriage, but the deception became increasingly more difficult to support. In his heart, he knew Allie basically used him for sex. They never did anything but have sex. She wasn't "into dating," as she put it.

That, she maintained, just opened a whole other can of worms for someone in her position. Once that might have been fine with him, but not now.

He wanted love. He wanted commitment. He wanted a marriage of equals. He wanted children to fill this old house. He wanted to hold up his head with the band and in church again. Allie declared his "marriage obsession" laughable. Yet, he kept hanging on and giving in, even when he increasingly felt bereft and dirty.

"So why do I keep doing it, boy?" he asked the dog, crouching to pet the broad head that lifted from the plump bed before the fire.

Trooper wisely offered no reply other than the patient devotion that radiated from his drooping eyes. He always looked so sad, but Champ sensed the contentment in his canine friend. Likewise, he sensed that, beneath the sophisticated veneer, Allie always seemed deeply discontented, even when she got what she wanted. Did she want him, he wondered, in any way except physically? She must. Otherwise, why be jealous of Mary Sofia?

He hated that he'd started to hope again, simply because she'd asked about sweet, innocent Mary Sofia. Maybe something was wrong with him, and no woman could truly love him until he figured out what he lacked as a man. Men, according to popular thought, were supposed to treasure their independence and hold the notion of true love in disdain. By that standard, he was a hopeless failure because he actually wanted to be married.

"What does it matter?" he asked the dog. "At least you love me, uh, boy?" He bowed his head, resting his forehead between the dog's ears. A thick, red tongue swiped across Champ's chin. Chuckling, Champ pushed up to his full height and wiped away the evidence of Trooper's affection with one hand. "Come on, boy. Let's go to bed."

Trooper heaved himself to his paws as Champ gathered up his discarded clothing, picked up his shoes, and set off through the darkened house. The big dog obediently followed, padding down the hallway past the kitchen and formal dining room to the expansive foyer. A pair of large, front parlors flanked the foyer. One contained a grand piano no one had played since his mother's death. Each overlooked the deep front porch that shielded the tall, leaded glass windows and enormous front door from the light of the street lamp. Darkness shrouded the big, old house, but both the weary man and the blacker-than-night beast could find their way around the familiar spaces with their eyes closed. Bypassing the first curving branch of stairs, they climbed the second.

The wide landing at the top ran the length of the second story, neatly bisecting the family rooms on the right from the "public" rooms on the left. The grand old house boasted a master suite, three bedrooms and a second bath on the family side and a parlor, library, study, and billiard room on the other. The "landing" itself, as large as the average ballroom of the era, contained a scattering of handsome antique chairs and tables, along with a trio of deep, padded window seats at the rear, overlooking the back garden. Stuart's indulgent parents had allowed him to play here, and he'd often created whole cities with his various toy sets, peopled by everything from action figures to Teddy Bears. As long as everything had been picked up before the housecleaner arrived for the weekly sweeping, vacuuming, and mopping, his play world could stay in place.

He'd been a happy boy, deeply loved and sure of his place in the world. Perhaps he'd been a bit shy, but his parents had always been willing to facilitate his social life and unfailingly supportive of every activity in which he'd participated. When his high school baseball team had won the regional championship, his parents had opened the house for a large, boisterous party to celebrate. As a taller than average fourteen-year-old freshman, Stuart had been a starter at shortstop and a backup pitcher with an excellent RBI. The name Champ had stuck when he'd hit the winning home run, with the bases loaded, to give his team the victory. He'd been so proud to host the event. This old house had not seen a real party since. In fact, other than Allie, few people had entered this house since he'd graduated college, over eight years ago.

As he turned into the open doorway of the master suite, rage abruptly seized him. Angry at Allie for not sharing his dream of marriage and family, angry at himself for the lonely, pathetic figure he'd become, angry at God for leaving him all alone these past years, he dropped his clothing then reared back and threw one shoe and then the other as hard as he could. The first hit the tall back of the chair in front of the bank of windows in the far wall. The other knocked over the reading lamp on the table beside the chair. It must have been a glancing blow, for he heard no sounds of breakage as he stood heaving out his distress.

Trooper's nails clicked on the polished hardwood of the floor as the dog calmly moved by Stuart and made his way to the big, four-poster bed. Leaping up onto the mattress with ungainly ease, Trooper plopped down on his side and stretched out, a black shadow of dog on the gold bedspread in the moon glow from the windows. Champ shook his head at both the dog's unshakably phlegmatic attitude and his own unpredictably choleric one. Then, with a sigh, he walked around to the side of the bed Trooper had left to him, stripped, peeled back the covers, and slid beneath.

Feeling the dog's warm bulk beside him, he

closed his eyes and pretended to sleep until he finally did.

Oddly, the last image his weary brain conjured was not that of the woman with whom he'd just had sex but the dreamy-eyed face of Mary Sofia Carter.

Chapter Three

Mary Sofia had come to enjoy church services. Even when she'd thought she was too cool for the "lame" youth activities, she'd enjoyed the music and more solemn rituals of "adult" worship. Not that the family church, an amalgamation of Spanish evangelicalism and mainstream traditions, could be called solemn. Far from it. Christ, as Pastor Albert often preached, brought grace and joy to this fallen, troubled world and so should be celebrated at every opportunity.

The past few years had impressed upon Mary Sofia how necessary celebration was to the human soul. With COVID still preying on the populace and her family's experience of losing their next-door neighbor to the virus, the simple, over-the-hedge wedding of her brother and JoJo had been an occasion of joy, if an unusual one. Since moving in with JoJo and Hugo, Mary Sofia had found a new appreciation for the delights of life, however modest. The end of the quarantine had brought more opportunity to celebrate, but in a somewhat truncated fashion.

Her recent college graduation provided a perfect example of that. Because she'd graduated in December rather than May, the ceremony would have been somewhat curtailed under the best of circumstances, but the attendance caps which followed the COVID lockdown meant that only Hugo and Gabi could attend her graduation in person. The rest of the family—her younger sister, Ana, along with JoJo and the triplets in Arkansas, and her oldest and youngest brothers, Rey and Tomas, her other sister-in-law, Della, young nephew, and baby niece in Tennessee— had watched on the computer. The graduation party Hugo and JoJo had hosted at their home afterward had been much more meaningful to Mary Sofia. Even Champ had put in a brief appearance, leaving a leather desk set as a gift.

Sadly, she'd begun to think she'd have no use for that handsome desk set. She seemed destined to wait tables for the rest of her life, which partially explained why she had accompanied Hugo and Gabi to this particular Sunday night prayer meeting. Now that she'd finished her degree, she'd increased her hours at the restaurant to full-time, which meant she had only Wednesdays, Sundays, and the occasional personal day off. She sometimes skipped the Sunday evening service just to have a little extra time to herself.

Her adamant refusal to work Sundays had never set well with her current employer.

Numerous times in these past months, she'd petitioned God to help her find favor with her current manager, Chet, because he routinely complained about her refusal to come in to work on the Lord's Day. He'd even hinted that she could be immediately promoted if she'd just consent to work the occasional Sunday. Knowing that "occasional" would eventually mean "every," she continued to stick to her guns.

Lately her prayers centered on finding a position in the business world rather than her current job. When the possibility of a college education had first appeared, she'd thought to pursue something in the medical field, nursing, perhaps. In the end, however, she'd opted for what her advisor insisted was the most versatile degree for her, business.

Maybe she should go to work for Hugo, after all. Or maybe she should take up Champ's offer to help her find employment with his company. Or maybe not.

Despite what she'd learned at the wedding reception, she still felt drawn to Champ, which was reason enough to keep her distance. No matter how much she chided herself, she couldn't seem to stop thinking about him.

Remembering that she sat in church, she resolutely turned her attention back to the pastor's remarks before focusing her mind on the prayer list that had been passed out at the beginning of the service. Appointed individuals voiced prayers for the concerns on the list, leaving time afterward for those present to lift up any personal concerns. When Hugo rose, placed his hand on Mary Sofia's shoulder, and asked God to guide her as she navigated her future, she felt a spurt of sisterly affection and hopefulness.

After the service, as the crowd dispersed, she caught sight of the new Youth Minister, Gavin Worley, hurrying in her direction. For once, she didn't try to evade him. That only seemed to spur him into dogged pursuit, so instead she greeted him with a polite smile. She'd already turned down several date requests from the man because she just didn't find him attractive. Gabi reported that all the kids liked him because of his sense of humor, but—given his short stature, receding hairline, round face, big ears, heavy eyebrows, and thin lips—that only made him seem clownish, in Mary Sofia's opinion.

Hugo appeared at her elbow. "Here comes Lover Boy," he teas   ed from the corner of his mouth.

Mary Sofia kept her smile in place and sent a short, swift jab to her brother's ribs. As her brother gasped, she said, "Hello, Gavin."

"Mary Sofia. Looking great. As always."

"Why, thank you, Gavin."

The smaller man frowned. "Hugo, are you okay?"

Shooting a glare at Mary Sofia, Hugo put out

his hand. "I'm fine, Gavin. And yourself?"

"Fine, thank you." Even as he replied to Hugo, Gavin's attention shifted back to Mary Sofia. "Youth group is expanding, I'm happy to say, and we're planning a ski trip for Spring Break. We'll be looking for adult sponsors. I was hoping you'd consider volunteering, Mary Sofia."

A week with Gavin and dozens of teenagers in a mountain hideaway? Not if she could help it, but she didn't refuse outright. "Oh, I don't know. It all depends on work. I don't have enough accrued vacation time where I am now, and that will only get worse when I start a new job. Which I hope is soon."

"Right, right." Gavin nodded, clasping his small, pale hands behind his back. "We'll pray about it then, and see if God presents a solution."

"That seems wise," Mary Sofia agreed, thinking she'd dodged a bullet, but then he took aim from another direction.

"Maybe we can discuss the details over dinner. I could use some help planning the trip, and I can't think of anyone better than you to assist me."

Blindsided, Mary Sofia could only blink for a moment, but then salvation seemed to come from another direction.

"I'm afraid the only evening she has off is Wednesday," Hugo said.

Undeterred, Gavin brought his hands around in a clap. "Excellent! Wednesday it is."

Seizing on the first excuse that entered her head, she blurted, "But Wednesday is Youth Night."

"That's not a problem," he insisted. "You can join us for pizza, and we'll talk afterward. In fact, I'll pick you up before I pick up the pizza. About six?"

She desperately wanted to refuse, but dinner with Gavin and forty teenagers seemed a lot safer than dinner with just Gavin."

"Uh, I suppose."

Gavin beamed. Then Hugo, bless him, came to the rescue once again. "That will save me multiple trips to and from the church with Gabi. She can ride along with the two of you."

It wasn't an out, but it meant Mary Sofia wouldn't be alone with Gavin on the drive to and from the church.

The dimming of his smile signaled Gavin's disappointment, but he acquiesced gracefully. "It's a date then." He chopped a salute in the air and left them.

"It's not a date," Mary Sofia whispered desperately to Hugo as Gavin went to greet the parents of a new teen.

"It is to him," Hugo replied softly.

Mary Sofia decided to beg her sister not to leave her alone with Gavin Worley for a single moment. She waited until she and Gabrielle were alone in the apartment above the garage of JoJo and Hugo's house. Mary Sofia could, and had, lived alone in the one bedroom apartment, but Gabi had recently declared their thirteen-year-old sister Ana a "complete snoop" and begged to share Mary Sofia's bedroom. That evening, as the sisters prepared for bed, Gabrielle listened intently while Mary Sofia explained her predicament, but then the teenager shrugged.

"Okay. I'll stick to your side like glue. But really, sis, I don't understand why you don't like Gavin. I think he's adorable."

"Puppies are adorable," Mary Sofia said, "but I wouldn't want to marry one."

"You mean you don't believe he's just looking for sponsors for the ski trip?" Gabi asked dryly. "And when did you arrive at that mind-blowing conclusion?"

At seventeen, Gabi wasn't nearly as stupid as Mary Sofia had been at her age. Much more pragmatic, Gabi called things as she saw them, with few filters in place.

"From the first moment he asked me out," Mary Sophia retorted, shaking Gabi's shoulder playfully. She suddenly realized her hand rested several inches higher than normal. That meant her baby sister now stood noticeably taller than her. When had that happened?

Gabi rolled her eyes. "You think just because you're beautiful every guy is out to marry you."

Shocked, Mary Sofia let her jaw drop. "I don't think any such thing."

"Well, you should," Gabi insisted, folding her

arms petulantly. "Because you are. Beautiful, I mean."

Mary Sofia smiled. "Why, thank you, Gabrielle."

Gabi wiggled her eyebrows. "And, of course, I look just like you." Affecting a sultry, sloe-eyed expression, she fluffed her hair, which was a shade lighter than Mary Sofia's.

They both erupted in laughter. Mary Sofia slung an arm around her sister's neck in a companionable hug, reaching up to do so. "Oh, Gabi, why do I always fall for the wrong guys?"

"Hm, maybe it's because you're more about the romance than the relationship."

Mary Sofia gaped at her sister. "What makes you say that?"

"History. You've picked some real losers in the past. Take that guy Faze for instance."

Horrified that Gabi even knew about that creep, Mary Sofia slapped her hands to her cheeks, "That was ages ago."

"True. But you came this close..." She held up her hand, the thumb and forefinger about an inch apart. "...to winding up as one of his many baby mamas."

Sighing, Mary Sofia shook her head. What a fool he'd made of her! "I know. I know. I shudder to think what might've happened if not for Hugo. I complain about how protective he and Rey are, but they're right to keep so close a watch on us. Me, at least."

"Oh, it's not as much about you as Mama," Gabi said. "They're just afraid we'll behave like her, so totally fixated on some guy we'd kill ourselves over him."

Mary Sofia scowled. "I wondered how much of that you picked up on."

"It's no secret. Mama couldn't live without Dad's complete attention. I always figured he took to driving trucks just to get some breathing room. When he died, I expected her to hook up with the first guy to come along. I never thought she'd…" Gabi let the words tail off.

"Commit suicide," Mary Sofia finished for her, taking her sister in her arms. "And in such a horrific way."

"Yeah, well, at least she waited until we were all gone to set the house on fire," Gabi said, hugging Mary Sofia back. "I just hope the pills worked before she burned to death."

Taking her sister by the face, Mary Sofia looked into her eyes. "Gabi, I'm so sorry you had to know all that about our mother."

Gabrielle stepped back, holding Mary Sofia by the shoulders. "I wasn't sure she even remembered we were there half the time, and that used to make me mad, but I'm over it now. And I know I'll never be like her. When the time comes, I want a solid man, like Rey and Hugo, and a sensible partnership like they have in their marriages. Meanwhile, I'm having plenty of fun. You should do the same. Just relax and date around. God's got a man in mind for you, and when the time is right, He'll bring him on."

"That's what I keep praying for," Mary Sofia admitted. "I'm afraid I'm too much like Mama, though. I seem to have no sense when it comes to men."

"Don't be so hard on yourself," Gabi counseled, heading to her bed. "Everyone's stupid when they're young. Except me." She grinned cheekily before going on. "Just leave it to God. It'll be fine."

"That, *querida hermana*, is exactly what I'm going to do," Mary Sofia decided, walking across the room to her own small bed. She climbed in and snuggled down beneath the covers, while Gabi did the same. An instant after Gabi turned off her light, Mary Sofia snuffed her own. Then she silently told God what she had told her sister moments earlier.

"I'm leaving it all to You, Lord. Everything. Job, romance, marriage, the future. Forgive me if I'm impatient. And please don't let me wind up like my mama."

***

For several days in a row, Champ woke with Mary Sofia Carter on his mind. As he dressed for work the Thursday morning following the wedding, he told himself that he really must set a day and time to help her with her job search. Nearly a week had passed since he'd made the offer, after all, and he wanted to help her if he could. Allie's reaction to him simply talking to the girl had made him hesitate. As much as Allie's reaction pleased him, he didn't want to deliberately make her jealous. A jealous Allie might become an angry Allie, and an angry Allie would be all too unpredictable.

On the other hand, everyone who knew Mary Sofia recognized her romantic nature. Rey had talked about it enough before departing Arkansas for Tennessee. He'd requested prayers for her on several occasions, either because he didn't approve of her current crush or because she so easily fell for every guy who came along. Of course, that had been several years ago, during her teens. She had undoubtedly matured since then. Many of the HOBBY RUN circle had mentioned it. Surely, Mary Sofia would call him when she felt ready for his help. Perhaps he ought to just let things be until then.

Pushing aside the guilt he felt for not setting up a meeting with her, he called the dog in, made sure the feeder and water dispenser were full, and left for work. He had much to do and quickly became engrossed with his current project. Yet, when his cellphone vibrated mid-morning, he instantly thought of Mary Sofia. When he picked up the phone he felt an unwelcome dread at the display of the caller's name. Dale Carmine, his Bible group leader at church.

The study group of single men and women met on Sunday evenings, rotating from home to home. Stuart had gladly welcomed them into his own home several times, but not in quite some while. For a long moment, he considered not answering the call, but he couldn't quite reconcile that rudeness with the kindness and concern Dale had always shown him. Finally, he tapped the green icon, put the phone to his ear, and injected as much enthusiasm as he could into his voice as he answered the call.

"Dale. How are you?"

"That's exactly what I wanted to ask you," came the reply. "It's been quite a while since we last saw you in Bible study or church. Everything okay?"

Stuart's heart sunk. Everything was not okay, but he couldn't very well say so. What was he going to do, tell his Bible teacher that he'd embroiled himself in an illicit affair and couldn't seem to get untangled? That he could no longer look the man in the eyes, not to mention the others in the group? Maybe he should say that every Bible lesson had begun to feel like a dark repudiation of him personally. Instead, he lied, telling himself that he could return to Bible study once he and Allie had made a firm commitment.

"Everything's fine, Dale. I've just been terribly busy with work and the band. And weddings," he added with a forced chuckle. "Seems like every time I turn around, one of my bandmates is getting married."

"We've had a couple of weddings in the group, too," Dale said, "so our numbers have dwindled a bit."

Stuart winced. He'd received invitations to those weddings, but he had attended neither. He'd intended to go. He'd even sent gifts. But in the end, he'd also sent his regrets, both times at the last minute. He couldn't remember now what excuses he'd used. For certain, he hadn't said that the very idea of attending another wedding alone made him sick at heart or that he couldn't be seen in public with the woman he was sleeping with, not as a couple anyway. So, once again, he lied obliquely.

"Yeah, I know. Wish I could've been there."

"Any chance we'll see you next week?" Dale asked.

"I sure hope so," Stuart replied heartily, knowing he wouldn't be anywhere near that Bible study next Sunday night, not unless he managed to resolve his situation with Allie.

After he and Dale briefly chatted about the newcomers in the group and ended the call, Stuart took a moment to reflect. He either had to make it clear that he wasn't coming back to the group or fix things with Allie so he could return with a somewhat clear conscience. He started seriously thinking about how he could convince Allie to marry him or at least to agree to an engagement.

He put thoughts of Mary Sofia on the back

burner. His guilty conscience could deal with only one problem at a time.

***

Mary Sofia remembered Wednesday's bedtime prayer when her cellphone rang on Thursday afternoon and the caller ID showed Justus Real Estate Development. Her first thought was that Bart must be using a company phone. Longhaired, heavily tattooed Bart had never shown the slightest interest in her, and neither had he intrigued her, but she couldn't think who else might call her on a phone belonging to Justus Real Estate Development.

Surprised and curious, she answered the call with a tentative, "Hello?"

A strange, rather curt male voice asked, "Is this Mary Sofia Carter?"

Definitely not Bart. Thoroughly confused now, she answered, "It is."

"Please hold for our CEO."

"CEO? What's this—" Mary Sofia began, only to realize he'd left the line. A few seconds later, Mary Sofia heard a click, then an all too familiar woman's voice spoke into her ear.

"Good morning, Mary Sofia."

Allie Justus. Weird just got weirder. "Uh. Good morning."

"Are you free to talk?"

"Um, yeah, I suppose."

"Try, 'Yes, ma'am.' If you're going to work for me, we might as well start off on the right foot."

Work for...? Was this Allie Justus offering her a job? Mary Sofia held the phone away from her ear and looked at it, half expecting to find the words, "Wake up, goofball!" blinking at her from the tiny screen. Nope. Apparently this was no dream. Heart hammering, Mary Sofia brought the phone back to her ear.

"I beg your pardon? H-have I missed something?"

"You are looking for a job in the business world, aren't you?

"Yes, but—"

"When Stuart mentioned it the other night... Or was it last night? I forget. Oh, no, it was the night of the wedding. Anyway, he said you were having trouble finding suitable employment, and as I am currently looking for a personal assistant, I thought I should give you a try."

Good grief. This was Allie Justus offering her a job!

The very idea boggled her mind. Surely this was answered prayer.

What else, after all, could it be?

Chapter Four

As Allie rattled on, Mary Sofia's whirling mind fixed on the first confusing tidbit of information she'd gleaned, and she automatically repeated it, interrupting the flow of Allie's words.

"Stuart?" The next instant, her befuddled brain offered up the answer to that query. "You mean Champ." Now everything started to make sense.

Allie chuckled. "Sorry. Silly nickname, but he's such a private person he prefers that most people use it rather than his given name."

"I-I see."

She saw a good deal actually. Champ and Allie were a couple, just as she'd imagined. Sometime when they'd recently, and apparently repeatedly, been together—visions of the two of them danced in her head suddenly—Champ, er, Stuart, no *Champ* had mentioned her in passing. Perhaps they'd been discussing Allie's need for a personal assistant, and he had recalled his promise to help Mary Sofia find work. In his estimation, this must have seemed like a great opportunity for her, but for some inexplicable reason, Mary Sofia felt only hurt and disappointment. She imagined watching Champ—she wouldn't think of him, let alone call him, Stuart without his permission—being affectionate with Allie on a daily basis, the way Hugo was with JoJo. The very idea made her stomach churn. Before she could refuse Allie's offer, if offer it was, her own words ran through her mind.

"I'm leaving it all to You, Lord. Everything. Job, romance, marriage, the future..."

A job was a good start. Besides, she had no claim on or expectations of Stuart Champion. A family friend, he'd never shown any personal interest in her. If she'd allowed herself to concoct a few foolish fantasies around him, she had only herself to blame.

Time to grow up, Mary Sofia, she told herself. *God has laid a golden opportunity at your feet.*

After pausing to suck in a deep breath, she said, "It was kind of Champ to recommend me."

"Mm, kind is not the word I most readily associate with Stuart," Allie replied. She laughed then, a throaty sound that managed to convey intimate knowledge. "Although, If this works out, we'll all benefit. You'll have a job, one that brings great experience and excellent contacts, if I do say so myself. I'll have an efficient personal assistant. And Stuart..." She dropped her voice to a sultry hum. "Let's just say I know exactly how to reward him for his…kindness."

Mary Sofia couldn't have replied to that if she'd wanted to. Her chest and throat felt stuffed with down. Fortunately, she didn't have to say a word. Allie seemed to assume that Mary Sofia would accept the job without reservation.

"Once Stu mentioned you, I realized you have all the requisite skills I need. You're the perfect hire, really."

It was Stu now, was it? May Sofia cleared her throat and modulated her voice. "What, um, what skills would those be?"

"You type, do you not?"

"Of course."

"Efficiently, I hope."

"Absolutely."

"And you're familiar with business software."

"Everything from time sheets to accounting," Mary Sofia confirmed.

"I can assume you're a quick learner. You have a college degree, after all."

"Would you like me to send you my GPA records? I only took so long to graduate because I had to work my way through school."

"We'll just say you're a hard worker and leave it at that."

"I am a hard worker," Mary Sofia declared. "My jobs thus far have mostly been in restaurants, I'm afraid. That is, *all* have been in restaurants of one kind or another. But any of my employers will tell you that I'm efficient, dependable, and hardworking. I can give you a list of references, if you like."

"That's not necessary."

"Oh. All right." Frowning, Mary Sofia asked herself what kind of employer didn't want references. Perhaps Allie considered restaurant work irrelevant.

"If you've worked in restaurants, you must've waited tables."

On the other hand, perhaps she considered it disqualifying. Mary Sofia wasn't about to lie, however. "Yes, of course. A-and in some very fine establishments. Most recently—"

"That'll come in handy," Allie interrupted, shocking Mary Sofia into a stunned silence. "I often entertain in the penthouse apartment of our building, and the chef doesn't like to serve at the table unless it's some new dish or something special. You must know how temperamental these trained chefs can be."

Forcing her brain to work, Mary Sofia managed a nod before muttering, "Uh, I do. Actually."

"Another important thing is that you look the part," Allie went on.

"The part of a waitress?"

"The part of my personal assistant. You may not be, well, particularly stylish, but you're presentable. In a sweet way."

Talk about damned with faint praise! Mary

Sofia gulped back an automatic "Thank You" as disingenuous and destructive. Polite was polite, but she wasn't going to sign up to be belittled and bullied. If Allie even noticed her lack of reply, however, she didn't indicate it.

"Now then, Selwyn will fill you in with all the details. Hold." Without so much as a *please* or a nanosecond's wait for a reply, Allie ended the call, her portion of it, anyway.

This time, Mary Sofia's "Thank you," died on her tongue.

She considered hanging up. Something told her that working for Allie Justus wasn't going to be all sweetness and light.

Then again, when had working ever been anything other than, well, work. She reminded herself she'd had no other opportunities dropped at her feet like this. Or any other opportunities at all. The few job interviews she'd had so far had been perfunctory, dismissive, and essentially over before they'd begun. Hugo's job offer didn't count. He didn't actually need her; he was just doing what overprotective big brothers do.

Determined to be excited about this, she stayed on the line. After a few moment, the same male voice she'd heard at the beginning of the call began abruptly speaking.

"If you don't have a pad and pen at the ready, I suggest you get them, and keep them with you until we issue you a company tablet."

Scrambling for pen and paper, Mary Sofia

remarked to herself that it wouldn't have hurt him to say hello. Instead, like his—their—boss, he forged right into the heart of the matter.

"I'll be emailing your personal password so you can go online and fill out the requisite forms electronically. First order of business is your email address. Go."

Blanching, Mary Sofia began reciting her email address, wishing she had something to offer him besides her old college account. "CartergirlUno…" When she got to "uniconnect.free," she could *hear* him rolling his eyes. Why, oh, why hadn't she opened a business email account after graduation? She felt like such an idiot.

"After your paperwork is approved," he informed her briskly, "your email address will be CarterMS at J-R-E-D-I dot org."

"J-R-E-I-D dot org," she muttered, scribbling it down.

"J-R-E-*D-I*," he corrected with a sigh. "That stands for Justus Real Estate Development International, or JREDI, if you prefer." He pronounced the acronym as "jay-ready."

"Jay-ready," she repeated. "J-R-E-D-I. I for International." Interesting.

"Now, then," he instructed, "When Ms. Justus is in the office, you will be in the office, and you should consider yourself on call twenty-four seven. Is that clear?"

Twenty-four seven? "Does that mean

Sundays, too?"

"Sunday, Monday, Tuesday, Wednesday, Thursday, Friday, and Saturday," he answered sharply. "That's seven days a week, twenty-four hours a day. Do you have a problem with that?"

"I go to church on Sunday," Mary Sofia answered meekly.

"No one cares what you do on Sunday. Or any other day of the week," he replied, sounding slightly less confrontational. "I'm not saying you'll work every Sunday. Chances are you won't work any Sundays, frankly. What I am saying is that you should consider yourself on call every day around the clock. Emergencies arise, and when you're needed, you're needed."

"I see."

She should have answered that she would pray about all this and get back to him, but she reasoned that God would not have allowed this opportunity if He didn't have a specific reason for doing so. That being the case, He would see to it that she could worship on Sundays and keep that day holy. Right?

Like Allie, this Selwyn person took Mary Sofia's compliance for granted. He once more began rattling off instructions. "In addition to the tablet, you'll be issued a company phone. Keep both charged and with you at all times. Ms. Justus or I will text you when she wants you to come in early. Otherwise, be at your desk by ten minutes of eight weekday mornings." He went on for twenty minutes, rapidly covering everything from the need for dependable transportation to what to wear. "Our clients and partners expect to see attractive, well-dressed individuals in this office. I hear you have long hair. Cut it or contain it for business settings. That's up to you. Just remember that social settings, and there will be many if you live up to expectations, require a certain...glamour. And I'm not talking high school prom."

Mary Sofia blinked at that. "Social settings?"

"Ms. Justus entertains often on behalf of the company, both here in the penthouse and her home. You won't be expected to attend on every occasion, of course, but when you must attend, you will be expected to present yourself in a fashion that brings credit to the firm."

"I see. All right."

She envisioned elegant soirees with international attendees at Allie's mansion, but when she got to Champ in a classy tuxedo, Allie on his arm in a sophisticated gown, she turned off her imagination and concentrated instead on the job being offered. If offered was the right word. This felt more like a command appearance, and apparently she'd be spending most of her paychecks on clothing, at least at first. That reminded her of a question she should have asked in the very beginning.

"What is the rate of pay, and when are paychecks sent out?"

"Rate of pay?" He paused. She realized later it was for dramatic effect. He needn't have bothered. When he named the figure she could expect as "base pay," she nearly fainted. And this was for an entry level position?

Her heart beating wildly, she sent up a quick prayer. *Thank you, Lord!* Then she began planning with one part of her mind what her initial purchases would be. Office wardrobe first, she decided, with evening wear coming later, after she got a good idea what she'd need. Meanwhile, another part of her mind took care of business.

"When would Ms. Justus like me to start?"

"Monday. Be there by eight-fifteen. Make sure the forms are filled out and returned by close of business today."

"I will. Anything else?"

She had scribbled three full, closely spaced pages of instructions before Selwyn hung up. Then she had to catch her breath and order her thoughts.

Something felt odd, but upon careful reflection she decided that she'd been handed a golden opportunity here. Doubts subsiding, she allowed her excitement to grow. She had a job! A well-paying job in her field of study. It had to be God's doing. After all, when she'd sat down with her university advisor to list possible employers, she'd never once considered Justus Real Estate Development International, or JREDI.

She'd tapped every other HOBBY RUN connection she could think of, including the soft drink manufacturer for which Samson Cody worked, a number of law firms recommended by Drew Camstock, a hotel in Branson, Missouri, suggested by Matt Polo, as well as several local hospitals where Amalie Harter's doctor husband could give her a recommendation. She'd even had Charlie Biggs send her résumé, such as it was, to a record label in Tennessee near her eldest brother, Rey.

Naturally her advisor had insisted that she should apply for jobs with the area's largest employer, also the world's largest retailer, and of course, she'd done so. At the time she'd thought idly that she might somehow wind up working with or near Champ, but she had never considered asking him for a recommendation. Why would she? He'd never been more than polite with her and only briefly so at that. Besides, why tempt fate? She already had a crush on the guy, and throwing herself into his path was no way to avoid the romantic fantasies her imagination so easily conjured. No. The more distance she kept from Stuart Champion the better.

She did owe him a debt of gratitude, however, and no one could say otherwise. That being the case, she decided she really ought to thank him for bringing her to Allie's attention. She couldn't couldn't quite bring herself to make the necessary phone call, however. Just the memory of the sound of his voice, low and husky, sent shivers up her spine. She actually considered writing him a formal letter of gratitude, but in the end she settled for a text.

"I got the job. Finally! And it seems perfect for me. Thank you so much for your kindness. And thank God for this opportunity!"

Stuart, uh, Champ—she had to get that Stuart business out of her head—immediately texted back.

"Excellent. Knew it would work out for you. Look forward to hearing all about it."

She assumed he looked forward to hearing about it from Allie. Ignoring the pang of envy, she told herself that was for the best. She didn't want or need the kind of man who would have an affair. When she married, it would be to an obedient Christian. Just to be on the safe side, she would henceforth consider Champ and Allie engaged. No doubt they would soon make it official, anyway.

Of course, she could be misinterpreting things between the pair. Her judgment about such matters had proved faulty in the past, after all. She shuddered to think how gullible she once had been and how close she had come to ruining her life. All because of her silly, romantic dreams.

No, no. She wouldn't let herself go down that path again. God had sent her a clear message here. Champ was not for her, no matter what the facts of his relationship with Allie were. God had even seen to it that she hadn't spent time in Champ's company looking for a job, so she would wisely keep her distance. She wanted only the right man, the one God would bring to her. Until then, she would concentrate on her career. From this day forward, she was a professional woman.

With that thought fresh in her mind, she adopted a determinedly delighted attitude before calling Hugo with the good news. She left out only Allie's remark about her appearance and that twenty-four hours per day, seven days per week part of the job requirements.

If God had brought her this job—completely out of the blue—then He would surely work out all the attendant details.

It never occurred to her to ponder that tiny *if*.

***

"Have you prayed about this?" Hugo asked, frowning. "Really prayed about it?

He'd said the same thing when she'd called him earlier with the good news. Mary Sofia pulled out a chair and sat down at the dinner table with her big brother and the rest of the family. They always ate around five P.M. so she could join them and still get to the restaurant by six. Relieved that she could give her brother a positive answer, she piled a Mexican rice dish onto her plate as she spoke.

"Actually, I prayed just yesterday for God to

show me His will, and today, out of the blue, Allie Justus calls."

Hugo pondered that while she tasted the dish.

"Mm. This is good, JoJo." Her sister-in-law had grown proficient at the type of meals that her family most enjoyed.

"Thank you. Found the recipe on the back of a can of tomatoes and chili peppers."

Hugo waved his fork. "She's right, sweetheart. It is good."

JoJo sent him the kind of look that made Gabi and Ana glance at each other with wiggly smiles. Before Mary Sofia could shake her head at them, Hugo turned his attention to her once more.

"I'm pleased for you, Sofi." He tended to use the nickname adopted by the family for their most private and heartfelt moments when he was most troubled about something she intended to do. This time, Mary Sofia chose to regard it as nothing more than affection. At least he wasn't forbidding her to take the job, not that he could make that stick.

"Thank you."

"What's next?" JoJo wanted to know. "Are you going to buy a new car? You always said that would be your number one priority."

"Oh, please, buy a new car," Gabi pleaded. "Then I can have yours and get my license. Right?" She glanced hopefully at Hugo.

"Don't rush her," he rumbled, glowering.

Mary Sofia hid a smile as Gabi collapsed into a pout, folding her arms.

"For starters," she said, "tomorrow morning I'm going through my closet to see what I can wear to the office. Then I'm going shopping." She leaned forward, addressing her little sister. "Want to come?"

Gabi immediately perked up, nodding enthusiastically.

"Me, too?" Ana asked.

"If JoJo can spare you."

"Go ahead," JoJo said. "I admit I couldn't make it through a week without you girls, but we manage here while you're at school, you know."

"Do you need money?" Hugo asked Mary Sofia. "You've got tuition loans to consider. I can front you a few hundred, and I'm sure Rey would do the same."

Considering her bank balance, Mary Sofia almost accepted, but then she shook her head. She'd been waiting tables at a good restaurant, beginning several months before her graduation, and she'd been full-time since then, so she'd built up a small reserve. Besides, she didn't have to start repaying her school loans for a while, so she'd have time to pay off anything she bought on credit. She didn't intend to be extravagant by any means.

"You and JoJo do more than enough by letting me live in the garage apartment rent free."

"Like we'd charge family rent," Hugo said, scooping up the rest of his chicken and rice with a tortilla chip, which Lizbet demanded and received.

"You and Rey paid my last semester's tuition, and you gave me JoJo's old car when you bought the minivan. Besides, I'll have plenty of income soon."

"I could use some money," Gabi put in hopefully.

"Me, too," Ana said, waving her hand.

"You both have savings accounts and allowances," JoJo pointed out with a smile.

"Speaking of your car," Hugo said to Mary Sofia, ignoring the girls. "When you're ready, we'll go down and to the dealership and see what we can find. I'll cosign, if necessary."

"Thank you, *hermano* dear, but it's time I grew up and got with the program. Gabi can manage until I can get a loan on my own. I'll be making good money, so it won't be long. Of course, I'll want your advice when it's time to look."

"You got it."

A rush of affection filled Mary Sofia's heart. Overprotective brothers weren't so terrible, really. "Have I told you lately how much I love and appreciate you, Hugo?"

For a long moment, he simply stared at her, but then he folded his arms against the edge of the tabletop and softly said, "You've told me every day since you moved in here, Sofi, with your behavior and hard work. I'm very proud of you and the example you've set for your sisters."

Gulping down a lump of emotion, Mary Sofia whispered, "It's difficult not to be good when your brothers are so wonderful."

He laughed, lightening the mood. "I'm going to remember you said that. And remind you often."

Feeling reassured, she rolled her eyes, got up from the table and left before they both wound up bawling. Despite his cautious nature, Hugo essentially had given the job his blessing. She could go forward with confidence. Before she could do anything else, however, she had to get to her current job and speak to her shift manager, Chet Hamlin.

He deserved to know that he could no longer count on her to serve tables.

Chapter Five

"You're quitting?" Chet demanded, dropping a stack of heavy, leather-backed menus onto the ornate table behind the reception desk. Broad and muscular with short medium brown hair and hazel eyes, he looked older than Mary Sofia, but they were actually about the same age. While she had just graduated with her Bachelor's degree, however, he was almost done with his Master's.

"Yes, and I'm afraid it's short notice," she told him. "I start the new job Monday morning, and it requires me to be on call around the clock, so I can't take any shifts after Saturday."

"Well, that's just great," he said but without the bite she'd come to expect from him.

A little confused, she continued to address the situation. "You wouldn't want me to have to leave in the middle of a shift, would you? I know you'll short-staffed, but this isn't an opportunity I can pass up."

Parking his hands on his hips, he gave his head a shake. "Nope. Wouldn't want that, and your leaving like this does create a big problem for me. But it solves another."

Surprised, Mary Sofia tilted her head. "And what's that?"

He smiled and leaned forward slightly, lowering his voice a notch. "Now I can ask you out. Well, after Saturday. Dating anyone under my management is against company policy, but once you're no longer an employee, we're free to do as we like."

Stunned, Mary Sofia babbled for a few seconds. "Uh...I never realized...that is, I didn't even think you liked me because I refused to work Sundays."

Refused. Past tense. She didn't have time to contemplate the ramifications of her own statement at the moment because she had to keep her mind on the conversation.

"On the contrary," Chet said, leaning back against the table behind him and folding his arms. "Management kept pushing me to get you to change your mind, but the truth is I absolutely admire you for sticking to your convictions."

Flattered, she had to consider the possibilities. The man was attractive enough, not particularly handsome, but certainly not ugly, and he'd been unfailingly professional with her. Until now. Could he possibly be the one?

"*Chet, Lord?*" she queried silently. "*But I don't think he's even a Christian.*" Was this God testing her sincerity and obedience? She decided not to chance it.

"The thing is, Chet, with this new job, I doubt I'll have much time to date."

"You're not dating anyone else, are you?"

"No, but like I said, I doubt I'll have time."

"Why don't I check back with you in a couple of weeks?" he suggested. "By then you should have a better idea what is expected of you. I mean, they can't really expect you to dedicate every waking minute to the company."

He had a point. "Well, as long as you understand that I can't make any promises."

I'll make you one, then. You'll be hearing from me after Saturday. Oh, and good luck with the new job."

The meeting left her feeling somewhat mystified. As she tied on her apron to begin one of her few remaining shifts, she wondered if Chet was a part of God's plan for her. She tried to picture Chet as her groom, waiting at the end of the aisle for her join him, but the image wouldn't quite come together.

Funny, she'd been able to place others there easily. Too easily. Suddenly, her mind's eye zoomed in on her dream groom. Tall, slender, elegantly attired in black and white with a pink rosebud pinned to his lapel, his pale blond hair gleaming in the candle light, she knew even before she looked into his brown eyes that he would be smiling in an intimate, secretive fashion that only the two of them understood. Then she realized the groom in her mental image was Champ. Immediately, she jerked herself back to reality.

"Give me strength, Lord," she whispered. "Give me strength."

She would put Stuart Champion out of her mind entirely. And every other man. Until God showed her otherwise.

Now that she'd set a definite course, her excitement built. Going through her closet the next morning didn't take much time. Her Sunday best comprised the only clothing she possessed that could translate to office work, so she laid out several outfits for the coming week, washed and pressed what needed it and polished two pairs of black heels that had seen better days but would be comfortable. Next, she prepared to pick up her sisters from school, a chore she would be unable to continue after she began working at JREDI. The girls chattered happily all the way home about going shopping together on Saturday.

Mary Sofia felt kind of funny about going to work with Chet again, but he'd been his usual, brisk, distant self the evening before, so she pushed any concerns out of her mind. She had too much else to think about.

The future had finally arrived, and she meant to make a success of it.

***

Stuart couldn't help being confused. Allie had not so much as replied to a text since she'd left him the previous Saturday night. On one hand, he felt a certain relief; on the other, he had to believe they could make each other happy if she would just admit that she loved him. She had to know he was totally committed to her. Didn't she? He just didn't know anymore.

He couldn't even figure out exactly why he'd felt a deep stab of disappointment when Mary Sofia had texted him that she'd found a job, especially after he'd put off helping her. Now, obviously, something had finally come through for her. He ought to feel glad that she'd landed a job to her liking, but he had to admit that he'd looked forward to helping her. Perhaps he had some deep-seated need to play the hero. Another reason he should be relieved rather than disappointed.

Though lovely, Mary Sofia was not his type, or so he told himself. Innocent and open, she possessed a romantic nature that he understood only too well. Unfortunately, he knew from experience that time would strip that from her. Reality would eventually set in. It had for him. As the years had passed he'd endured one disenchantment after another, until he'd given up on the idea of finding a "soul mate."

Now, if he could just stop feeling as if he'd missed another opportunity with Mary Sofia. Nothing about that made sense. He'd barely spoken to the girl over the years, watching from afar as she'd matured from a sulky teen to a lovely young woman, still innocent yet ripe for love. That innocence made him feel old at twenty-nine and dirty because of his involvement with Allie. Perhaps his turmoil stemmed less from the need to play the hero for Mary Sofia as much as it did from a nostalgic longing for the innocence he himself had lost.

Not that it mattered. None of it mattered. He told himself to stop moping, but his preoccupation had been noticed. Late on that Friday afternoon, his boss, Harry Purdle, stepped into his cubicle and parked himself on the corner of Stuart's desk.

"Something wrong, Champ?"

A good manager Harry always had an eye out for his subordinates. Friendly without being intrusive, kind without being a pushover, efficient without being cold, he had earned the respect of everyone in the department. A couple inches shorter than Stuart, fortyish and fit with a blocky build and short, nut brown hair just beginning to go gray at the temples, Harry had one of those unremarkable faces that belied the intelligence and shrewdness with which he operated. More than once he'd obliquely invited Stuart to confide in him, but Stuart didn't feel comfortable letting anyone in on his private life, let alone the boss.

Knowing well how to play the corporate game, Stuart put on a tired smile, leaned back in his chair, and swiveled slightly to appear more open. "Been a tough week, new initiative and all."

"That seems to be coming along well," Harry pointed out.

"Time will tell," Stuart hedged, rocking his chair back into its upright position. The latest feedback on the new project had been very positive, but Stuart liked to have figures to inform up his conclusions, and those hadn't come in yet, so he changed the subject. "I'm just trying to get in the proper frame of mind for tonight's performance with the band."

Harry looked down, pinching the crease in his navy slacks. "Everything going all right there?"

"Oh, yeah. Band's still popular. We've got our sound down to a science now."

To Stuart's surprise, Harry stayed with the subject. "What, exactly, would you say your sound is?"

Stuart lifted a hand to the nape of his neck. Harry had asked a few questions about the band before, but never with this intensity. "Well, it's an eclectic sound. You know, the best of several different disciplines. I mean, we combined a rock band with a jazz band and two duets, one into folk music and the other...hm. I have to say Charlie Biggs and Matt Polo play everything from classical and easy listening to pop and country and western. They're our two true professionals."

Harry chuckled. "Guess that explains the Variety in HOBBY RUN Variety Praise Band."

"Yeah, it does," Stuart agreed, grinning.

"The praise part," Harry pressed, looking Stuart in the eye, "is that serious?"

"What do you mean by 'serious?' Not sure what you're getting at."

Harry shrugged. "It's just that putting 'Praise' in the name makes it sound like a Christian band."

Was Harry implying that being a Christian was a bad thing? Stuart frowned. More and more anti-Christian sentiment had crept into public spaces. Could his job be on the line here? He briefly considered his options, but then he told himself that the least he could do was acknowledge his own faith.

"Yes," he said, hoping he didn't sound as belligerent to Harry's ears as he did to his own. "Everyone in the band is a Christian," he went on in a more moderate tone, "and we play mostly praise songs written by Charlie Biggs or occasionally someone else. Charlie happens to be a very successful songwriter and an accomplished musician."

Nodding, Harry slid off the desk to his feet. "Good to know. The wife and I will have to take in a show sometime. Well, you have a good weekend. I'll see you Monday morning."

Stuart waved a hand in farewell. "Sure thing, boss."

Harry returned his wave and disappeared into the warren of cubicles.

A few minutes later, Stuart shut down his computer and left the office, turning his mind to dinner. He didn't have time for cooking, so he'd have to pick up something on the way home. He'd just turned the corner onto the side street next to his house, a burger and fries cooling in the paper sack on the passenger seat, when his phone rang.

The speaker in the dash of his truck announced, "Allie Justus." Surprised, he hit the connect button on the in-dash screen.

"Hey. What's up?"

"Just thought I'd see what your plans are tonight after the performance."

Wow. Imagine Allie employing normal etiquette. He fought to keep his tone normal as he replied. "Got none really. Why do you ask? Are you wanting to come over?"

"Maybe." Her voice dropped into that sultry, suggestive tone he knew so well, and his body responded accordingly. "What time do you think you'll be home?"

Warring with himself, Stuart took the time to turn into his accustomed bay in the carport and put the transmission into park before he answered. He knew, of course, exactly what'd she's expect, what would happen, if she came over. He just didn't know if he could live with himself if he indulged in one more night of purely recreational sex, but surely if their relationship culminated in marriage, his guilt would dissipate. Wouldn't it? Chilled, he gave her the only answer he felt he could.

"Won't be until late tonight. Too late."

"Tomorrow then."

He set up a little straighter. What was going on here? Allie never gave warning. She just showed up whenever the mood struck her.

"Well, I was thinking about going out to dinner tomorrow evening," he said, just to see what she'd say next.

"Alone?"

He lifted his eyebrows. Talk about odd. "Yeah. Alone."

It hit him then. This was Allie angling for a date. He rubbed his hands over his face, mind whirling. Perhaps the time had come to let go of his few remaining scruples and give her the public acknowledgement she wanted. Maybe then she would admit to loving him, even if she remained adamant in her refusal to marry. It would be best, of course, to begin this public acknowledgment of their involvement away from the band.

Throwing caution to the wind, he asked as casually as possible, "Wanna come along?"

Several seconds of silence passed before she spoke again. "Might as well. I don't have anything else planned at the moment."

He put his head back against the headrest. Would wonders never cease?

"I'm thinking Golucky's. Food's good, and it's

convenient." Plus the owner was a friend from college, someone he might be able to introduce to Allie. Best of all, he'd never seen another band member there.

He held his breath until she said, "Okay. Meet you there at seven?"

Letting out a silent, jittery breath, he said, "Parking's not great around the square, so why don't you stop here and ride with me?"

With both a smile and a challenge in her voice, she retorted, "Why don't I swing by and pick you up? You can ride with me."

He knew just by the way she spoke that she was planning something, but so be it. He'd stepped off the cliff. Too late to worry about the landing.

"Try to be here by six," he told her. "I want to get in before the dinner rush begins in earnest."

"Six it is."

"See you then." She hung up before he could ask if she was coming to tonight's performance, but at least he'd taken that first big step.

One step at a time, he told himself.

He should've known that if he gave Allie an inch she'd take a mile.

She did not show up at the performance, but when six o'clock came around on Saturday evening, she pulled up to the curb in front of his house in her expensive sedan and honked the horn. Shaking his head, he went out the back as usual and walked around the side of the house to the front. She wore a long, satiny black coat and high, stiletto heels. He got in on the passenger side, wearing his customary slacks and a pullover beneath a casual coat.

"Looks like I'm underdressed," he said.

She shrugged, as if it was of no concern to her, and maneuvered the car back into the traffic lane. "How'd the performance go last night?"

"Oh, we had a minor glitch. Bart's mic cut out and had to be replaced. Didn't he tell you?"

"Haven't seen him."

Stuart said nothing to that. Brother and sister avoiding each other in six thousand square feet of house couldn't be that difficult, after all.

She parked the car in the lot of a church about half a block down a side street, so they got out to walk briskly through the cold to the restaurant. The door hadn't even closed at their backs before she peeled off the coat, revealing a black leather dress, sleeveless and absurdly short, with a side slit that reached her upper thigh. At least the neckline cut straight across her collar bone in front. Unfortunately it plunged to her waist in the back. She seemed to be showing yards of skin. He made no comment but let his hand hover in the small of her back as the waiter showed them to a booth.

Stuart asked if the owner was present and felt an awkward sense of reprieve when told that he wouldn't be in that evening. Both Stuart and Allie ordered the special, lobster with a small beef filet, rice au gratin, and asparagus with mushrooms and capers salsa. Allie ordered hers with wine. He asked for iced tea. She put on a pout, leaning against him and complaining while the waiter gathered up the menus.

"A glass of wine won't kill you, you know."

"I know. I just don't care for it."

"You never drink," she went on petulantly, looping her arms around his neck, "not even when I bring over champagne."

"Haven't developed a taste for it," he muttered, alarmed when she started to kiss his neck and ear. The seatbacks were high and the lights fairly low, but they were still in a public place. Then he realized what she was doing and forced himself to relax.

She wanted him to understand that just showing up together in public wasn't enough. Clearly, she wanted no doubt in anyone's mind about the extent of their relationship. He placed his hand on her knee under the table and turned his head for a quick kiss before launching into a conversation about his current project at work. That worked surprisingly well. First and foremost a businesswoman, Allie queried him about the project design and the reasons for it.

"So, by offering endorsements and prime placement for these products, the company gets mentioned on TV and in print, and the logo is shown along with the product."

"And the company pays little to nothing,"

Stuart confirmed, nodding. "There are costs involved, of course. Shelves have to be rearranged, and a special team is formed in each store to make sure the endorsed products get prime placement. Also, the sell-through has to be carefully tracked and reported to prove the return is worth the ad space for the other companies involved."

"That is genius," she told him. "Wish I could think of a way to implement such a thing in my business."

"Hm, maybe by working from the opposite angle. Make a deal with suppliers to mention them and use their company logos for a cut in price."

"Brilliant!" she exclaimed. More than one head turned their way. Just before she looped her arms around his neck again and planted a big one on his mouth.

He felt heat rising to his cheeks from a combination of the compliment and the public display of affection. Breaking the kiss, he quickly reached for his water glass, murmuring, "Just logic."

"No, it's much more than that," she insisted as he gulped water, hiding behind his drink. "I'm serious, Stuart. Would it be possible for you to come by the office and help me lay out some details? I'm definitely going to pursue this, I'm just not sure how to word the offer."

Setting down his half-empty glass, he made

a quick decision. "How does Monday sound?"

A slow smile spread across her face. "We could make it a working lunch."

He nodded, quite certain he wouldn't be running into any HOBBY RUN folks in the offices of Justus Real Estate Development International. "It's a date."

He'd never seen her look quite so pleased.

Yes, he told himself, *this is the right move.*

Hopefully, by the time anyone whose opinion really mattered found out about the two of them, they would be engaged.

That thought made his heart pound.

With hope and excitement.

What else, after all, could it be?

Chapter Six

A t work on Monday morning, Stuart told the boss he'd need extra time for lunch. Allie texted that he should enter her office building by the main lobby and that she'd have Selwyn waiting for him.

When lunchtime came, he found himself surprisingly nervous. Determined, he left his own office twenty minutes early and drove over to the Justus Building, where the much mentioned Selwyn met him practically at the door. Obviously Selwyn had no problem recognizing Stuart, even though they had never before met. Tall, fit, expertly tailored, and with a shaved head, Selwyn could only be described as a very handsome man. His caramel-colored skin stretched tautly over a square chin, strong jaws, high cheekbones, sculpted nose, and slightly slanted eyes as black as the slashes of his eyebrows. He might have been twenty-something or forty, and he didn't balk at making his opinion of Stuart known. With one look, he told Stuart he had been found wanting, that he wasn't quite muscular enough, handsome enough, well enough dressed, or imposing enough to withstand Selwyn's influence or garner his respect. Stuart immediately wondered if Allie had slept with or was sleeping with the man.

Irked at both himself and Selwyn , Stuart put on his friendliest smile and thanked the arrogant dandy for meeting him, before saying, "Let's not keep Allie waiting. I know how much she hates that." Then, without a handshake or waiting for Selwyn to lead the way, Stuart strode toward the elevators.

After he entered the empty elevator car, he saw the button with the shiny new brass plate next to it identifying the twelfth floor as Justus RDI. He also saw an elevator button marked "Private" with a key slot in its center. Allie had mentioned more than once that they could meet in private at her office. She'd even implied that they could "enjoy" themselves without anyone knowing, but Stuart had to wonder just how private that meeting could be. Selwyn surely had a key that would fit perfectly into that slot.

And how many others? he asked himself. Allie had made no promises of fidelity, after all. She could be sleeping with half the town.

Nevertheless, he stuck to his plan. He meant to make a public statement in Allie's world, to show her that he was willing to meet her more than halfway.

When he stepped from the elevator onto

the twelfth floor, Stuart expected to be eyed with interest, but surprisingly, hardly a soul paid him any attention. The receptionist, an attractive brunette with short, spiked hair, sent him a polite smile, saw that Selwyn accompanied him, and went back to whatever she'd been doing. Meanwhile, others came and went from luxurious wood and glass cubicles or talked on phones at their open desks. One striking fellow with a full head of unusual charcoal gray hair, stood propped against a marble pillar, talking on his cellphone in what sounded like Italian. To a person, the employees of Justus Realty and Development International presented as attractive, well groomed, and youthful. Most of the women had short, expertly styled hair, though a few wore their longer hair in sophisticated rolls and buns.

Selwyn walked him through the maze of offices, cubicles, and open desks to the very back of the floor where an entire wall of glass revealed a huge office with a large sitting area furnished classically with expensive sofas and chairs arranged before a stately fireplace, where even now a cheery gas flame flickered around a realistic pile of fake logs. The heat couldn't possibly have reached the large, ornate, desk where Allie sat perusing a computer screen that clearly rose and lowered through a slot in the marble top, but the fireplace did provide a cozy ambiance. Selwyn tapped on the glass door, and she looked around. Then she smiled and waved them inside, rising to come around the desk in greeting.

Stuart smiled back and went to meet her, knowing what would happen even as he walked across the deep pile of an enormous, and probably priceless, Persian rug. True to Allie form, as soon as he drew near, she seized him by the lapels and pulled him in for a hot kiss. He shocked her by sliding his arms around her and giving it his best. Always liking to call the shots, she almost pulled back, but then he felt her soften, and she slid her arms around his neck, pressing against him. When next he looked around, Selwyn had disappeared.

"I'm so glad you came," she said, leaning back to perch on the edge of her desk. "I have a surprise for you."

Quite certain what that surprise would be, he gave her a regretful smile. "I can't stay much longer than an hour," he warned. "So if you really want to discuss business, we'd better get to it."

"Right. Let's head on upstairs then. You can leave your overcoat here, if you like."

He peeled off the long, heavy, camel hair coat and draped it over a chair as she rose to full height again. Catching him by the hand, she led him toward a paneled door at the opposite end of the room from the fireplace.

Only as she swung the door open did he realize a small elevator waited behind it. She tugged him inside and pushed a button. As the steel door slid closed, she wrapped herself around him. Another steamy kiss followed as they swiftly rose to the next floor. When the elevator stopped and the door slid open, they remained entwined for several seconds before she pulled back slightly, glanced outside, and grinned.

"Surprise," she whispered.

He turned his head. Mary Sofia Carter stood there, her cheeks ruddy with embarrassment, dark eyes staring with sad disillusionment at the tableau he and Allie presented. Her long hair had been coiled into a tight knot at the nape of her neck, and he saw at once that her skirt reached several inches lower than Allie's, not to mention those of the other women in the office. Her pale pink blouse buttoned all the way to the top, and the jacket over it, though stylish, did not fit like a second skin. The dusky rose color of her suit flattered her dark hair and eyes, and the wide, pale pink belt emphasized her impossibly narrow waist. Her shoes, high stiletto heels, were very nearly the same shade as her suit, but not quite, just as the pink belt *almost* approximated the pale pink of her blouse. These details, he knew instinctively, had not gone unnoticed or unremarked by Allie and, most likely, her staff. He felt a white hot flash of anger at Allie for subjecting Mary Sofia to certain ridicule and embarrassment, but a deep, paralyzing shame quickly followed.

He'd stepped off the edge of the cliff, and the landing had been catastrophic, indeed. Still, he had no choice other than to pick himself up, dust himself off, and move forward.

Offering what he knew to be a lame smile, he disengaged from Allie and nodded at Mary Sofia.

"I think you know my new personal assistant," Allie said, her voice dripping with honey.

He dropped a hard glare on Allie, but her cat-in-the-cream smile didn't falter. "I thought Selwyn was your personal assistant."

"Selwyn is my right hand," she told him, smiling archly. "I wouldn't demean him with the title of Personal Assistant."

In other words, she had hired Mary Sofia for the express purpose of demeaning her. Stuart bit back a heated reply, pushed aside his qualms, and tried not to look as guilty as he felt, wondering what other mischief Allie had planned. No doubt she had arranged this farce merely because he'd spoken to Mary Sofia and offered to help her find employment, but to what end?

He desperately reasoned that Allie obviously cared more for him than he'd realized. Otherwise, she wouldn't have gone to such lengths to make sure Mary Sofia knew about them. Surely, when his temper and mortification cooled, he would be glad of it. Wouldn't he?

"Your lunch is ready," Mary Sofia announced

shakily, waving her arm at a round, elaborately laid table before a wall of glass at the back of the large room.

For the first time, he noticed the opulent furnishings. A pair of massive sectional sofas covered in white leather took center stage, with various cassocks, oversized chairs, and tables scattered across the space between them. A flat TV or movie screen measuring at least a hundred inches had been mounted on the front wall, with doors on either side of it. A wet bar that would have done any nightclub proud took up a good portion of the other side of the room. A pair of swinging doors behind and to the side of it evidently opened onto the kitchen, while various credenzas and a small desk filled the wall with the elevator in it. Feeling as if he'd stepped into an alternate universe, Stuart allowed Allie to pull him across the room and over to the table, where shallow china bowls of crisp green salads waited on silver charging plates.

He took no notice of the view and barely remembered to pull out Allie's chair for her before taking two hesitant steps to his own. Eyes averted, Mary Sofia expertly snapped open a heavy linen napkin and laid it across Allie's lap before moving down to do the same for him. He beat her to it, appalled that she had entered the business world only to find herself still waiting tables. Murmuring his thanks, he trained his gaze on his salad.

"Let me know when you're ready for the main course," Mary Sofia said in a soft, deferential tone before moving out of sight.

He looked up and saw Allie's smug smile. She didn't even try to hide her pleasure at seeing both him and Mary Sofia discomfited. For an instant, Stuart imagined himself launching across the table to shake Allie and demand apologies from her. In that moment he realized the bald truth. Realized and accepted it.

He didn't love this woman, could never love her, let alone shackle himself to her for the rest of his life.

Even if she should love him in some twisted, demented fashion, he could never respect or honor her as his wife, not that she'd accept a marriage proposal from him. With Allie, wild sex and domineering games were all he'd ever have.

And that was not enough, not even for a sinner such as he had become.

What magnificent irony. He had just outed himself for nothing. Mary Sofia would surely speak of this, and soon everyone he truly held dear would know that he'd indulged in a torrid but pointless affair with a bandmate's sister. He wondered if they would ask him to quit the band, and the bleakness of that possibility washed through him like a bitter waterfall of tears.

Only one good thing would come of this day's doings. He and Allie were over. He'd never again take her to bed. He didn't even want her in his house, if he could help it, let alone his life.

But first he had to get through this lunch with some small measure of dignity and get out of here. Later, in private, he would tell Allie that he never wanted to see her again. Fat chance of that, with Bart now singing lead in the band, but he couldn't think of another way to handle this without diminishing himself even further in Mary Sofia's eyes, if such a thing could be possible.

With shame turning every bite to ashes, he worked his way through the salad, French onion soup, and a remoulade of tender beef wrapped around a filling of truffles. He spoke little, ate as much as he could force himself to swallow, ignored Allie's angry glares and attempts to discuss business, then took his leave after a single bite of sliced apples baked in a high, flaky crust drenched with caramel cream. So angry she made no move to accompany him, Allie sat mute as he thanked her for the lunch. She watched with narrowed eyes as he stepped into the elevator alone.

He let himself into her office, shrugged into his overcoat, then walked through the busy outer floor, avoiding all eye contact. By the time he reached his vehicle in the parking lot, he had himself under control well enough to return to work, but his boss again commented on his distraction as he headed out the door for home at the end of the day.

"You haven't been yourself for a while, Champ. Can I help at all?"

Stuart shook his head. "It's just personal junk."

"That's the worst kind," Harry said, coming forward to clap a hand on Champ's shoulder. "I truly am here to help, you know. If not as your boss, then as your friend."

"I appreciate that, Harry, but this is something I have to handle myself. I'll get it straightened out soon."

"Just know I'll be praying for you."

Stuart nodded, sudden tears burning the backs of his eyes. Harry couldn't know just how much he needed those prayers, how badly he'd screwed up his life, or how helpless he felt to fix it. If only he felt able to seek God's guidance for himself.

* * *

Sick at heart, Mary Sofia put on a brave face, once again determining to make the most of this opportunity with JREDI. She didn't know why seeing Champ and Allie—Ms. Justus, rather—entwined in an ardent kiss made her want to cry. She'd already known about their involvement, after all, and she had no hopes of Champ ever looking her way. Still, she'd almost burst into sobs when that elevator door had opened and she'd seen them together like that. She'd been embarrassed, for herself as well as them. Why that should hurt so, she refused to contemplate.

As she cleaned the small, industrial-style kitchen after Champ's departure, she reminded herself that what he and Allie did together was none of her business and, in the larger scheme of things, didn't matter a whit. No doubt they'd soon announce their engagement, and when they did, she would be happy for them. Meanwhile, she'd perform every task to the best of her ability, however menial, and earn Allie's —Ms. Justus's—respect. Soon, she felt sure, Ms. Justus would assign her more meaningful work.

With the kitchen spotless, Mary Sofia gathered up the tablet and stylus with which Selwyn had replaced her notepad and pen and walked through the door to the right of the media screen. She passed through a short hallway to the public elevator, and pressed the down button to the twelfth floor, then walked past the receptionist, who smirked as if she knew what Mary Sofia felt and thought. Perhaps, Mary Sofia mused, all new employees were assigned table service and kitchen chores at first, not just those with experience waiting tables. She moved through the general office to her desk in the cubicle open to both Selwyn's office and Allie's, er, Ms. Justus's. Oh, phooey! She couldn't be disciplined for calling Allie Justus by her given name in her private thoughts.

As she took her seat, Selwyn walked out of Allie's office, tapping on his tablet. Mary Sofia had noticed earlier that his office contained a private door that opened into Allie's, so he must be off on some errand. He stopped at her desk, but then he just stood there until her own tablet dinged with an incoming message.

"That's your next assignment," he informed her. "Ms. Justus made notes concerning some revisions needed on pending contracts before they go out. You'll find the document names there. You can open them with your personal access code. Clear?"

"Clear," Mary Sofia affirmed, wondering if she was Allie's assistant or Selwyn's. She quickly looked over the revisions, which were minimal. The number of contracts requiring revision was lengthy, however. Before she could comment, Selwyn did so.

"You can go home when you're finished. I'll check your work first thing tomorrow. If it's passable, we can send the contracts out for completion."

Shocked, for this could take hours, she tried not to react with more than a nod. Obviously, they intended to get a full day's work from her, even though she'd spent the morning at her desk learning the company rules and the federal regulations by which she had to abide.

"By the way," he went on brusquely, "Ms. Justus want you to have that suit tailored before you wear it again. The skirt's too long and the whole thing is too large. You look like your grandmother dressed you." Her mouth ajar, she watched him scrape her with a cool, assessing gaze before he said, "You have a nice figure. Learn to use it to your advantage."

"But—" Before she could complete the thought, he simply walked into his office and closed the door.

Deflated and self-conscious, she pulled in a deep, silent breath and went to work. The office gradually emptied as she toiled. She'd realized after the second time she'd typed in the new wording that she'd do better to cut and paste, so she created a separate document with the necessary changes, and thereafter the work went more quickly. Selwyn and the boss lady were the last to leave, excepting Mary Sofia herself, of course.

Allie stopped by long enough to glance down as she slipped on her expensive fur coat.

"Be here by a quarter of eight in the morning. Selwyn will show you how to make the coffee and where to find the day's schedule."

So she was expected to make the coffee, too. So be it.

"Yes, Ms. Justus."

Allie strode away before Mary Sofia could get out a "goodnight." Sighing mentally, Mary Sofia went back to the computer terminal. The time showed 6:17 PM. She'd barely opened the next document before Selwyn appeared, a cashmere coat folded over one arm.

"Don't forget to log out. You won't need to

turn off the lights or lock up. The lights shut off when the last person leaves, and the elevator to this floor stops operating at five-thirty."

Appalled, Mary Sofia blurted, "You mean I have to walk down?"

He gave her a derisive look. "You can ride the elevator *down* by scanning your key card, but without an override code it won't bring you back *up* until seven-thirty in the morning. And the doors to the stairwells lock behind you, so you can't get back in that way without your key card, either. The system records who comes and goes, by the way." With that he shrugged into the coat and walked away, shaking his sleek head.

"How was I to know that?" she muttered under her breath, going back to work.

Another twenty-two minutes passed before she could call it quits. She made it home about ten minutes after seven o'clock, due to having left the office after the rush hour traffic between Bentonville and Fayetteville. Hugo, as expected, opened the front door of the house just as she got out of her car, his standard poodle, Bitsy, at his side.

"You're late."

"Killer first day." She pulled her handbag and tablet from the car's passenger seat.

"We held dinner for you."

"Oh, you shouldn't have done that," she protested, just then realizing how hungry she was. "But I am starving."

"Come on in and tell us about it."

Reluctantly, she followed him into the house. Relatively large and comfortable, the place had originally belonged to Amalie Harter and her two sons before her marriage to Dr. Tate Golden. She'd practically given the house to JoJo, who had previously lived in the garage apartment that Mary Sofia now shared with Gabi. Hugo and JoJo had acquired the more formal house next door after their former neighbor Horace Everett had passed away. He'd willed his house and every other material possession he owned to JoJo and given Bitsy, a standard poodle with an uncanny way of knowing when the triplets got into something they shouldn't, to Hugo. So, the big, tough Marine had himself a poodle that left his side only to corral the triplet toddlers that made mayhem of the house.

JoJo, who had never returned to her job as a print shop manager after the COVID lockout, sold the Everett property and invested the proceeds. She and Hugo had disobeyed the retired college professor's edict that they not name anyone after him and called their son by Hugo's middle name and the irascible neighbor's surname. Marc Everett, wearing pajamas, waited just inside the door for her.

He lifted his thin arms, greeting her with, "Sofi, hold."

As tired as she felt, she couldn't deny the

boy. Laying her capacious handbag containing the ubiquitous electronic tablet on the hall table, she shucked her coat, hung it over another one on the hall tree, bent, and lifted the boy into her arms. He laid his head on her shoulder.

"He's ready for bed, as you can see," Hugo told her, "but we had to coax him into the bath by promising he would see you before he goes to sleep."

Bitsy suddenly darted into the hallway, an instant before an angry toddler shrieked in protest from another part of the house. A pitiful wail followed.

Mary Sofia heard JoJo say, "Oh, good grief. Give me that. The toothpaste goes on the toothbrush, not your sister's hand. I can't take my eyes off you girls for a single moment."

Hugo called, "I'm coming," before offering Mary Sofia an apologetic smile and taking Marc Everett from her. "Head into the dining room while I help JoJo brush teeth. Gabi's getting the food out of the oven. The kids have eaten," he went on, carrying the boy past her, "but she insisted on waiting for you with JoJo and me."

Touched, Mary Sofia walked into the large dining room. The dining table, the natural cracks in the dark wood inlaid with precious metals, never ceased to awe. Hugo had outdone himself with the design and construction of this particular piece, not that everything he designed and built wasn't unique and beautiful. Gabi had just arranged the platter of chicken breasts to her satisfaction when Mary Sofia entered the room.

Surrounded by quartered potatoes and long, elegant green beans, the slow-cooked chicken breasts were Mary Sofia's favorite dish. Placed frozen in a crockpot with large slices of onion on the bottom and the potatoes and green beans on top, JoJo seasoned the pot with salt, pepper, and minced garlic, then left everything to cook for three or four hours. Not only did the results taste delicious and the chicken all but dissolve in the mouth, the dish was so simple to make Mary Sofia had added it to the recipe book hidden in the hope chest Hugo had made for her.

That hope chest held everything of great significance that she owned. When her mother burned down their house, she'd also burned nearly every heirloom and photograph in their possession. The exception was the scorched Spanish Bible that her *abuela*, or grandmother, Ana Sofia, had given Mary Sofia on the day of her baptism. Ana Sofia had also made an elaborate veil, which she hoped her three granddaughters—Mary Sofia, Gabrielle, and Ana —would each use in turn. Not to be outdone, her *abeulo*, or grandfather, had carved each of his granddaughters a jewelry box from Mesquite wood. The pearl necklace belonging to her paternal great-grandmother, whom Mary Sofia had never known, now rested inside Mary Sofia's box.

Having no children of her own, Aunt Mildred, her father's only sibling, had sent the pearls to Mary Sofia. Aunt Mildred had also sent pieces of jewelry to the other girls and tokens belonging to her late father to each of her nephews, Rey, Hugo, and Tomas. Besides the Bible, veil, jewelry box, pearls, and recipe book, Mary Sofia's hope chest included a delicate lace tablecloth that had supposedly passed from eldest daughter to eldest daughter through the Carter family for six generations. Aunt Mildred, who had no children of her own, had confessed that she hated to part with it but that it belonged with Mary Sofia, the eldest granddaughter. She'd hoped someday to lay the table with it for the first meal she cooked and served her husband.

She wondered if she would ever have that honor.

Meanwhile, she had reason to celebrate with the meal laid out before her here and now.

She would not fail to thank God for it.

No matter how trampled her silly heart felt.

Chapter Seven

Gabi shyly offered the bread basket, saying, "They're just canned crescent rolls, but I rolled them up myself."

Mary Sofia went to hug her sister. Suddenly, she felt so tired she thought she might collapse. Realizing what was happening, Gabi quickly pushed her big sis onto a chair. She slid an arm around Mary Sofia's slumped shoulders.

"Are you okay?"

"You know what? I forgot to eat lunch," Maria Sofia said, just now realizing it. The Justus Building contained a sandwich shop on the lower floor, but most of the staff went out to eat. She hadn't had time or inclination for either prospect. From now on she'd take her lunch. Propping her elbow on the table, she rested her forehead in her upturned palm. "And it's been a trying day."

"If the work's too hard for you," Hugo said, coming into the room, "then quit. You can find another job."

"No, no, it's not that," Mary Sofia told him, lifting her head and squaring her shoulders. "It's not physically tiring." Although she had spent a good part of the day on her feet. "It's just a lot to absorb." She smiled wanly and attempted to change the subject with, "Champ stopped by today." Hugo's gaze sharpened, and she immediately regretted the words. "To see Allie. In fact, they had lunch together." She neglected to say that she'd served them or that she'd had to wash up the dirty dishes afterward. Hugo relaxed somewhat.

"So it's true then. Champ and Allie Justus are seeing each other."

Mary Sofia made herself smile and nod. Did everyone suspect? Had she been the last to realize what was going on?

JoJo walked in. "Are you still gossiping about that, Hugo?"

"It's not gossip," he defended with feigned smugness. "It's fact. Mary Sofia just confirmed that Champ and Allie are an item."

"They had lunch together today," Gabi said, folding her arms. She looked sympathetically at Mary Sofia, who wished a hole would open in the floor and swallow her. Apparently, her little sister could read her like a book. She had to hope that no one else could.

"That doesn't mean they're a couple," JoJo said dismissively.

"Oh, but they are," Mary Sofia heard herself say.

JoJo sent a sharp gaze her way. "Are you sure

about that?"

Wincing inwardly, Mary Sofia tried to make light of her next words. "Well, the lip lock they were in seemed pretty convincing." She added a chuckle, but no one seemed amused.

Hugo actually frowned. "That doesn't mean it's serious."

"Oh, it's serious."

Hugo lifted his eyebrows. "And how do you know that?"

Mary Sofia shifted in her chair. "Um, Allie as much as told me so at the wedding reception. In fact, I wouldn't be surprised if they announce their own en-engagement soon."

The wrinkles on Hugo's brow smoothed. "Ah. That's all right, then. A bit unexpected, but if they're happy together..."

JoJo shrugged and moved to her chair, which Hugo pulled out for her. "I guess it makes sense."

"I thought he had better taste," Gabi grumbled, plopping onto her own seat.

"That," said Hugo, taking his place at the head of the table, "makes two of us."

JoJo lightly admonished them both. "Now, now. None of us really know Allie that well."

"I know she's snooty," Gabi said.

"That's an unchristian thing to say," Hugo scolded mildly, "and the word is pretentious."

"What she is is vastly successful," JoJo insisted, "and we really don't know anything else about her, other than she's divorced."

"And beautiful," Mary Sofia said, trying not to sound envious. She must have failed, for the others stared at her. "It really isn't any of our business, though, and I shouldn't be telling tales outside of work." She put on a smile, which she spread around the table. "Thank you all for dinner. Let's pray and eat. I'm hungry, and it smells so good."

"Amen to that," JoJo said, "and we'd better hurry. Ana's reading to the triplets."

"Which means anarchy will soon reign," Hugo put in happily, reaching for his napkin. Linen, in Mary Sofia's honor.

The mood sufficiently lightened, Hugo prayed over the meal, and they ate. If Mary Sofia seemed a little too cheerful and praised the meal a little too highly, everyone tacitly refused to notice. They finished the meal and even managed to start on pieces of the store-bought apple pie Gabi insisted the occasion merited before squeals and screams sounded from the back of the house.

JoJo sighed, and Hugo instantly stood. "This is a dad job."

"Mmm," JoJo hummed, winking at Mary Sofia and Gabi. "Just don't wrestle them to the point they're too hopped up to sleep."

On his way out the door, Hugo grinned at her. "Just save me another slice of that pie."

Fresh screams sent him scurrying. Gabi snickered, and Mary Sofia laughed, while JoJo cocked her head.

"That particular scream means Lizbet pulled Caro's hair. For the tenth time today." Smiling, she went back to eating her pie. Envy stabbed Mary Sofia so deeply that she couldn't breathe for a moment. She pushed away the remainder of her pie, declaring that she couldn't eat another bite.

After the dessert dishes were stacked, Mary Sofia offered to help clean up the kitchen, but neither Gabi nor JoJo would allow it.

"It's a one-dish meal, as you know," JoJo pointed out. "Besides, I used a liner in the crock pot."

Mary Sofia allowed herself to be sent off with smiles. She slung her coat over her shoulders and picked up her bag before going out to climb the stairs to the apartment, both energized and warmed by the meal and the company. Telling herself that she had too much to be thankful for to let herself become depressed over a man with whom she'd never had a chance, she mechanically got ready for bed. Only later, beneath the concealing covers of her small bed, did she cry. Speaking to God through the silence of her tears, she asked that He help her put away the dream of Stuart Champion once and for all.

Thankfully, sleep claimed her a few minutes later, and she at last found rest.

**

Stuart did not rest easily that night. He

kept seeing Mary Sofia's stricken face when that elevator door had opened. The disappointment in her eyes made it all the more necessary that he formally end his relationship with Allie.

After their somewhat public luncheon, he'd expected Allie to show up before bedtime, gloating over her little surprise that day. Not only had Allie failed to show, however, she'd ignored his texts asking her come over. Finally, writing that they needed to talk, he'd offered to come to her, something he'd never before done.

She'd texted a terse reply. "Not tonight."

Knowing that she'd have been thrilled to welcome him to her palatial home any other time, he reasoned that she must realize how unhappy he was with the situation. On the other hand, Allie didn't always seem sensitive to the feelings of others, so he decided to give her the benefit of the doubt. Perhaps she thought he was fine with Mary Sofia witnessing that passionate kiss, or she could have a business thing going on tonight. He wouldn't know because she rarely apprised him of her schedule. Their relationship had never called for that.

Regardless of why she stayed away, he shamefully admitted to himself that he felt more than a little relief at not being able to confront her that night. He urgently wanted the breakup over and behind him—if it could even be called a breakup—and he'd prefer to do it in private. At the same time, he dreaded the confrontation.

Allie didn't like being called to account, so the chances were better than even that she'd make a scene.

He could always ghost her, simply go silent and unresponsive. She'd eventually get the idea, especially if he didn't answer the door when she next showed up at his house. He'd have to change the locks to make that work, though. Besides, he couldn't bring himself to do it. He'd taken the coward's way out long enough. He might be a terrible sinner, but he could still make some claim to being a gentleman.

Small comfort that. Too small to allow him to relax and sleep well, despite his unusual exhaustion.

At some point, he finally nodded off, only to dream of that horrified look on Mary Sofia's face when that elevator door had opened. It didn't matter that he hadn't actually seen her face at that particular moment; what he'd seen moments after the door opened was bad enough. He could imagine all too well what she must have looked like at the moment of exposure. Jerking awake, he mentally banished the image, only to drift off again and dream of a screaming showdown with a vengeful Allie.

Filled with dread, he hovered the rest of the night in that netherworld between sleep and wakefulness, his mind churning up images of his bandmates when they found out about the affair. In his mind's eye, he saw their disappointed, contemptuous expressions. He felt their censure and the deep well of loneliness that threatened to imprison him, holding him forever apart from the love and companionship he craved.

Then his thoughts circled back to Mary Sofia, and a sense of loss he didn't understand overwhelmed him. He saw her placing dishes on the table in front of him and Allie, then withdrawing them again as unobtrusively as possible, her dark eyes bruised with pain. He'd wanted to take her by the hand and lead her out of there, but she needed the job, and he had no right to influence her life or decisions.

He did owe her an apology, if only for mentioning her job search to Allie, maybe even for having an affair with a jealous, vindictive woman and blowing his Christian convictions all to hell. If Allie abused her in any way, it would be his fault.

Suddenly, he couldn't stand that bed one second longer. Jolting into full wakefulness, he threw back the covers and leapt to his feet. Alarmed, Trooper lifted his massive head with a deep, growling, "Ooof."

"I'm taking a shower," Champ barked at the dog, as if the mutt could understand him. Sensing nothing dangerous afoot, Trooper laid his head down again and blew out a deep breath, as if settling in for another long nap. Champ tried not to resent that as he banged into his bathroom.

Once there, he felt an almost overwhelming need to drop to his knees, but the idea of facing God felt even more daunting than the idea of confronting Allie. He quickly turned on the water in the shower and let it heat up to the point of stinging before stepping inside. Only afterward, sitting at the kitchen table with a cup of rapidly cooling black coffee, did he think of taking a long run, but that should have taken place before the shower, not after. He dropped his head. He couldn't even get that much right.

His appetite absent, he chugged the coffee and got to his feet. It wouldn't hurt to go in to work early.

He arrived at his office a full hour before the official start of the workday, only to find Harry and three other members of their forty-person department huddled together over Bibles in the breakroom. Unaware of his presence, they laughed and talked together, while he stood back and watched, contemplating how to get past a wall of glass without being seen. He heard someone mention the second chapter of First Peter.

"Grow up in your salvation," another man, Bill Beck, quoted. He patted his protruding belly. "Well, I've grown out. Don't suppose that counts."

Everyone chuckled, with Harry quipping, "I wish." He glanced around then and spied Stuart trying to slip past to his cubicle. Smiling in welcome, Harry waved a hand, calling out, "Champ! Join us." He waved again. "Join us."

Champ backed up a step to the open doorway. "Didn't mean to disturb you. I, um, have some work to catch up on."

"Stay," Harry urged. "Just for a moment. We have welcome news."

"And donuts," Bill added, pointing to a box on the counter next to the table. That brought more chuckles. Bill reached back and pulled a chair from another round table to theirs, while everyone else scooted closer to make room.

Reluctantly, Champ stepped through the doorway, draped his overcoat over the back of the chair Bill had pulled up for him, and sat.

"The four of us meet once a week for Bible study before work," Harry explained, getting up to pour Stuart a cup of coffee. Selecting three donuts, he stacked them on a paper napkin. "We usually meet on Mondays, but Coop had to be out of town. As I'm sure you know." Turning, he set the coffee in front of Stuart. "So, we shifted to Tuesday for this week." Using both hands, he carried the donuts to the table and set them beside Stuart's coffee before retaking his seat.

Well aware of Al Cooper's mission, Stuart sipped his coffee and smiled at the other man. "How'd that go?"

"Well," Cooper answered. "From now on, every New Man commercial will include a line saying that their latest razors are now available at…" He wiggled his well-groomed eyebrows. "…the nation's largest retailer."

"That was a great idea you had," Harry said, smiling at Stuart, "and Coop obviously did a great job presenting it." He spread the smile to the other man. "So, I've let the top brass know and recommended you both for bonuses."

Cooper pressed his hands together and looked to the ceiling. "Thank You, Lord." Straightening in his chair, he winked at Harry, adding, "The wife will be pleased."

Stuart couldn't help thinking that he had no wife, or anyone else, to be pleased for him. He didn't even have anyone to tell. Trooper certainly wouldn't care. Nevertheless, he approximated a smile and accompanied it with a nod of gratitude for Harry and the others. As for thanking God, he very much doubted God had anything to do with him being included in the praise report and recommendation. Harry, after all, couldn't very well spotlight Cooper's service without mentioning Stuart's when everyone knew he had proposed the advertising scheme. He'd even come up with the list of initial products to be highlighted and the companies to approach.

The whole thing was a no-brainer. Shelf space at the world's largest retailer came highly contested, especially premium shelf space. This new advertising scheme could save the company millions of dollars in promotional costs, so the acquisitions department had granted eye-level placement for the products from vendors who agreed to the cross promotion. Cooper, a seasoned salesman and negotiator, had secured that agreement on both ends, first pitching the idea to the necessary departments within the company, then selling it to the vendors.

A look passed between Bill and Harry.

"You oughta join us next week for Bible study," Bill suggested to Stuart.

"You and Coop sure make a good team," Harry pointed out. "Bible study will bring you closer together. I know you're a Christian because you play with that praise band."

Cooper beamed at Stuart, who wished he could crawl under the table. These men wouldn't dare invite him into their weekly Bible study if they had any inkling of his true nature.

Shoving back his chair, he gathered the donuts into one hand, tossed his overcoat across one shoulder, and picked up his coffee with his free hand. "I'll think about it," he said as congenially as he could manage. Then he simply bolted, calling out, "Gotta get to work. Thanks for the donuts, guys."

He didn't realize he'd failed to thank Harry for the commendation until he reached his desk, where he sat down, put his head in his hands, and tried to gather his wits. Somehow, the idea of being singled out for attention and recommended for a bonus made him feel even worse, but he shoved aside all thoughts and feelings to concentrate on work.

Powering up his computer terminal, he signed in and began searching out the particulars of the next vendor who might be willing to mention the world's largest retailer in their commercials. Because premium shelf space was limited, he had to cast aside those already with favorable spots, concentrate on the newest products, and research the price point of each unit. The work was detailed and painstaking, and it didn't help that his mind kept wandering. He ate the donuts and downed the coffee by rote. When he rose to refill his cup, he found the office populated and the morning well underway. He hadn't even noticed the growing activity around him. Neither had he accomplished much of anything.

Buckling down, he had lunch delivered and ate at his desk, determined to make progress, but quitting time arrived without any notable results. Tonight being Tuesday, the night reserved for weekly practice with the HOBBY RUN band, he couldn't simply stay late to make up for it, though he would've preferred that. His friends and bandmates must all know of his involvement with Allie by now. Surely Mary Sofia had made mention of it, if only in passing. Why wouldn't she? The idea tied knots in his stomach.

Suddenly he felt an overwhelming need to talk to Mary Sofia. He not only needed to apologize, he had to warn her to beware of Allie's intentions. Given the situation, it seemed wise to speak to her face-to-face. She might not answer a phone call from him, but she was too sweet and polite to ignore his physical presence. He decided to drive through the Justus Building parking lot to see if he could catch her there for a moment of private conversation.

Thankfully, he saw Allie's empty parking space as soon as drove up to the lot, and to his relief, he recognized Mary Sofia's little coupe, parked off in the far corner. He'd seen her climbing in or out of it more than once. Checking the time, he estimated that he had an hour or so to spare before he had to find something to eat then drive over to Centerton for practice. He parked near Mary Sofia's vehicle and waited.

People were already coming out of the building in varying numbers, some in groups, some alone. Before long, the parking lot sat essentially deserted. Finally, Mary Sofia exited through the front door, along with a few stragglers. Quickly, he got out of his truck and walked over to lean against the driver's door of her car. The instant she spotted him, she came to an abrupt halt. Then she ducked her head and continued to move forward.

"Hello," Stuart said as soon as she drew near, his voice sounding too hearty even to his own ears. "How are you?"

"Fine," came the reply. She seemed a little tentative, a bit wary.

Sighing inwardly, he abandoned all pretense and got right to the point.

"Look, Mary Sofia, I owe you an apology for that display yesterday. I know you were shocked. I could see it on your face, and I want you to know nothing like that will ever happen again."

"You don't owe me an apology," she said quietly, her gaze on the keys in her hand. "It's just...I didn't know you were the guest. I was told it was business."

"It was supposed to be business. Partly, anyway. If I'd known you were going to be there, I'd certainly have behaved with more decorum."

"It's not your fault," Mary Sofia insisted, looking past him into the distance. "If she'd told me to expect you, I'd have known there was going to be...personal stuff, and kept out of your way."

That didn't sound right. Stuart tilted his head, trying to make sense of what he'd just heard.

"What do you mean you'd have known there would be personal stuff? What would make you think that?"

After a slight pause, she slowly said, "Well, Allie as good as told me."

"Told you what exactly?"

"Um, that the two of you are...involved."

"And when did she as good as tell you this?" he asked, trying to keep a grip on his temper. "Before or after she hired you?"

"Before. At the wedding reception. I mean, she didn't come right out and say...that is, it was the way she said it more than anything else."

"Say what?"

"Ah, she was talking about long hair looking unprofessional in a business setting. She said it was too much trouble to put it up every day. A-and that short hair went easily from the boardroom to the...bedroom."

"And from that you deduced we were involved?"

Her gaze finally met his. "Was I wrong? I-I mean there were other, um, hints."

He shook his head, unable to hold her gaze. "You weren't wrong. I'm just sorry she mixed you up in our private business."

"It did seem somewhat...um, calculated."

"It was. It's all about her jealousy of you."

"Jealousy? She's jealous of me?" Mary Sofia chuckled dryly. "That makes no sense."

"Oh, but it does," he told her. "She knows you're beautiful in a wholesome, endearing way that she can never be."

"B-beautiful?" Mary Sofia stammered. "Me?"

"Your inner beauty outshines even your outer beauty," he told her softly, realizing the truth of that as he spoke the words. Clearing his throat, he told himself to get a grip. The last thing he should do was come off as flirtatious; that wouldn't be fair to either of them. Even if he hadn't given her a complete disgust of himself, he wasn't the right man for her. Her brothers would never approve, and he couldn't blame them. He got back to the point of this meeting. "I need you to promise me something."

"Oh? What's that?"

"I need you to promise me that you'll let me know if she fires you or embarrasses you or mistreats you in any way. Do you understand?"

"I...I think so."

"Promise," he insisted. "Please, Mary Sofia. I won't rest easy until you do." And probably not even then.

"All right," she said reluctantly. "I promise I'll tell you if any of that happens."

He rubbed a finger over one eyebrow. "Good. I'll let you go and get out of this cold now. But I meant what I said. I'm sorry for letting you get mixed up in my messed up relationship with Allie, and if you suffer for it, I'll put it right, whatever it takes."

"Don't worry about that," she told him. "It's fine."

But it wasn't fine. Allie had no business involving Mary Sofia in this. Then again, he'd had no business getting involved with Allie in the first place, so however he cut it, he was to blame. That being the case, he would do whatever he must to protect and aid Mary Sofia.

Of the three of them, she alone was innocent, after all.

And he would not have her suffer the

slightest indignity.

For any reason.

Chapter Eight

W ith the engine of her little coupe idling, Mary Sofia watched Stuart slide into his truck and drive off. She rubbed her hands together absently, having decided not to bother with gloves as she'd left the building, but then she hadn't counted on meeting him in the parking lot and standing outside in the cold to talk. She couldn't decide quite what to make of his apology, let alone his insistence that she notify him of any problems she might encounter on the job. For some reason, she couldn't seem to concentrate on either aspect of the conversation, because what stuck in her mind, what repeated incessantly in her inner ear, were undoubtedly the words she probably should dismiss and forget.

"She knows you're beautiful in a wholesome, endearing way that she can never be...your inner beauty outshines even your outer beauty."

To have Stuart Champion say such things to her not only astounded her, it confused her. How could he be in love with Allie and compliment another woman in such a fashion? The only reasonable conclusion was that he saw her as a little sister, and wasn't that just what she needed? Another big brother.

The apology itself made some sense. After all, her emotions must've been as plain for him to see as that kiss had been for her. She'd been embarrassed and disappointed to see the two of them like that. But she shouldn't have been. She had known already that he and Allie were deeply involved, so she shouldn't have reacted as she had. Her immaturity and lack of sophistication couldn't have been more obvious, so it was no wonder he felt somewhat responsible. He'd helped her get the job with Allie, only to realize that she wasn't quite ready for it. Perhaps she never would be. At this point, she wasn't even certain that she wanted to be. Yet, what other option did she have, other than taking a pity position with her brother's fledgling company?

Perhaps God was trying to show her that what she thought she wanted wasn't what was best for her. Or was this meant to be a step toward the maturity she obviously lacked? God certainly had a purpose here. After all, she'd prayed for a job and His will, and suddenly a job had been dumped right in her lap, a job Champ had helped her get.

She realized suddenly that she had never really thanked him for that. Here he was taking responsibility for any inadvertent harm he might have caused her, and she hadn't even had the decency to thank him for his help.

The car's heater finally started blowing warm air, and as the chill left her, she reasoned that God would eventually reveal His purpose in placing her at JREDI. It didn't matter what that purpose might be, Champ had obviously played a significant role in it, and she hadn't thanked him. She hadn't even thanked him for his compliments!

His words ran through her mind again, but this time certain words stood out, their significance unmistakable. Wholesome. Endearing. Inner beauty. That didn't exactly put her on a level with Allie, and maybe that was the whole point. Maybe God wanted her to understand that she could not, should not, aspire to the kind of glamour that came so easily to women like Allie. Maybe she should learn to be content with any wholesome and endearing beauty she possessed. Certainly, as a Christian, she should value inner beauty over physical beauty.

Bowing her head, she whispered a prayer. "Thank You, Lord. I know I should be content with how You made me. Help me not to try to be anything other than what You want me to be. Instead, make me grateful for all that I am and all that I have, for every blessing You have so generously bestowed."

Resolved, she decided not to put off thanking Champ for his part in landing her the job at

JREDI. She also needed to let him know that he shouldn't worry about her. He wasn't responsible for her wellbeing, and she certainly didn't want to cause problems between him and Allie.

"I give up my romantic notions about Champ," she said, looking up at the ceiling of her car. "I yield them to You, Lord. In the holy name of Christ Jesus. Amen."

Feeling much more settled, she put the transmission in gear and began the drive home.

***

Stuart felt better after speaking to Mary Sofia, more able to meet the coming confrontation head on. Now that he thought about it, he always felt better after speaking to her, however minor or short the conversation. She just had that effect on people. As he wolfed down a burger and fries at a fast food joint, he pondered what awaited him. Mary Sofia would never stoop to actual gossip. Still, he couldn't expect—and would never ask—that she not mention to others what she had witnessed with her own eyes yesterday. He had to expect that she'd say something, if only in passing, and that undoubtedly would be enough to get the ball rolling. He worried that Bart would hear from others about his affair with Allie before he had a chance to tell Bart himself. He felt he owed Bart that much.

The old Bart might well put in an appearance and sock him in the jaw once he confessed;

Stuart almost hoped that happened. A blow to the chin would be preferable to seeing the disdain in Bart's eyes, and it might help blunt what Stuart feared most, the censure of the rest of the band. Given that, missing practice felt like a possibility for a while.

Others had missed practice, even performances, but not Stuart. That being so, his absence would undoubtedly draw attention and result in speculation, and if Allie happened to be there, as she often was, she wouldn't hesitate to confirm and inform every innuendo. Even those who wouldn't join in the talk would wonder, and it would all be waiting for him the next time he showed up. Besides, he deserved whatever he got, so he might as well go and be done with it. Time to set the record straight. Surely he had the gumption to do that, at least. He just hoped no unexpected visitors would be at practice that evening.

Stuart alone had never brought a guest to practice, or a performance, for that matter. Several of the women he'd dated had seemed interested in him only because of his association with the band, so Champ had balked at bringing them around the others. A couple times he'd contemplated introducing a particular female to his friends, but the relationships simply hadn't lasted long enough for him to follow through. Mostly, he just hadn't felt close enough to the women he'd dated to endure even the good-natured ribbing he knew he'd get from the rest of the gang. The sad truth was that the band was the closest thing to family he had, and he wanted them to think well of him.

Faint hope that.

He actually sat in his Jeep outside the Ogilvie place for several minutes, trying to pray for courage, when a tap on his window jerked his head around. The sight of Mary Sofia smiling at him through the glass made his heart leap. He fought the urge to press his hand against his chest.

"We seem destined to meet in parking lots," she said, her voice muffled by the closed door. "Didn't mean to startle you."

Bracing himself, he rolled down the window and managed to get out the words, "No, it's okay. I'm just surprised to see you again so soon."

Hunching her shoulders inside a billowy, pearl pink coat, she tilted her head. "I wanted to come because I didn't have an opportunity to thank you earlier."

Stuart tilted his head. Had he heard that right? "Thank me?"

"You know, for the job. I don't want you to feel responsible for how it might turn out just because you recommended me to Allie."

Recommended? Dumbfounded, he gaped at her for several heartbeats before he could formulate a reply. "Mary Sofia, I didn't recommend you to Allie. I didn't even know she had an opening to fill."

Surprise flitted across her face, but then the smile returned in rather determined fashion. "For mentioning me to her, then. Now that I think of it, that's exactly what she said, not that you'd recommended me but that you'd mentioned I was looking for a position."

That he had surely done, and now he regretted it. Deeply. "So she was scheming all along," he muttered, more to himself than Mary Sofia. "She hired you to make sure you knew about us."

"Well, I like to think I do have some skills to offer," Mary Sofia said lightly, sounding a bit aggrieved.

Appalled, his gaze snapped to hers. "Of course you do. I didn't mean to imply otherwise."

He watched her suppress the negative emotions and put on her smile again. "T-To be fair, most of the work is new to me."

Not the waiting tables part, however. He bit back those words and instead said, "You promised to tell me if she mistreats you in any way." He could imagine Allie firing Mary Sofia in a huff once he broke off things with her.

"I will," Mary Sofia promised again, "but I really don't think that's likely to happen." Her smile looked strained now.

Compelled to set her mind at ease, he hurriedly said, "And remember, I can always look for a place for you with my company. In fact,

I've gained a little influence since we first spoke. My boss recommended me for a bonus." Maybe that was why God had let Harry call him to the attention of higher-ups, for her sake. Why, after all, would God go out of His way to bless a sinner like him?

"That's wonderful!" Mary Sofia crowed. "Congratulations." She sounded sincerely pleased, despite the clacking of her teeth.

Realizing that he was keeping her standing out in the cold again, he opened the car door, paused to roll up the window, and got out.

"It's not that big of a deal," he told her. He opened the rear door and retrieved his electric guitar in its case. "Another guy and I worked out an advertising venture with a new vendor. Looks like it could save some serious money, so..." He shrugged, depressing the button that locked the vehicle, and pocketed his keys before using his free arm to turn her toward the building. "We're both getting bonuses."

She beamed at him. "Stu—" Abruptly breaking off, her steps slowed, and she ducked her head. "I mean, Champ. I'm so happy for you."

As she'd fallen behind him, he stopped and turned to face her. She wouldn't meet his gaze, tucking her chin into the collar of her coat, her hands buried in the pockets.

Stamping feet shod in fur lined, vinyl ankle boots, into which her brown leggings had been tucked, she murmured, "Sorry."

He seemed to keep missing parts of the conversation. Why would she apologize to him? "Sorry for what?"

"I-I know you prefer for most people to call you Champ."

Puzzled, he shook his head. "Don't be silly. What gave you that idea?"

She looked up then. "Allie told me."

"Allie?" He couldn't fathom why she'd say such a thing, but without a doubt her lies had a purpose. Angry that she would involve an innocent like Mary Sofia in this tug-of-war between them, he immediately tried to mitigate the damage. "Listen, Mary Sofia, about Allie. I want you to know—"

"Oh, you don't have to explain anything to me," Mary Sofia interrupted, wagging her hand back and forth. "I know how complicated relationships can be."

He frowned. "Do you?"

She seemed to gather her thoughts before saying, "My mother was sixteen when she married my father. Sixteen."

"Boy, do I feel old," he quipped sourly. "Here I am nearly thirty and still alone."

"There. That's it," Mary Sofia said. "It's feeling alone, even in a relationship, even in a houseful of family, that can make you desperate and... well, in my mother's case, obsessive. She always seemed to feel abandoned unless my dad was there to shower attention on her, no matter how busy or chaotic our household was. Or maybe because it was so busy and chaotic." Shaking her head, Mary Sofia sighed. "All I really know is that I never want to be like my mother. All the same, for a while there, I was so afraid of winding up alone that I latched onto some real doozies. Or let them latch onto me."

His frown deepened into a scowl. "I don't understand that. You must have had your pick of guys, a girl like you."

She laughed, the sound hollow and self-deprecating. "If I did, I kept picking the worst ones. Thankfully, my brothers are smarter than I am, and they were always looking out for me."

And without a doubt would continue to do so, Stuart mused. "Apparently, I need someone to look out for me."

She laid a hand on his forearm. "God looks out for us. If we let Him. He's the one Who gave me two overprotective big brothers, after all. I used to be mad about that, but now I know what a blessing my brothers are."

"I didn't get any brothers. Or any siblings at all. In fact, I don't have any sort of family. Guess I slipped His notice."

"That's not true," she insisted. "The only thing God ever forgets is our sins after we confess them."

"Yeah? Well, in my case, that's a big ask. I mean, I've made some huge mistakes, and I don't see how confessing them makes any difference.

It's not like God doesn't already know what I've done."

Mary Sofia lifted one slender, shapely eyebrow. "I doubt your mistakes are any bigger than the Apostle Paul's. Before he met Jesus, he persecuted Christians. You can even say he murdered them. And what about King David? He stole another man's wife and killed to hide that fact. Or Zacchaeus. He stole tax money from poor people. They were all forgiven. Believe me, you've done nothing unforgiveable," she insisted, "and I'm going to pray for you to figure that out."

Before he could reply to that, headlights swept the parking area, casting shadows over the pale gravel as they moved. Stuart recognized the newly arrived vehicle as Bart's, a black Toyota Sequoia TRD. His heart gave a hard knock inside his chest when he saw that Bart was not alone. Looked like the much dreaded confrontation had arrived. So be it. Better to get this over with now. But not in front of Mary Sofia. She'd already been involved enough—too much—in something in which she had no part.

He swiftly shoved his guitar case at her. "Take this inside for me, will you? Please. I need to have a few private words with Bart."

"O-of course." Gripping the handle of the case with both hands, she glanced behind her as she trudged toward the tall, weathered building.

"Thanks." He started toward the big SUV, formulating in his mind what he would say.

As Bart slid from behind the steering wheel, the passenger door swung open and Allie got out, wearing skinny jeans, black knee boots, and a black turtleneck sweater beneath a long, supple, black leather coat. The light turned her perfectly coifed hair into spun gold. Unmoved by the sight of her, Stuart trained his determined gaze on Bart.

Once Stuart and the other members of the Young Rockers had shared a love/hate relationship with their lead singer, whose wealthy, indulgent, adopted parents had convinced him he should have whatever he wanted whenever he wanted it. Time, experience, the influence of his natural parents, and his growing Christian faith had changed Bart very much for the better. He still looked more like he belonged to a motorcycle gang than a praise band, but his entire demeanor had softened and opened. He'd become a good friend, and Champ hated to disappoint him. Nevertheless, the reckoning had arrived, and Champ knew that if he had any hope of surviving it, he would have to be honest.

"Bart, would you mind if I spoke to your sister alone? I have something important to say to her."

Slinging a glance his sister's way, Bart answered. "Sure."

Before Bart could move or Champ could speak, Allie launched a verbal sortie, hoping, no doubt, to put Stuart on the defensive.

"I see my personal assistant is moonlighting. I know what she does for me, but I can't help wondering exactly what services she's providing you."

Bart let out a disgusted, "Al-lie."

Revolted, Stuart turned a scowl on her. "Mary Sofia is a complete innocent, as you know."

Allie rolled her eyes and snapped, "You say that like it's a good thing."

Ignoring her, he again addressed Bart. "I'd appreciate it if we could have a few minutes of privacy. It won't take long."

"Anything you have to say to me, you can say in front of my brother," Allie declared.

No doubt she thought that would stop him from speaking, but Stuart pulled in a deep breath and nodded. "All right. Have it your way." He turned back to Bart, looked him squarely in the eye, and confessed. "I'm ashamed to say I've been sleeping with your sister."

Bart brought a hand up and briefly covered the lower half of his face before letting his hand fall to his side once more. "Yeah, I thought that might be the case. She's not exactly subtle, my sister."

Stuart felt his jaw drop. "You knew? And you said nothing?"

"What did you want me say, Stu? I love you like a brother, man, but I'm not your conscience. I guess I just hoped it would work out between the two of you. I mean, she needs a good man like you."

His words hit Stuart like blows, fueling his shame. "But I haven't been a good man. That's what I'm trying to tell you. And I'm so sorry. I never should've let this happen. I need you to know..." Pivoting on one heel, he pulled Allie in with a glance and proceeded. "I need you both to know that it's not going to happen again."

She laughed. She actually laughed. That husky, throaty sound had once reduced him to slavering lust, but now it just saddened him.

"Oh? Are we about to be treated to another marriage proposal then?" she asked, both delight and disdain coloring her voice. "Because I warn you. If passionate declarations can't sway me, pressure from my brother certainly won't."

"No marriage proposal," Stuart stated, surprised by the calm relief flowing through him. "It's over. Whatever was between us is over. We are over."

She stepped directly into his line of sight, eyes blazing. "Really? Then what were those public displays last weekend and yesterday?"

Nothing but the truth, he decided. From now on it would be nothing but the truth. "I admit I first thought that if I gave you a public acknowledgement of our relationship, you'd give me what I thought I wanted." He shook his head at his own foolishness. "But then I realized that it would never work between us, Allie. We're just too different."

Her ice blue eyes all but shot angry sparks at him. "And when did you come to this great realization? When you saw innocent little Mary Sofia at the wedding looking like a candy waiting to be gobbled up?"

"No," he answered evenly, although Mary Sofia had looked extraordinarily appetizing that night. "I realized I couldn't continue what we were doing when I saw myself in her eyes yesterday in the penthouse. They said exactly what my conscience has been saying all along. I can't keep on with you and live with myself." He shook his head, adding gently, "I tried to believe it was love, Allie, but it wasn't. Not for either of us."

Vibrating with fury, Allie folded her arms and swept him up and down with a look of disgust. "I've had better, you know," she sneered. "And with much less angst."

He didn't point out that she'd kept coming back night after night with apparent enthusiasm. Instead, he let her spin away without a word in his own defense.

She held out her hand to her brother, demanding, "Keys!"

Bart dug into his pocket and produced the key ring.

Snatching it from his fingers, she flounced to the driver's door, unlocking it remotely as she went, and threw herself inside, snarling, "You're going to regret this, *Champ*. Mark my words. You're nobody's champion."

Steeling himself, Stuart finally looked Bart in the eye again. The affectionate pity he saw there brought a rush of relief so great his knees weakened. Swallowing down a doughy lump that had suddenly risen in his throat, he croaked, "I can drive you home. Unless you'd rather—"

To his shock, Bart stepped in close, lifted both his hands to clasp Stuart's shoulders, and brought their foreheads together.

"Bro," he said, "I'd be happy to ride with you." He grinned then and lifted his head, adding, "The problem is, she left with my house keys. I'll have to hope she doesn't change the access code before I get home."

Near tears, Stuart chuckled softly. "If she does, you can stay with me. Plenty of room."

Bart pointed a finger at him. "I'll hold you to that."

Stuart nodded. Then he whispered, "Thank you. I don't deserve your friendship after what I've done. So...thank you."

"Dude," Bart said, backing up a step, one hand still resting on Stuart's shoulder, "I know my sister, and I know how easy it is to get caught up in these things. You don't realize until later that there's nothing easy about the sex. It always comes with strings, no matter how hard you ignore them. Besides, it sounds like you tried to make it right. Would you really have married her?"

"At one point, yes. But that doesn't mean what I did wasn't wrong."

"Okay, it was wrong," Bart acknowledged. "Now it's done, and if God can forgive you and so can I, then you can surely forgive yourself. Right?"

Stuart licked his lips. "You really think God can forgive me?"

"I know so." Bart lightly shoved his shoulder, and this time Stuart let himself be turned toward the building. "When we repent, confess our sins and turn away from them, He forgives us. Isn't that what you just did?"

Pondering, Stuart fell into step beside his friend. Finally, he said, "Yes. I never again want to repeat the mistake. Even if it means being alone from now on."

"Good," Bart said. "But I can't believe God means for you to be alone. Frankly, though, I'm glad you didn't marry Allie."

Stung, Stuart slid a glance at Bart. "Why? Didn't you just say you thought I'd be good for her?"

"More or less," Bart admitted. "What I'm telling you now is that I don't think she would be good for you. The thing about my sister is that she's walking wounded, and she refuses to even acknowledge how badly she's messed up. She doesn't have faith to fall back on, so she tries to patch the wound with things like money and success. And sex." He shook his head. "Breaks my heart for her, but I wouldn't wish her on any of my friends. Not now. Maybe one day. I have faith that she'll yield at some point, and then He'll have her. Jesus, I mean."

"I hope so," Stuart said. A fresh gush of shame forced him to confess all. "I did nothing to help her find God, just took what she offered and tried to justify it to myself."

Bart smiled. "Maybe that's true and maybe it's not, but I can tell you how to make amends."

"Please do."

"Pray for her to come to Jesus."

Stunned, Stuart froze in his tracks. "You really mean that."

"Absolutely."

"You're asking the man who sinned with your sister to pray for her salvation."

"I'm asking my repentant Christian brother to pray for my sister's salvation," Bart corrected.

Then he smiled and simply walked on, leaving Champ to ponder such generosity with tears in his eyes and gratitude in his heart.

Chapter Nine

A fter leaving Stuart's guitar in its case against the wall just inside the door to the practice area, Mary Sofia took the last seat in the front row behind the big glass window in the visitors' section. She didn't want to wait with the guitar in case that caused trouble for him with Allie. Perhaps, she mused, she shouldn't have come to watch practice tonight, but when Hugo had announced that he was going to stay home to help Gabi with a mountain of homework and the triplets, Mary Sofia had impulsively decided to accompany her sister-in-law.

She hadn't expected to find Stuart sitting alone in his Jeep in the parking lot, but she'd welcomed the opportunity to thank him for helping her get the job at JREDI. In addition, she hoped to dispel any negative feelings or assumptions between them. It wasn't her place to judge, after all, and neither Stuart nor Allie owed her a thing. She'd been silly to let that kiss upset her, and Stuart—she couldn't seem to think of him by any other name now—shouldn't feel guilty about her foolishness. What was between him and Allie was between him and Allie. Period.

At first she'd been confused when he'd denied recommending her for the job, but she'd quickly realized her mistake. Allie hadn't stated that he'd recommended her. Perhaps she had implied it, but she hadn't said it. Besides, however it had come about, he'd been instrumental in getting her the position. It did seem odd that he hadn't known about the opening, but God didn't see fit to make her privy to the details of anyone else's life, so why should He make Stuart aware of Allie's business dealings?

Bart walked into the practice room just then, derailing Mary Sofia's train of thought. He raised his hand in greeting to the eight other musicians already tuning up and otherwise getting ready to start, then turned to wave at those there to observe, all family of band members. A minute or so later, Stuart walked into the studio, his head bowed. Shucking his overcoat, he walked right past the guitar, so Mary Sofia tapped lightly on the glass to get his attention. When he turned toward her, she saw at once the emotion in his reddened eyes.

She had no idea what had transpired after she'd left him, but she couldn't help wondering about it. Concerned, she waved to get his attention then pointed to the side, indicating where he could find his guitar. He glanced that way, nodded to her, smiled wanly, and went to retrieve the instrument. She leaned forward to look out the visitor's room open door for Allie. Instead of her boss, however, she saw Maggs Ogilvey, the band's manager and wife of the band's senior member, Wyatt, upon whose property they all now congregated. Maggs stepped into the observation room, pulled the door closed behind her, and climbed the shallow steps to the third row of seats, passing out greetings and smiles as she did so.

Immediately Maggs began talking about Rey's latest music video and the song it promoted. Most of those gathered there had seen and heard it, and many naturally turned to Mary Sofia for comment. She told them everything she knew about her eldest brother's recent release, who had written the song, who had produced it, and that it would be the title song on Rey's new album. Some folks were surprised Charlie Biggs hadn't written the music, but everyone nodded knowingly when Mary Sofia told them that Charlie had recommended that a fellow songwriter offer the ballad to Rey. Charlie was generous to a fault and cared about everyone who came into his orbit.

With the door closed, the room quickly began to warm up. Mary Sofia shucked her thigh-length coat just before the overhead speakers came on and the sound tech announced they were ready to begin. From there, Wyatt took over, opening the practice session with prayer. Mary Sofia bowed her head and listened.

She always enjoyed watching the band rehearse. These practice sessions felt much more intimate than performances, and the process of working out the best rendition of each song fascinated her. As the band members assumed their assigned positions and prepared to play, she couldn't help noticing that Stuart smiled more readily than usual and seemed in especially good humor with Bart.

Relaxing, Mary Sofia sent up a silent prayer of thanks, quickly following with a prayer for herself.

"Help me not to hold on to my feelings for Stuart. He's obviously promised to Allie now and would never be interested in me even if he wasn't.. Besides, I work for Allie, so I owe her respect and loyalty, not to mention gratitude. Help Stuart find his way back to You, Lord. And Allie, too."

She didn't have to say that she was working hard on the respect part or that her loyalty in this case had limits. God surely knew her heart better than she did herself.

Her treacherous, romantic, troublesome heart.

***

As always, practice started with prayer. As always, Stuart stood and joined hands with the others as they expressed personal concerns and then Wyatt prayed aloud. Although he routinely went through the process at every practice, Stuart had felt for some time now that he somehow stood apart from the group, that he merely watched from the outside, looking in, while the others prayed. Now, suddenly, he felt united with the whole band again. The warmth and relief of that nearly brought him to tears for a second time that evening. Samson Cody, the band's drummer and an original member of the Young Rockers, noticed.

Looking straight into Stuart's eyes after the prayer ended, Sam asked, "You okay, Champ?"

Smiling, Stuart nodded. "Getting there, anyway."

Wyatt called attention then, so Sam climbed into the phalanx of drums he played so effortlessly, and Stuart took up his usual position to Sam's far right with Bart between and slightly in front of them. Amalie Golden, their keyboardist, moved behind her instrument to Sam's left, directly across from Bart, while JoJo Carter assumed the position slightly behind her on Sam's extreme left, placing her on a parallel with Stuart. Everyone else stood behind Sam on a slightly raised platform, mimicking the elevated positions of the actual stage in The Milking Barn, the venue owned and operated by Maggs, where the band played every other Friday evening.

They'd been learning a new song written by Charlie Biggs, an extremely prolific talent.

Charlie had made a key change in order to better tailor the song to Bart, so the entire group stumbled for a while, but soon they all got the music down. Bart continued to have difficulty with the vocals, however. Stuart didn't understand it. Singing background as usual, he found the new key change very easy and melodic. The lyrics were simple but moving. Obviously frustrated, Bart abruptly broke off in mid bar, shook his head, and waved an arm for silence before pointing directly at Stuart. For one horrified moment, Stuart thought Bart was blaming him for the difficulty. Then Bart spoke.

"Honestly, guys, Champ ought to be singing lead on this. The style's just too smooth and lyrical for me."

For a moment, Stuart froze, unable to react to such an unexpected suggestion, but then Wyatt called out, "How about it, Champ? We all know you can do it. You have a fine voice."

Others called out encouragement, too.

"You've already got it nailed, man. Give it a go."

"It's about time you took the spotlight, Champ."

"Great idea. Those smooth tones are just right for you."

Charlie decided him. The big bear of a man set aside his violin and walked down to Stuart. Clapping him on the shoulder, Charlie smiled.

"To tell you the truth, Champ, I wrote

this with you in mind. That's how it happens sometimes. God gives me the words and melody, and He puts a voice in my head to sing it, but for some reason I didn't feel I ought to bring it to you until now." He glanced at Bart, adding, "Bart obviously picked up on that. This one's yours, Champ. You gonna take it?"

The hair stood up on the back of Stuart's neck. He had put an end to his sinful affair with Allie and confessed to Bart. Now God seemed to be calling him back home. Could it really be that simple? He only knew that a great weight had been lifted from his shoulders, and he now felt an eagerness to follow God that he hadn't felt in far too long. What could he do but agree?

"I'll give it a go, at least."

"Good man," Charlie said, thumping him on the back hard enough to make him rock forward. With that, Charlie went off to talk to the technician behind the glass wall of the mixing room.

After Charlie resumed his position and picked up his violin again, Wyatt took over, calling the beat to launch the music. Stuart held his usual place and sang as he always did, but this time his voice took precedence over the others. The words, firm in his memory, flowed effortlessly. His own voice surprised and encouraged him with its purity and depth, a trick, no doubt, of the sound system.

"God of love, God of Grace,

"Heaven knows You took my place.

"Who am I that You died for me?

"What greater love can there be?

"The Spotless Lamb of Calvary,

"Was crucified to set me free.

"I praise You, Lord, with every breath.

"My endless life for Your pain and death.

"God of love, God of Grace,

"Heaven knows You took my place..."

A smiling Bart sang Stuart's usual part, and this time their familiar harmony melded perfectly. Afterward, applause broke out among the musicians. When he looked to the visitor's booth, something he'd avoided until just then, he saw everyone there on their feet and clapping. All but Mary Sofia.

She stood with her hands clasped just below her chin, a broad smile on her face, tears sliding down her cheeks. An impulsive prayer suddenly broke into Champ's mind.

"Thank You, Lord."

Humbled and overjoyed, he closed his eyes and silently prayed again.

"Thank You. Oh, thank You. I don't deserve any of this, and I'm so sorry. Please forgive me. Please help me to follow You more closely from now on. Thank You."

They went over the song several more times, and Stuart grew increasingly comfortable with his performance, but he knew he'd be nervous Friday after next, the night of the show.

Meanwhile, he felt clean again. Perhaps he would always be alone, but he privately vowed he'd never indulge in another liaison like the last. It would be marriage or nothing for him from this point onward.

His gaze went back to Mary Sofia, who had retaken her seat, along with the other listeners, but he held no hopes there. She deserved better, someone as kind and pure as she was. And her brothers would no doubt see that she got it.

After the rehearsal, the whole band gathered around to congratulate and encourage him, as did many of the onlookers. Mary Sofia, he noticed, hung back, watching JoJo pack up her flute. After that, the two had a brief conversation. JoJo left, calling out her farewells, and still Mary Sofia lingered. Sensing that she waited to speak with him again, he did his best to ignore her as he packed his own equipment and the congratulatory crowd thinned, but then he turned and there she stood, a big smile on her lovely face. He quickly spoke first, hoping to deflect any praise. God knew she had no reason to admire him.

"Thanks for bringing in the guitar."

"Oh, Stuart," she gushed, completely ignoring his gratitude, "your song was so beautiful it made me cry. You have an amazing voice. Why haven't you sung lead before?"

He hunched his shoulders in a shrug. "It just never came up before."

"It should have," she told him, "but you're too shy to put yourself forward." She clapped her hands to her blushing cheeks. "No, that's not what I mean. You're too..." She shook her head. "You're so humble. That's what I mean."

Now it was his turn to blush. "I have a lot of reasons to be humble, as you put it." Stepping closer, he softly said, "Listen, about yesterday," but she again shook her head, her lovely hair undulating about her face and shoulders.

"You don't have to explain anything to me."

"You don't understand." He briefly closed his eyes, determined to speak the truth. "You thanked me earlier for something I didn't do." He met her gaze then and said, "Now I want to thank you for something you don't even know you did."

She blinked at him. "You're right. I don't understand."

He sucked in a deep breath and let it out again. Flattening his lips, he took a moment to order his words. "Deep down, I've known all along that my relationship with Allie wasn't going where it should."

Mary Sofia looked up at him from beneath the gentle sweep of her brows. "You're going to marry her, aren't you?"

He shook his head. "No. That's what I'm trying to tell you."

"What do you mean?"

He looked down, keeping his voice low. "Allie made it clear from the beginning that she didn't want marriage, but I thought…" He let that trail off, reminding himself that he was going to be honest from now on. "I used the idea of our eventual marriage as a way to justify what I was doing. Then, when I couldn't sustain that illusion any longer, I had to look at things honestly, and I didn't like what I saw. So I broke it off with her just before practice tonight."

"I see." She looked away, bowed her head. "I get what you're saying. Because I've done that more than once, tried to believe something was real when it wasn't. It took someone else, my brothers usually, to make me face the truth."

"That's exactly what happened," he said. "Someone else made me see the truth."

"Who? Was it Bart? I mean, he seems to have matured a lot, and he is her brother."

Stuart waited until she settled her gaze on him once more. "It wasn't Bart. It was you."

Her mouth dropped open. "Me? How can that be?"

Seizing her by the upper arms, he kept her firmly planted, saying urgently, "When I saw the look in your eyes yesterday, I saw the disappointment and the disgrace, the whole ugly truth. For me, Allie and I ended right then. I just couldn't hold my shame at bay any longer. Until that moment, I hadn't even realized Allie had hired you, but I knew instantly why she'd done it. Of course, it didn't work out the way she'd planned. I think she expected your disgust of me to eliminate you as any possible competition and also push me to completely abandon the convictions I'd tried so hard to ignore."

"But I've never been any competition for her. Not with you or anyone. And I wasn't judging. Truly I wasn't."

"I know. I know," he hastily replied. "You're not like that. As for you not being competition for her, I think she realized the night of the wedding reception what a lovely young woman you've become. In a way, you're everything she is not and at the same time, so much of what she is, the attractive parts, I mean. She has to see that, and it must make her feel lost and cynical. I always knew that about her, of course, but I hoped..." He dropped his hands and shook his head. "It's just too much of a mess. And you made me see that without ever saying a word."

To his surprise, Mary Sofia stepped up and tenderly hugged him, whispering, "I'm sorry it didn't work out for the two of you."

Astounded that she would seek to comfort him for what had been a great folly on his part, he stood immobile for several long seconds, desperately warning himself not to read too much into it. This was sweet, kind, virginal, nonjudgmental Mary Sofia.

She was not for him.

Or to be more precise, he was not for her. She deserved someone with an unstained soul. And that could never be him. It was much too late for that.

***

Stuart once again gently took Mary Sofia by the upper arms, but this time, much to her dismay, he firmly set her back.

"No, no, sweet girl. Don't feel sorry for me. It was wrong, and I'm glad it's over." He let out a deep sigh. "I'm relieved. And ashamed that I..." He broke off, grimacing. "Enough said on that score. I just wanted to thank you for opening my eyes."

"I can't take credit for that."

"I don't know who else could."

"Don't you? If you think about it, you'll realize that it was God Who really opened your eyes."

Stuart smiled. Of course. "But He used you to do it. Because you are so sweet and innocent."

"Not as sweet or innocent as you seem to think," she muttered.

He just smiled at that, but if he knew how many times she'd built romantic fantasies around the wrong sort of guys, even him, he wouldn't be so certain of her character. She knew all the facts of life, after all. How could she not? And she'd spent plenty of time wondering what intimacy would be like with certain men. Especially him.

"You don't even know what a treasure you are," he said fondly, sounding like an indulgent older brother now.

She deflected her disappointment, and a smidge of irritation, with, "What I do know, from personal experience, is that you're relieved. I can see it in your face. You've made a wise decision."

"Wise?" he scoffed. "My own personal experience tells me otherwise."

"You're too hard on yourself."

Looking down into her dark eyes, he shook his head. "You don't know, Mary Sofia. You just don't know."

She folded her arms, growing miffed. He seemed determined to treat her as a child or, worse, as a baby sister. "I know you're a good man."

"I'm not," he stated bluntly. "If I were..." Again, he shook his head. "You're a delightful girl, Mary Sofia, a complete innocent, and I'm sorry to say you'll eventually understand."

Frowning, she dropped her arms and stepped back, tartly correcting him. "Stop treating me like a child. I have enough big brothers, Stuart Champion, and I'll have you know I'm twenty-three years old. That's hardly a girl."

He seemed amused, saying indulgently, "All right. I stand corrected."

Irritated—and more than a little hurt—she nodded crisply and turned to make a dramatic exit, only to freeze in place. A livid Allie stood in the open doorway. Resigned to an ugly scene, Mary Sofia glanced around. At least nearly everyone had left. Besides she and Stuart, only the Ogilvies, Bart, and Sam remained.

Her icy glare boring into Stuart, Allie flew across the room and slapped him hard enough to snap his head to the side. He didn't make a move to defend himself, but without a thought to the possible consequences, Mary Sofia immediately did so.

"Stop it! You have no right to attack him like that!"

Allie dropped a malicious glare on her, snarling, "That's quite enough out of you, little Miss Goody Two Shoes. Now get out of my sight."

Mary Sofia folded her arms. "This is not the Justus Building. I am not your employee here. And neither is Stuart."

"Stuart, is it?" Allie snapped.

Surprised that she'd called him that, Mary Sofia dropped her arms just as Allie's hand began to rise once more. Without a word, Stuart captured Allie's wrist to keep her from striking Mary Sofia. After a stunned moment, Allie jerked free. At the same time, Maggs and Wyatt rushed forward.

"That's enough," Wyatt decreed in his gravelly voice.

"More than enough," Maggs put in sharply.

Realizing she'd gone too far, Allie jerked her gaze to her brother, barking, "Get in the car or walk."

Spreading around an apologetic look, he lifted his hands in a placating motion. "I'm coming."

She whirled away, her heavy leather coat belling around her, and stomped toward the open door, arms outstretched as if the building itself had to be moved aside so she could leave.

Bart turned, walking backward, and said to the room at large, "Sorry about that. I'd better get her out of here before she wreaks more havoc." Once through the door, he hurried out of sight.

Pinching the bridge of his nose, Stuart sighed and made his own apologies to those in the room. "I'm sorry about that. Allie and I have been...seeing each other. And I broke it off earlier tonight."

"You don't owe anyone apologies or explanations," Mary Sofia told him defiantly.

As if suddenly too exhausted to maintain his posture, he let his head fall forward into his palms.

Reaching for Maggs's hand, Wyatt said, "We'll be back to lock up later." Then the two of them diplomatically slipped out.

Stuart dropped his hands and nodded. Mary Sofia sent him a sympathetic look, smiled wanly, and said, "JoJo has been waiting all this time. I'd better go, too."

"I hope everything goes okay at work tomorrow," he said as she moved toward the door. "Remember. You promised to let me know if it doesn't."

"Don't worry about that."

"I will worry about it," he said.

"Okay. Fine. I'll let you know if work doesn't go well tomorrow."

"Good. By the way, feel free to call me Stuart anytime you want." He grinned, shaking his head. "Or anything else that pleases you."

Glancing back over her shoulder, she smiled and moved toward the door. "I look forward to hearing you sing again. Bye. And... Bye." She left before she could say anything she shouldn't.

The romantic part of her exulted. He'd broken up with Allie, and then protected her from Allie's anger. In her mind's eye, Mary Sofia saw again the stern expression on his face, the unblinking determination of a true protector, as he'd kept Allie from slapping her. She may have lost her job tonight, but at the moment, she didn't care. Stuart had protected her. If Allie fired her over that, so be it. God would provide another job.

A more mature part of Mary Sofia urged great caution. She mustn't let herself think Stuart—or anything else she pleased to call him—had any romantic interest in her. He seemed to think she was little more than a child, as pure as the driven snow, and completely untouchable. She couldn't think of a thing that might change his mind. No, Stuart Champion could not be the man for her because she had no way to win his regard. She might as well face that fact and trust God to show her who He had in mind for her.

As she got behind the wheel of her car, JoJo asked from the passenger seat, "What's going on? Allie and Bart just tore out of here like the devil was chasing them."

"Mm, well, Stu, er, Champ broke up with Allie tonight."

JoJo gave her a sardonic look. "You don't say?"

Shrugging, Mary Sofia started the car and backed it around. "I thought they were getting engaged, but turns out I was wrong."

"And I can tell how brokenhearted you are about it."

Mary Sofia put on an innocent face. "It's nothing to do with me."

"Isn't it?"

"No. Why would you think so?"

Smiling, JoJo turned to look at the night-blackened window. Deciding it best to just let the subject drop, Mary Sofia drove onward. She could just imagine the conversation her sister-in-law would have with Hugo later, but she had bigger problems.

What on earth could she say to her brother if Allie fired her tomorrow?

Chapter Ten

Watching Mary Sofia leave, Stuart brought his hands to his hips and bowed his head. His cheek felt as though it had been hit with a blow torch, aching and burning at the same time, but that was nothing compared to how his heart felt.

"I am twenty-three years old...hardly a girl."

"And I am not the man for her," he muttered to himself. His own actions and stupidity had ruled him out before he'd even realized he might have a chance. For one thing, it was too late to win the approval of her brothers. Allie had almost hit her because of him, for pity's sake. He could just imagine Hugo's reaction to that, not to mention Rey's. Nope. He'd blown it before he'd even begun. Maybe he should be alone for the rest of his life. Maybe that would be best for everyone.

A hand landed on his shoulder. He'd completely forgotten about Sam. Whirling, he managed a limp smile.

"Oh. Hey."

"Looks like you could use a word of prayer,

my friend."

Gratefully, Stuart nodded. "I could."

"Let's sit down," Sam suggested, pulling around two folding chairs that stood against the wall. Stuart sat, leaned forward with his forearms propped against his thighs and waited for Sam to speak. "Am I right in assuming that you and Allie have been in a sexual relationship?" Sam asked calmly.

Stuart gulped and nodded, hanging his head in shame.

"Well, that's over now. Yes?"

"Yes," Stuart managed, breathing roughly. Closing his eyes, he came clean. "But it's not the first time I've done that."

"It can be the last time, though," Sam said, not a whiff of judgment in his tone. "Until you marry, that is."

"I don't know if I'll ever marry," Stuart muttered miserably, his voice filled with regret.

"I think you will. You want to, don't you?"

"Yes. I have for a long time now."

"Then that's what we'll ask God for."

Sam placed his hands on Stuart's slumped shoulders. As he prayed, tears leaked from Stuart's eyes and rolled down to drip off the end of his nose. He felt shattered and whole at the same time. In the silence of his own mind, he asked for forgiveness and thanked God for such friends as Bart and Charlie and Wyatt and Maggs and Sam. And Mary Sofia.

Though nearly seven years younger than him, Mary Sofia had achieved much more in her life that he had, a solid character, for one thing, not to mention a caring soul. He thanked God that she seemed heart-whole and unbroken by life. That he laid at the feet of her older brothers. But who could he blame for his failures? Certainly not his parents, good, loving, God-fearing people both.

Something his mother said to him as she lay in her hospital bed, a small, wounded husk of her former self, came to him then.

"*Son*," she'd said, "*God's perfect light shines through our brokenness, and it always heals, one way or another.*"

She'd gone on to say that if God didn't heal her earthly body, He would give her a perfect one afterward.

At the time, Stuart had thought that nothing more than an attempt to prepare him for her imminent death, a death that hadn't come for some months yet. By the time it had, numerous strokes had taken her speech and everything else but her ability to make eye contact. He'd marveled to see the smile in her eyes every time he'd entered the room at the convalescent home, but he'd felt helpless and inadequate to the task of letting her go. In the end, she'd died quietly in her sleep. He'd hated that he hadn't been there with her and felt shaming relief at the same time.

Suddenly, the image of his loving, indulgent mother materialized before his mind's eye. Then he remembered a picture of her as a young woman. For a moment, he couldn't recall the photo itself, but then the whole thing came to him, and he saw his parents on their wedding day. His dad looked so tall and handsome, his light brown hair thick and wavy. Beside his father, barely reaching his shoulder, stood his beautiful mother, smiling brightly in her old-fashioned wedding gown and veil. He realized for the first time how dark her hair and eyes had been. He'd only known her after her hair had softened to a slate gray and then gradually given way to silver. He'd never seen his father with hair of any sort, except that on his face, which had gone from a glistening blond to a bright white mustache and goatee.

Did he imagine that his mother looked like Mary Sofia? Oh, not in the way of twins. That would be absurd. For starters, Genevieve Champion hadn't had a drop of Mexican blood in her. She'd been proud of her Scots heritage and her maiden name of Stuart, and yet she resembled Mary Sofia in some way he couldn't quite put his finger on. Perhaps it was only the dark hair and eyes, but he didn't think so. There was something else.

As if God tapped him on the shoulder, he suddenly felt catapulted back into prayer. Somehow, he'd heard every word Sam had said, even as his thoughts had ventured elsewhere, but his mind felt strangely clear and engaged now. He nodded in agreement as Sam thanked God for His many blessings and ended the prayer in the name of Christ Jesus. Echoing Sam's "Amen," Stuart straightened, feeling Sam's hands fall away.

Sitting back, he realized his tears had dried and he felt immeasurably better.

"Thank you, Sam. For the prayer and for being my friend."

"Anytime for the prayer," Sam said, smiling. "And always for the friendship."

Stuart realized how greatly he had underestimated his bandmates. They were upright and moral, yes, but they were also forgiving and supportive. He didn't deserve such friendship, but he was thankful for it.

They rose to gather their coats and instruments, which in Sam's case amounted to several pairs of drumsticks because the drum array here remained in place all the time. He kept another identical set at The Milking Barn. As they turned toward the door, Stuart saw that Wyatt had returned and now waited patiently in the observation room. Stuart gave him a grateful wave, and Wyatt nodded in understanding.

The cold night air felt fresh and clean when Stuart stepped outside, despite the wisps of fog that gathered in the lowest lying areas.

"Looks like we're going to warm up for

a bit," Sam commented, turning up his collar. Stuart smiled. Somehow, Sam's collars always got turned up.

"Take care going home. And give my best to Holland."

Named for the country in which she'd been born, Sam's wife, Holland, was a popular local newscaster.

"Will do," Sam called, walking to his car.

Stuart sucked in cold air and rolled his shoulders. Such a weight had been lifted from them he wondered how he kept his feet on the ground. After carrying his guitar case to the Jeep, he stowed it in the back seat, then got in behind the steering wheel. Wyatt must have been watching, for the bright lights aimed at the parking area went out as soon as Stuart started the engine and the truck's lights came on.

As he turned the Jeep pickup toward home, he mused that he would sleep well tonight. He prayed that Mary Sofia, Bart, and Allie would all do the same.

He prayed.

Literally and easily, as if a call had rung through or a pipeline had suddenly opened.

And then he prayed again in thanks.

***

What was the deal with older brothers? Mary Sofia wondered. Did God give them some sort of sixth sense when it came to their baby sisters? It didn't even take a private conversation for Hugo to grasp the evening's significance. JoJo made a simple, off-hand remark about Champ singing lead that night, and Hugo instantly pounced on Mary Sofia.

"Oh, swell. I suppose you'll be mooning over him forever now."

"I am not 'mooning' over Champ. Or anyone."

Hugo ignored her automatic defense as if she hadn't even spoken. "Just remember that he's with Allie now."

"Uh, not exactly," JoJo put in. Mary Sofia winced at Hugo's dagger sharp glare.

"What do you mean by 'not exactly?' Just yesterday she said they were an item."

"They were," Mary Sofia mumbled. "Champ broke it off tonight."

Hugo's eyes narrowed. "I see."

"Don't look at me like that," Mary Sofia huffed. "I had nothing to do with it."

"Oh, really? Yesterday they were about to get engaged, and tonight he breaks up with her? After you saw them kissing. I suppose that's just a coincidence."

"Yes."

"Did he know you saw them kissing?" Hugo pressed.

Mary Sofia gulped. "Well, I was standing right there when the elevator door opened, so yeah, he knew I saw them. I mean, he had to. I-I was standing right...there."

Hugo stroked his chin. "Huh. Guess they weren't that deeply involved, after all."

"Look," Mary Sofia said reasonably. "Maybe I misunderstood what Allie was getting at. It's not like she gave me details. A-and I don't want any. Not my business. Besides, Allie is my boss now." For the moment. She had every intention of showing up for work in the morning, but that might be the last time she did so.

"You're quite right," JoJo agreed, nodding. "We shouldn't be gossiping about someone else's private lives."

Relieved, Mary Sofia changed the subject back to Stuart's surprising performance as a lead vocalist.

"I couldn't believe it when Charlie said he'd written the song with Champ in mind. Who knew he could even sing like that?"

"Everyone in the band knew," JoJo informed her. "But he always seemed unwilling to step out from behind Rey. Even after Bart insisted tonight, Champ waffled. Then Charlie took over, and that was that."

In Mary Sofia's private opinion, Stuart had a better voice than Bart for sure, and could sing at least as well as her big brother Rey, but she didn't say so, and the subject died a natural death. Looking at Hugo's cloudy, brooding face, she breathed a surreptitious sigh of relief. Thank God that JoJo hadn't been present when Stuart had stopped Allie from slapping her! No telling what Hugo would take from that. Mary Sofia told herself that Stuart would've done the same thing if it had been JoJo or Gabi or anyone else standing in the path of Allie's rage at that moment. But it hadn't been anyone else; it had been her, and she forever would secretly treasure that moment when Stuart had caught Allie's hand, his face a stony mask.

Pleading exhaustion, Mary Sofia said goodnight and went upstairs to take a hot, relaxing bath before going to bed. Selwyn had ordered her to be in the office at seven in the morning to receive a hand-delivered contract that had already gone astray once, and she meant to be there fifteen minutes early in order to have coffee made before anyone else showed up. Then, if Allie fired her, everyone would know it wasn't because she hadn't performed her job conscientiously.

As it turned out, Allie sailed by Mary Sofia's desk the next morning with nothing more than a breezy "Hello," and she remained the pleasant boss lady all that day. She even let Mary Sofia leave an hour early because all her work had been completed.

That gave her plenty of time to prepare for her non-date with Gavin. He showed up precisely as arranged, politely greeted Gabrielle, and effusively complimented Mary Sofia's appearance.

"You make even jeans and a sweater look

glamorous."

She wondered wryly if she made a ponytail look glamorous, too, but she smiled impersonally and thanked him for the compliment, ignoring Gabi's laughing eyes. By taking her time locking the door, Mary Sofia made certain that Gavin went down the stairs first and Gabi followed. Nothing, however, could get her out of riding in the front seat of Gavin's sensible sedan.

He tried in every way to be considerate, opening the car door for her, asking what kind of pizza she preferred, making sure she had a comfortable seat at the meeting, eliciting her comments and advice. He even introduced her at the teen session, as if nine out of every ten kids there didn't already know her. Impressed with how he handled the study session and group activities, she had to admit that he had a great sense of humor, a solid grip on Scripture, and a gift for communicating with teenagers. By evening's end, he even looked less clownish to her. Gavin Worley, she had to admit, was a fine man with a firm calling.

That didn't make her any more amenable to his interest, however, so when he asked Gabi to give them some privacy after walking the two of them to the apartment door later, Mary Sofia braced herself. He began with a bright smile and a light tone.

"Thanks for your help tonight."

"I don't know how much help I actually provided, but you're welcome."

"So..." He rocked back on his heels. "When can you have dinner with me? Just me."

Mary Sofia smiled gently and delivered her previously determined reply. "Gavin, I'm flattered, but I'm not interested in dating just now. I've started a new job, and I owe it to my brothers, who helped pay for my degree, to concentrate on that until I've established myself."

He bowed his head. "I see."

"I hope so," she told him, "because you're a nice guy, and I do like you." In fact, she liked him more than she'd expected to, but Gavin was not the sort of fellow a girl could date casually. Within a month, he'd be looking for an engagement ring and planning a wedding, although he wouldn't actually propose until an appropriate amount of time had passed.

Nodding, he took one of her hands in his, and said, "Feel free to call me anytime." He smiled and added, "I almost said, 'if you change your mind,' but the truth is I'll be happy to hear from you anytime you want to talk. About anything. For any reason."

She squeezed his fingers and slipped free. "Thank you, Gavin. You're a good friend."

He leaned forward and kissed her lightly just below her hairline. "Good night, Mary Sofia."

"Good night, Gavin."

He moved quickly down the stairs. She stepped into the apartment and closed the door, relieved and a little sad. Why couldn't she go for the Gavin Worleys of the world? What was wrong with her? What more did she need than a good, godly man whose fidelity and feelings she'd never have to doubt? Why, she wondered, did she have to pin her hopes on someone like... She immediately turned off that thought and dropped down onto the sofa, looking up to find Gabi standing with her shoulder braced against the wall, grinning at her.

"What?" Mary Sofia demanded.

"Oh, nothing. Except everyone in the Youth Department is already thinking you're Gavin's girlfriend."

Mary Sofia closed her eyes. She should have realized that would happen. Groaning, she got up from the sofa, brushed past her sister and went to the bedroom for her night clothes, already silently apologizing to God for being such a dunderhead.

It wasn't the first time, she privately admitted.

And sadly, it probably wouldn't be the last.

***

The days passed quickly for Stuart, so quickly he didn't have time to think about the upcoming performance with the band. For one thing, the weather had warmed enough to inspire him to begin a new routine. Every morning, he got up early enough to take Trooper on a run. That meant going to bed earlier than had become his custom. It also meant that he slept better. Work had become a round of departmental and unit meetings focused on collating the data they'd gathered on the new promotion. Encouraged with the results, Stuart put forward another proposal.

"What if we take the same deal to other vendors but with end cap promotion?"

Currently, they used the end of aisle space for sale items and small impulse buys. After some minor tweaks, everyone not only praised Champ's idea but tossed out suggestions for the types of vendors who might go for the plan, primarily big manufacturers with large advertising budgets. Harry instructed him to put together a study of how much space they had to offer and how many special displays could actually be up for grabs. That meant designing and conducting a nationwide survey of product placement in stores throughout each country throughout the world, a herculean task, calling for coordination between several departments.

"You'll need a team for that," Harry decided. "Pick three people to work on it."

"Anyone interested let me know privately," Stuart said, realizing he'd just been given his first leadership role.

He essentially worked around the clock until he had his team in place, outlining the project and talking with everyone who volunteered to help out. He studied employee profiles at home, eating commercially delivered dinners at the desk in his study before stumbling into bed in the wee hours of the morning for two nights in a row. So, when quitting time came on Friday of the performance, he realized with a shock that he had to hurry to get himself ready for the evening. On his way out the door, he explained to Harry why he couldn't stay late.

"So there's a performance tonight," Harry commented.

The too casual tone brought Stuart to a stop. He looked back over his shoulder at his boss, who sheepishly slid his hands into the pockets of his slacks. That was not like Harry. Backing up a step, Stuart let the hydraulic arm on the door close it.

"Yeah. Eight P.M. At The Milking Barn, just over the state line on highway ninety-four."

Harry nodded. "Didn't realize it was that close."

Stuart impulsively said, "I'd like for you to come. In fact, if you want, I can have the box office hold tickets for you and your wife. I mean, if you're interested." To his surprise, Harry readily accepted.

"We'd love that."

"Great," Stuart exclaimed. "Try to be early because I can hold tickets for friends but not save seats."

"We'll see you there."

Stuart rushed out, drove home, took the time to text Maggs and request that tickets be held in the box office for Harry Purdle and wife, then gulped down a sandwich and took the stairs two at a time up to his bedroom to change. Outfitted in his standard black jeans, black cowboy boots, and a black shirt with pearly snaps beneath an open black leather vest, he threw on a heavy, black leather jacket and a white muffler then rushed out, forgetting both gloves and cap. The last to appear in the Green Room at The Milking Barn, he arrived with cold fingers and ears. The teasing began immediately.

"He didn't run out on us, after all."

"Better late than never."

"You don't suppose he lost his voice between here and there, do you?"

Stuart took the ribbing good-naturedly and went through his usual pre-performance preparations. He felt sufficiently warmed up when Maggs entered the Green Room through the stage door. Her arrival usually signaled the group to gather for prayer.

"Five minutes, everyone," she announced. Then she looked squarely at Stuart and said, "Your party's here, by the way. They came early and grabbed seats near the front. Not all ten are together, though."

"Ten?" Champ shook his head. "I'm sure I texted you for *two* complimentary tickets."

"You did, but they showed up with eight other people claiming to be coworkers of yours."

His jaw dropped. When he could speak again, he asked, "You didn't give them all free passes, did you?"

Maggs shrugged. "Why not? Seemed reasonable, given that you've never asked for a complimentary ticket before."

Champ blinked, stunned. He'd never before invited anyone to attend one of the band's performances, especially not anyone from work. The idea hadn't even occurred to him. Yet, with only a nominal invitation, they'd shown up in numbers he'd never imagined.

You're not as alone as you thought.

The words ran through his mind with the certainty of an epiphany. With it came a calmness and confidence he hadn't felt in years. He thanked Maggs for her generosity to his friends, and as he linked hands with the others and bowed his head in prayer, he privately thanked God, too, especially for those with whom he now stood. His world, his life, suddenly felt peopled with caring, supportive friends and family, for HOBBY RUN had become more than a mere collection of bandmates and acquaintances. If he had felt somehow apart in the past, he knew now that he had held himself at a distance.

How foolish he had been, how blind and ungrateful. He silently vowed then that he would be more mindful of the blessings God had already bestowed upon him and that he would be alert from that moment on for every blessing and purpose God brought his way.

After the prayer, he got in line with the others and walked quietly up the hidden ramp to take his place on stage in the dark. By rote and the convenience of tiny hidden lights, he took his guitar from its stand and slung it over his shoulder. Waiting with the others for fog to build up to his knees, he turned his face toward Heaven and whispered a promise to God.

"For Your glory and honor, never my own."

The announcer made the usual introduction. The lights came up, and a cheer rose from the audience.

For the first time, Stuart felt that the cheers were at least partly for him.

Chapter Eleven

Because the stage lights tended to be blinding, Champ had learned never to look directly into them. That kept him from paying much attention to the those who sat beyond the footlights. It was easier to look inward or to the side and up into the sizable private box Maggs provided for the family and close friends of the performers. The first—the only—face he saw was Mary Sofia's, who grinned ear to ear. She seemed to be staring straight at him and even gave him a little wave. He managed a kind of salute before Wyatt began calling out the beat. Then, at the appropriate moment, he added his bass notes to the tune. After that, the music transported him to a place of complete absorption, which was the very reason he kept picking up the guitar and filling himself with song.

This time felt different from previous performances, however. This time he felt a holy presence, a sort of pleasure raining down on him, as musical praise rose beyond the space containing the players and listeners.

Lord Jesus, forgive me, he thought. *I'll never just go through the motions again. From now on, I praise You with every note.*

The music seemed to flow effortlessly from his fingers and tongue, until suddenly the spotlight hit him and the moment had arrived for him to take the vocal lead. Without a qualm, he opened his mouth and sang.

> God of love, God of Grace,
> Heaven knows You took my place.
> Who am I that You died for me?
> What greater blessing can there be?
> The Spotless Lamb of Calvary,
> Was crucified to set me free.
> I praise You, Lord, with every breath.
> My endless life for Your pain and death.

As he began the second verse, tears filled his eyes, but his voice remained steady.

> God of love, God of grace,
> Heaven knows You took my place.
> You reached low and touched my head.
> 'I will pay the price,' You said.
> No more death. No more fear.
> My life is His. My eyes are clear.
> No more guilt. No more shame.
> I am forgiven, whole again.
> God of love, God of grace,

Heaven knows You took my place.
Covered and washed clean
By Your sacrifice for me,
It's forgiven. It's forgotten,
As if it never even happened.
God of love, God of grace,
Heaven knows You took my
place...

Well before the last musical notes faded away, he heard the applause and whistles of the crowd. Through the haze of light, he saw that everyone in the audience has risen to their feet. Bart, who had stepped back to give Champ the limelight, elbowed him lightly and whispered, "Bow."

Champ immediately bent at the waist, bobbing up and down over his guitar two or three times. He straightened and looked up to the VIP box. Most of those there were reclaiming their seats, but Mary Sofia remained standing, her hands clasped over her heart, her smile beaming, her gaze locked to his. He laughed, happier than he had felt in a very long time, and almost missed the new beat count as the band swung into the next number.

Only in the midst of the latest song did he think of his friends and coworkers in the audience. When the number ended, he shaded his eyes and peered beyond the glare. A hand went up. Then Harry briefly popped up out of his seat. Smiling, Stuart gave him a wave as Wyatt and Drew began one of their humorous routines.

Laughing along with everyone else, Stuart thoroughly enjoyed their antics. In the past he'd merely marked time during their tomfoolery. Now, suddenly, he appreciated their comedic genius, and it gradually dawned on him that most of their stuff was extemporaneous, adlibbed on the spot. He tried to recall if he'd ever heard the same bit twice. They must come up with new material constantly to mix into their bag of gags and spoofs. And he hadn't even noticed.

Had he been sleepwalking through life, ignoring all the joyful moments and blessings God had provided? He wanted to kick himself, but the words of the song he'd sung minutes earlier came back to him.

No more guilt. No more shame. I confessed. I'm whole again...No more death. No more fear. I am His. My eyes are clear...

His eyes had been cleared. He could see truth again. He could see the love and compassion all around him. God had filled his life with beauty and creativity, given him talent and the opportunity to reach others with his praise. He had a magnificent home, a great job, friends as close as family, even a slobbery dog that adored him. Then Charlie's statement at the last practice came through the laughter.

"I wrote this with you in mind. That's how it happens sometimes. God gives me the words and

melody, and He puts a voice in my head to sing it, but for some reason I didn't feel I ought to bring it to you until now."

Until, Stuart realized, he had stepped away from sin and asked for forgiveness. He now knew that the very thing he'd thought would bring him pleasure and companionship had instead brought darkness and angst. Truthfully, he'd felt more alone while involved with Allie than he did at this moment.

Stuart performed that night with a kind of joy he hadn't known existed. He silently promised God that he'd stay on the right path from here on out. Now that he saw things as they truly were, he never wanted to blind himself with sin again.

"I want what You want for me, Lord."

A single word whispered through his mind and lodged in his heart.

"Joy."

His Lord wanted joy for him.

***

After the performance, Mary Sofia tried to talk herself out of going back to the Green Room with Hugo, but she just couldn't let the moment pass. She'd traded Gabi for tonight. One or the other of them stayed home with the kids on performance Fridays so Hugo could be there for JoJo, and tonight had been Gabi's turn to accompany Hugo to the show. That meant it would have been two weeks before Mary Sofia could next see the band, and who knew if Stuart would ever sing lead again? They usually retired a song after Charlie sold it. That being the case, Mary Sofia set aside her concerns about Hugo's disapproval and followed him backstage. She greeted and congratulated JoJo first, then saw to it that she did the same with several others before she approached Stuart.

Still beaming, he locked the clamps on his guitar case. He then jerked his head toward the door and lifted a hand, saying, "Walk with me? I need to slip out for a minute."

Mary Sofia glanced at Hugo, saw that he was engaged in conversation with Charlie, and nodded. She avoided Stuart's hand as they moved to and through the door, just in case Hugo looked their way. Once in the hallway, Stuart turned and quickly walked toward the lobby, explaining that some friends and coworkers had attended the performance and he wanted to try to catch them.

As they drew near the crowd working its way out the front doors, he called out a name. "Harry! Over here!"

A tallish, fortyish man built like a brick wall lifted a hand in acknowledgement then ran it through his thick, sandy brown hair as he looked around him, speaking to others. A number of people began making their way toward Stuart. As they drew nearer, Mary Sofia counted ten, including Harry. Seven men and three women made up the group. They all reached out to shake hands with Stuart or pat his shoulders.

"Y'all should be touring," gushed a short, stout woman with long, blonde hair.

Harry, who stood behind her, clamped his hands atop her shoulders and said, "Now, now, Angie. Don't go giving them any ideas. I already thank God that Champ hasn't left us for a career in music."

"You could win one of those singing contests on TV," another man said.

Yet another remarked, "I didn't know you could sing like that."

Mary Sofia heard herself say, "I don't think he knew it, either." Instantly, all eyes turned to her, making her wish she'd kept her trap shut.

Harry stuck out his hand for Mary Sofia to shake. "Harry Purdle, and this is my wife, Angie. Champ and I work together."

"What he means is that he's my boss," Stuart put in, beaming. "And my friend." He looped his arm loosely around her shoulders and added, "This is Mary Sofia Carter, another friend. Her sister-in-law, JoJo, plays flute for us."

"The whole band is all so good," Angie said to Mary Sofia. "You make sure they know I said that."

"I will," Mary Sofia promised, smiling.

After thanking everyone for the compliments, Stuart introduced the other people standing there, all but one. Tall and stylish, with short, artfully spiked, strawberry blonde hair, she looked fit and confident in a tailored gray-green pantsuit, a double-breasted, navy blue coat draped over her shoulders.

"This is my wife, Tamara," said the man identified as Coop, looking on her with proud eyes. A slender, tidy man with closely cropped dark brown hair and dark eyes, he matched his wife in height.

Tamara reached out and clasped Mary Sofia's hand. "Pleased to meet you." She then looked to Stuart. "When Al said we were going to hear a variety praise band, I asked, 'What is that?' Well, now I know, and I'm thrilled I got to hear ya'll."

"Thank you," Stuart said. "I'm so glad you all came."

"Do you ever play in churches?" Tamara asked.

"Some of us do," he answered, "but the whole band is quite a production to set up in most churches."

"Hm. Who do I talk to about that?"

He gave her the name and number of the band's manager, Maggs Marko Ogilvie, explaining, "This is her place."

"Huh. I wonder if she ever rents it out for special performances."

Before Champ could answer in the affirmative, Al Cooper sighed. "Might as well get ready for it. Once Tamara fixes an idea in her head, she's going to see it through, no matter what anyone says."

"Aloysius Cooper! That's rich coming from you," Tamara objected. She ignored the hoots and remarks of those around her. Looking to Mary Sofia, she confided, "That man can sell snow in Alaska."

Meanwhile, her husband's coworkers teased him about his name.

"No wonder you've kept it a secret. Aloysius!"

"And Harry's kept your confidence all this time."

"I'd be going by my last name, too."

"I know you didn't use that name in grade school," said another.

"I didn't even learn to spell it until college," Al Cooper joked, to the laughter of the others.

Harry took control then. "All right, all right. I could tell tales on all of you, and Coop didn't pick his own name."

"No, that was my mother," Al Cooper opined, looking crestfallen. "I don't know why she didn't like me." He shook his head then broke into a grin as everyone else laughed. "Actually, I'm named after my grandfather."

"I think it's a fine name," Mary Sofia put in. "Unique."

"That's what I said," Tamara Cooper agreed.

"After you stopped laughing," her husband quipped out of the corner of his mouth, again eliciting hilarity.

"We all know what a fine salesman he is," Stuart said to the woman, "but he must be better than we even knew if he convinced you to marry him with that name."

She bit her lips before giving in to a grin and admitting, "We didn't use it in the wedding ceremony."

Laughter erupted yet again. Cooper took it all in stride. Though considerably younger than Tamara, Mary Sofia liked the woman and thought they could be friends, given the opportunity.

Just then, Hugo called out from behind the gathering. "Mary Sofia! Time to go."

Cringing inwardly, she put on a polite smile and passed it around the group, saying, "Nice to meet you all."

Champ's arm tightened in a sideways hug. "Thanks for coming," he said softly.

Without thinking, she went up on tiptoe and kissed his cheek before starting off in Hugo's direction. "Bye, and congratulations. You did a great job."

He turned, watching her go, and waved when she reached Hugo and JoJo. She waved back, painfully aware that only JoJo copied the move.

The door to the back parking area had barely closed behind them when Hugo growled, "Getting kind of familiar there, aren't you?"

JoJo, thankfully, came to her defense. "What d'you mean? They've known each other for years. Besides, it's not like they slipped off alone together. They were with a big group."

"Champ's boss and a bunch of his coworkers, with a couple of wives thrown in," Mary Sofia said lightly.

"And just how did you get included in the group?" Hugo wanted to know.

"I followed Champ out to congratulate him on his performance. He killed it tonight."

"He certainly did," JoJo enthused, latching onto the subject.

They theorized about Stuart's future role with the group, giving Hugo no chance to chime in, until they were all in his double-cab truck. Then they could complain about the cold, even though it felt significantly warmer than only a day or two ago, and JoJo groaned that her feet hurt, which prompted Hugo to promise her a massage after they got home. The topic of Champ effectively buried, Mary Sofia relaxed and let herself doze in the backseat as her brother drove.

She slid into a dream that replayed the parting scene with Stuart and his friends, but instead of kissing his cheek, he turned his head, and they kissed on the lips as naturally as if they'd done so a thousand times before. In her dream, she'd been unaware of her brother looking on until he erupted into anger, raging at her.

"You fool! What were you thinking? He's a known womanizer. He can't be trusted! Don't you

remember what happened last time with that nut job Faze!"

Jerking awake, she recalled in horror the night she'd let Faze pull her down to the ground in the backyard of their previous home. He'd pleaded with her to "make love" with him. She'd instinctively known that pleading would soon turn to demand. If Hugo hadn't happened upon them, yanked Faze off her, and broken Faze's arm in the process, she might actually have given in just to maintain the fiction that Faze loved her. She had been a fool, but she would never be a fool again.

Blinking bleary eyes, she realized they were turning into the driveway of their mutual home. Practically baling out of the pickup, she rushed away before the garage door lifted far enough for Hugo to pull the truck inside.

"What about your sister?" he called. "Aren't you going to wait and walk her up?"

"Bathroom!" Mary Sofia claimed, thankful that she did have a need. She could only pray that Hugo wouldn't take it upon himself to walk Gabi upstairs and stay to grill her about her supposed relationship with Stuart.

To forestall interrogations or lectures, she hid in the bathroom for some time, removing her makeup and brushing her teeth, all to avoid the topic of Stuart Champion.

Alas, that could not last forever.

As Mary Sofia pulled the bedcovers up, barely

an hour later, Gabi spoke out of the darkness of their shared bedroom.

"Hugo said you kissed him."

The him in question, of course, could only be Stuart. Mary Sofia didn't waste breath trying to argue the point.

"On the cheek. In front of a group of his friends. And Hugo. And JoJo. It was no big deal."

"You ought to have better sense than to do that in front of Hugo," Gabi said. "Especially if you like the guy as much as I think you do."

"Of course I like Stu...er, Champ. Who doesn't?"

"I'm not sure Hugo likes him at the moment."

Mary Sofia flopped over and punched her pillow. "Oh, for pity's sake, I don't like Champ any more or less than anyone else."

She heard movement as Gabi repositioned herself in bed. "Do you mean that you don't like Champ more than anyone else or that everyone likes Champ?"

"Both! Now, will you go to sleep?"

"Yup. Sweeet dreeeams," Gabi crooned in an irritating voice.

Mary Sofia rolled her eyes, but she couldn't help feeling troubled. Remembering how Stuart had draped his arm about her shoulders and the thrill that simple contact had given her, she knew she was in danger of building castles in the air again, this time about a man who had been carrying on a sexual affair with another woman. In the silence of her mind, Mary Sofia prayed that God would take away her feelings for Stuart.

She remembered that prayer on Monday morning when she found a coffee mug filled with a small bouquet on her desk. The words on the side of the mug made her catch her breath.

"Here's to beautiful mornings for a beautiful woman."

Picking up the bouquet, she glanced around and saw Grant Leonardo leering at her through the glass half of her cubicle wall. She'd been warned by some of the other women in the office to avoid him at all costs. At his insistence, everyone called him Leo. Apparently he thought Leo a sexier name than Grant. She immediately dropped the posy, mug and all, in the trash can. Laughing, he turned and walked away. Only later, when she looked up to find another fellow lounging on the corner of her desk, did she begin to wonder if she'd made a mistake.

Taken aback, she stammered, "H-hello. Didn't notice you come in."

She'd seen him around the office, but this wasn't the friendliest place she'd worked, and no one had offered to introduce them. Handsome in the same polished, stylish way as the rest of the men around here, he wore his conservatively cut, light brown hair in a careless tousle, which drew attention to tawny eyes ringed and mottled with warm brown. He gave her a frankly appraising, bright white smile.

"Thought it time to come by and introduce myself. Name's Jackson Dillman. Pleased to make your acquaintance."

She nodded in greeting. "Mr. Dillman. I'm Mary Sofia Carter."

"Call me Jack. Mary Sofia. Lovely name for a lovely woman. Didn't care for my flowers, I see."

Horrified, she slapped her hands to her cheeks. "Those were from you?" She immediately scrambled through the trash for the mug and bouquet.

"Just a little welcome gift. No biggie."

"I'm so sorry." She carefully placed the mug and its posy on her desk. "I thought Leo left these here."

"Leo?" Dillman echoed, shaking his head. "Good grief, you want to stay away from him. You know he's married, don't you?"

"Yes, but my understanding is that doesn't stop him from hitting on all the women in the office."

"True." Jack smiled, his tawny eyes sparkling with secret mirth. "I hope you don't think I'm the same way."

She quickly replied, "Oh, uh, no. No, of course not."

His smile grew into a grin. "Good." He reached out with his manicured hand and picked up her left one, squeezing the second knuckle of her ring finger. "I see you're single."

She gently pulled her hand away. "Yes."

He held up his own left hand, fingers wiggling. "Well, that makes two of us."

She said nothing to that, just sat there while he smiled at her. After a moment, he tilted his head.

"You're not like the others."

"What others?"

"The other women here. Or the men, for that matter."

"I don't know what you mean."

He got up from the corner of her desk and turned, placing his hands flat on the desk top and leaning toward her. "Between you and me, this whole office likes to play musical beds."

Recoiling, Mary Sofia felt the blood drain out of her face. She briskly pivoted her chair to face the computer monitor. "I wouldn't know about that, and I prefer not to."

"That's what I mean," he said, straightening. "You're not like that."

"No," she stated firmly. "I am not."

"And I, for one, am glad to know it, Mary Sofia Carter." He thumped his fist on the desk, grinning. "Any reason you can't go out to lunch with me?"

Lunch. That was quick. Instinctively, she shook her head. "Sorry. I brought my lunch."

He shrugged lightly. "Ah, well. Some other time then. Maybe we can make it a group outing, an informal welcome lunch."

As he moved away, she thought better of her refusal. Maybe she'd misjudged his intentions. Besides, what if this was God giving her someone other than Stuart to concentrate on? What if Jackson Dillman was the man for her?

"You could always order in," she said, thinking quickly. "We could eat here. In the breakroom." There, that made it lunch with a workmate rather than a near date, with nothing private or particularly personal about it.

His smile bloomed anew. "Good idea. Give me fifteen minutes to run downstairs to the deli, then meet me in the breakroom."

As he hurried away, she nodded, pleased with herself. Nothing untoward could happen in the breakroom, after all, and she'd left space for God to work, if He so willed.

After all, she wanted the man God meant for her.

Who would surely then become the man of her dreams.

"Ah, Lord," she whispered, "I hope You know what I'm doing because I don't."

Chapter Twelve

S tuart showed up early to work on Monday morning specifically to join the guys for Bible study.

Bill Beck, who had not attended the previous Friday's HOBBY RUN performance, greeted him with, "I hear I missed a great time on Friday night. Wish I could've been there."

Explaining that the band performed at The Milking Barn every other Friday evening, Stuart went on to say, "Maggs can't comp every friend of the band that shows up, but I'm sure I could secure complimentary tickets for you and your wife if you want to make one of the shows."

Bill made a face that Stuart at first interpreted as free tickets not being enough, but then Bill said, "My wife's not well. Cancer. She has to keep away from crowds."

"Oh, Bill, I'm sorry. I didn't know."

"That's okay. No reason you should."

Stuart couldn't help feeling that he'd had every reason to know about the serious illness of the wife of one of his coworkers. His wife's illness explained Bill's frequent absences from work.

Recalling that one of his old projects had been reassigned to Bill, Stuart looked to Harry.

"Listen, I'll have the new product placement survey up and running by week's end. After that, the next push won't come until the information has been fully compiled. Why don't I go ahead and work the seasonal accounts until then? With Valentine's and President's Day behind us, St. Patrick's and Easter already in the bag, and the National Teacher's Day and Mother's Day promotions largely settled, there's no reason I can't put the finishing touches on Flag Day, Father's Day, and the Fourth of July."

"But those product placement surveys will be coming in from all over the world," Harry pointed out.

"Yes, and they need to be received, slotted, and graphed, but the team can do that. I'll just make sure they do it correctly. I mean, as long as all the info is in place when we begin compilation, it doesn't matter who receives and slots it."

Harry looked to Bill. "What do you think?"

"It would help," Bill admitted. "I already have plenty on my plate, but most of that can be done while I'm sitting beside my wife's bed."

"Okay. If you're sure, Champ," Harry decided.

"Absolutely."

"Thanks, Champ," Bill said, a look of utter relief on his face. "I sure appreciate this."

"You'd do the same for me."

"I pray to God I never have to," Bill told him.

"Speaking of prayer," Coop interjected, "let's get to it."

Along with the others, Stuart bowed his head and joined in the prayer. He had never before felt so comfortable in this building, so sure of his place in the scheme of things. That feeling carried over into Tuesday and Tuesday night's band practice, right up until the moment Allie showed up.

Fearing another scene, he quietly asked JoJo if Mary Sofia had complained about work at all. JoJo whispered that Allie had apparently been her usual detached self but pleasant enough. Reassured that Allie had returned to her cool, controlled self, he took a chance and approached.

"Allie, I owe you an apology."

She raised her chin, nose in the air as if he'd brought a bad odor with him. "No kidding. But for what exactly?"

"I insisted on a private affair," he admitted, "but I didn't end things between us privately. That was poorly done of me, and for that I apologize."

She shrugged a fur draped shoulder. "Private, public. Why should I care?"

"Because I embarrassed you. I didn't intend to, but I just couldn't live with it anymore. The whole thing was wrong, beginning to end, and I always knew it."

Fixing him with a cold glare, she huffed, "So

much for your gallant talk of marriage."

"Did you want to marry me, Allie?" he asked quietly, already knowing the answer.

That perfect nose rose another notch. "Of course not. I said so repeatedly, didn't I?"

"You did."

She rounded on him then, hissing, "So why persist with your proposals and show up at my office in front of everyone if it wasn't to make a spectacle of me?"

He looked down at his feet. "I truly thought that if I gave you what you wanted, public acknowledgement, you'd eventually agree to marriage. Only later did I realize that the possibility of marriage was just a patch to cover my guilty conscience. I used it as justification for what cannot be justified."

"Later?" Allie demanded. "You mean when virtuous little Mary Sofia saw you for what you are."

After considering for a long moment how to reply, he met Allie's angry gaze with his and nodded. "Yes. When I saw myself in her eyes, I had to face facts."

"And that's why you humiliated me," Allie snapped.

"I didn't mean for that to happen," he told her, but she was already walking away from him.

Sighing, he turned and saw Mary Sofia watching from across the room, concern on her lovely face. He turned away, in case she thought to come over to speak to him. That would only set off Allie once more. He'd heard nothing thus far to make him think that Allie had taken out her ire on Mary Sofia, so it seemed best just to drop the matter and get on with life.

The rest of the week and all of the next passed without incident. Allie attended the Friday night band performance at The Milking Barn, but Mary Sofia did not. Stuart sang the new song again, but Allie did not congratulate him afterward or comment in any way, so far as he knew. Gabi, however, could not contain herself. After the performance, she rushed into the Green Room and straight over to Stuart, loudly proclaiming her approval.

"Wow! Champ, you blew me away out there tonight. Mary Sofia said you made her cry with your song, but I didn't cry. I'm not a crier. She was right, though. It was great. Oh, she asked me to give you this." With that, Gabi bounced up on tiptoe and kissed his cheek.

Chuckling, he made a silly bow, rotating his hand in an exaggerated flourish. "Many thanks, my lady, to you and your fair sister."

Gabi clapped her hands and laughed. Straightening, he caught sight of Allie standing beside her brother. If looks could kill, he'd have gasped his last breath. He stood for several minutes, listening to Gabi gush.

"It was my turn to come last week," Gabi confided, loud enough for the entire room to hear, "but Mary Sofia traded dates with me so she could be here the first time you sang lead."

Stuart felt a startling pang of hope that he tried to mask with politeness. "That was nice of her."

"I wouldn't have traded," the girl rushed on. "I mean, she owed me anyway. For ruining her date with Gavin. That's our Youth Minister at church. But she wanted to be here *so* bad and, you know, she's my sister."

"I'm not sure I understand," Stuart told her, unable to make himself abandon the subject. "Why did you ruin her date with...your Youth Minister?"

"Because she asked me to. I don't see why. He's a very nice guy, kinda funny looking, but why should that matter?"

Stuart found that he hoped it mattered a lot to Mary Sofia. But then he realized that not being keen on this Gavin guy didn't mean she wasn't hung up on someone else. As Gabi prattled on about Gavin and someone named Davina Shelley, who had accompanied Gavin to the youth group's St. Patrick's Day party, Stuart clamped his jaw hard to keep from asking if Mary Sofia was dating anyone else.

"She's like third-generation from Ireland and knows all the legends about St. Patrick," Gabi hurried on. "It was fun hearing about the folklore, but Gavin made sure to give us the off cap."

"Off cap?" Stuart asked, puzzled.

"You know, the facts."

"Ah. And it was this Davina Shelley telling you about St. Patrick?"

"Who else?"

"Uh, I just thought Mary Sofia might've been there."

Gabi laughed. "No way. She'd have enjoyed it, though. Davina says…"

Stuart tuned out again, telling himself firmly that he had no business prying into Mary Sofia's private life. Besides, she would never consider him as a dating partner. Or any other kind of partner. Why, if she so much as sat down to a cup of coffee with him, Hugo would surely tear him limb from limb. And who could blame him? Given his own behavior and Mary Sofia's age and innocence, Stuart shouldn't allow himself to be anywhere near her. Maybe later, once he'd made it apparent that he was determined to live a life pleasing to God, he and Mary Sofia might… No, no.

Turning off the thought, he told himself that he'd just be asking for heartbreak if he even considered pursuing Mary Sofia. He couldn't ask her to sit around waiting for him to prove himself. She deserved better, and her brothers would see to it that she got it. Period. From now on, he would forget Mary Sofia and concentrate on Bible study, work, music, and whatever else God brought to him.

As he half-listened to Gabi going on and on about St. Patrick, he told himself that he had no right or reason to feel as if he'd lost something precious. Finally Hugo called to the girl.

"Time to head out. Ana says the twins are giving them trouble."

Gabi rolled her eyes and quickly confided, "If Marc Everett would stop hanging all over Mary Sofia all the time, the twins wouldn't get so upset."

"The boy does seem awfully attached to her."

"All three of them adore her," Gabi said glibly. "She's really good with them and even talked about becoming a professional nanny for a while. But the gups talked her out of that." She lifted a hand to cover one side of her mouth, confiding, "It's just that she wants her own family so much."

Stuart ignored that last part about Mary Sofia wanting her own family and the pang that came with it. "The, uh, gups?"

"Grown-ups." She pointed at Hugo. "That one's about to blow a gasket. Bye!"

Before Stuart could even thank her for coming, Gabi hurried toward her glowering brother. Stuart caught a calming breath, as if he had been the one talking a mile a minute, then quickly finished stowing his guitar. He'd made arrangements for a late meeting with the Ogilvies and the Coopers. Tamala had some sort of fundraiser in mind to aid the Becks so their daughter wouldn't have to come home from college to help care for her ailing mother. Apparently, Bill's wife was losing ground and needed around-the-clock assistance now, but the family didn't want her in a hospice facility and insurance wouldn't cover full-time in-home care. Champ felt compelled to help all he could, and he knew the rest of the band would, too, once the matter could be put to them.

He glanced around to see if Wyatt and Maggs were ready to depart the Green Room, when Allie stepped into his line of sight, her hands on her hips, pale eyes snapping.

"What's the matter, Stu? Mary Sofia not young enough for you? Now you're hitting on high schoolers?"

"Don't be absurd."

"Absurd is a man your age flirting with teenagers."

"I wasn't flirting."

"I saw her kiss you. And so did everyone else in the room."

Stuart kept a firm grip on his temper. "That kiss was from Mary Sofia, not Gabrielle."

The instant he said it, he regretted the words.

A feral gleam lit Allie's cold eyes. "But of course. I should have known."

She started to flounce away, but he caught her in midstride, his hand clamping onto her forearm. At the same moment, Wyatt signaled that he was ready to leave, pointing to the door. Stuart raised his chin in acknowledgement, then switched his attention back to Allie.

"There is nothing between me and Mary Sofia."

"Not yet, you mean. What's the matter, Stu? Doesn't Miss Virginity consider you husband material? Can't say I blame her."

"Neither can I," he gritted out. "Mary Sofia is a sweet kid just trying to make her way in the world. That's why I'm warning you. Don't you dare take out our problems on her."

Allie put on a surprised face that he knew to be fake. "Why would I do that? She's actually quite good at her work. Besides, I expect there'd be open rebellion if I fired her. She has all the men in the office slavering over her like wolves at a lamb convention." Jerking her arm free of his grasp, she bee-lined for her brother, who looked concerned.

Stuart gave Bart a quick shake of the head and a lame smile, then he followed Wyatt to Maggs's office, where the others already waited. He did his best to concentrate on and contribute to the discussion that followed, but a part of his mind remained on Mary Sofia and what Allie had implied about the men in her office.

No matter how many times he told himself that Mary Sofia had the good sense to take care of herself and that she had her brothers to call on if she needed shielding, he couldn't shake his concern.

Or was it jealousy?

"Please, God," he prayed, *"not jealousy. My days of hooking up with the wrong women are over."*

All the same, he couldn't help feeling responsible for Mary Sofia's situation.

If only he could so something besides pray.

***

By week's end, lunch with Jack had become a daily occurrence. Mary Sofia felt a little self-conscious and uncomfortable about it, even though he'd begun praying with her over the meal. That gave Mary Sofia the impetus to invite Jack to church. Surely that would tell her something. He arrived looking comfortable and well turned out in a navy blue suit and tie. Hugo, to her relief, greeted him amicably, with just the slightest narrowing of his eyes.

The Davina person Gabi had been going on and on about also attend the service that Sunday morning. Surprisingly, she stood at least a couple inches taller than Gavin, not counting the height of her thick, curly red hair. Her round, freckled face seemed almost featureless, but she had a killer figure and a laugh that brightened the entire room. To her, Gavin was evidently the funniest man on the planet. Mary Sofia hoped things worked out for them, because the two of them together were delightful.

Jack seemed to find them an affable pair. In fact, he seemed in charity with the whole world, shaking hands with the pastor and accepting Hugo's unexpected invitation to join the family for Sunday dinner. Mary Sofia set aside her misgivings and silently congratulated herself on finally finding a man her brother didn't hate on sight.

For once, the triplets sat quietly, staring at Jack as if they'd never seen a stranger. JoJo even joked that he should come around daily to quell their worst behaviors. The only blight on the day came with Gabi's frown. She made it known in subtle ways only family would pick up on that she didn't much care for "Smiling Jack," as she later called him.

"Too sure of himself," she muttered, alone in the apartment with Mary Sofia after Jack politely took his leave.

"You don't even know him," Mary Sofia pointed out.

"What about Champ?" Gabi asked.

Mary Sofia's heart skipped a beat, the way it always did when she thought of Champ, but she did her best to present a calm, unmoved façade. "What about him? We're friends. End of story."

"I don't believe you."

"Champ is not the guy for me," Mary Sofia insisted, a tad tartly that she'd intended. "He's... too old and too... experienced."

"He's not any older than Smiling Jack. And if you ask me, Jack is way too smooth and polite. All that 'sir' and 'Mrs. Carter' stuff. What's up with that?"

"Horrors! So he wanted to make a good impression. He's just a nice man. And he likes me."

Gabi folded her arms mulishly. "Well, I don't like him."

"But I do," Mary Sofia countered, "and that's what counts."

"You like him better than Champ?" Gabi asked, pouting.

Shaken by the question, Mary Sofia struggled to find an honest but suitable answer. "I didn't say that. I've known Champ much longer, after all. But there's nothing serious between me and Champ. Or me and Jack, for that matter."

Gabi "humphed' doubtfully and flounced into the bedroom. Mary Sofia gladly let her go, but just to prove her point, when Chet Hamlin called that evening, she accepted a dinner date for Thursday night. Chet worked weekends, of course, so it had to be a weeknight. Something of a foodie, he suggested a restaurant in downtown Bentonville called Golucky's.

It turned out that the popular restaurant offered a two-for-one discount on Thursdays, with wait times of over an hour.

***

Doing his very best to enjoy his solitary dinner, Stuart sliced another piece off the Chicken Papillon on his plate. Baked in parchment with sliced mushrooms and curled strips of bell pepper, the meat all but melted in his mouth. Eating alone had never been one of his favorite things to do, however, especially in a crowded, busy restaurant. Why hadn't he recalled that Thursday was two-for-one night at Golucky's? He should've turned around when he saw the crowd, but the owner was on hand and wouldn't hear of his good friend Champ leaving or waiting. After immediately being shown to a table, Stuart had begun to feel like a pig in the hen yard, hogging a table for four all to himself —until he looked up and spied a bright, bouncy Mary Sofia waving at him from the other side of the welcome station.

Delighted, he laid aside his utensils, stood, and waved her over. Only as she started forward did Stuart realize she wasn't alone. But of course she wouldn't be. His heart sank as he comprehended that the beefy fellow following in her footsteps could only be her date. Both carried their coats, and Mary Sofia had a roomy canvas bag slung over one shoulder.

"Fancy meeting you here," she greeted him brightly.

Stuart smiled. "Hello. I come here often. Place belongs to an old college friend, but I usually try to avoid Thursdays. Seems selfish to take up a whole table by myself with all these couples and families waiting for seats." He waved a hand at the throng in the holding area.

"No kidding. Is it always so crowded? This is

my first time here."

"I come here now and then," said the man with her. "Just didn't expect Thursday to be this busy Guess it's the milder weather."

Stuart smiled, aware that he'd been rudely ignoring the fellow. Young and fit, he stood a couple inches shorter than Stuart but was twice as wide and several years younger.

Mary Sofia hurried to make the introductions. "Oh. Sorry. Stuart Champion meet Chet Hamlin." As both men reached out to shake hands, she added, "Chet and I used to work together."

"And now we don't," Chet stated significantly, maintaining his grip on Stuart's hand.

Mary Sofia quickly changed the subject. "Champ works in advertising, and he plays with the same band as my sister-in-law."

"Mm. The hobby band," Chet said off-handedly, finally relinquishing his grip.

"HOBBY RUN," Stuart corrected mildly, trying not to let Chet grate on his nerves. Just because the guy was with Mary Sofia was no reason to despise him on sight. Clearing his throat, Stuart said, "Thursdays are always busier than any other weeknight, but the weekends can be just as packed. At least they take reservations on the weekends. Why don't you two join me? You won't have to wait for a table that way, and I won't feel so guilty for taking up this one all by my lonesome."

Mary Sofia looked to Chet, who shrugged and pulled out a chair for her on Stuart's right. She hung her roomy handbag over one corner of the chair and draped her coat over it before sitting.

Stuart signaled the waiter. "Could we have a couple of menus, please?"

As Chet walked around and took the chair at the end of the table on Mary Sofia's right, Stuart resumed his seat. Chet dumped his coat on the one empty chair, sat, and immediately appropriated Mary Sofia's hand. He didn't let go until the menus arrived.

"I highly recommend tonight's special," Stuart said, studiously ignoring the handholding. Bracing his elbows on the tabletop, he steepled his hands over his plate.

"Oh, please go on eating," Mary Sofia urged. "We don't want your food to get cold."

"Yeah, go ahead," Chet said, as if the sooner Stuart finished the happier they'd all be.

Smiling, Stuart began slowly cutting into his chicken again, one small bite at a time, and choking it down. Mary Sofia and Chet ordered. She had the special. He asked for a steak. The waiter brought fresh, hot rolls, which Stuart took his jolly good time buttering and eating. Meanwhile, Mary Sofia kept up a steady stream of chatter, mostly about the band. Even after their food arrived, she babbled on, and Stuart happily joined in, finally relaxing a bit. To his surprise, he was enjoying himself, but when he ordered dessert and coffee, Hamlin looked as if he would blow his top. Staring daggers at Stuart, the other man contributed nothing more than grunts and growls to the conversation.

Eventually, Stuart could delay his departure no longer. As compensation for horning in on their date, he picked up the check for all three dinners. Mary Sofia rose when he did to embrace him fondly and kiss his cheek.

"Thank you. We'd have been waiting forever if you hadn't invited us to your table."

"My pleasure," he told her, not daring to return her kiss. He didn't trust himself to keep even a kiss on the cheek friendly when it came to her. "Will I see you on Tuesday?"

"I hope so."

"Me, too."

The gaze that met his, broke his heart. She was worried about him. He could see it in her eyes. Sad and a little wistful, they asked if he was all right. For her sake, he reactivated his smile.

"Enjoy the rest of your dinner."

Chet grumbled his thanks as Stuart moved away from the table. Stuart managed to leave without looking back, but once on the sidewalk, he couldn't help one last gaze through the window. Mary Sofia sat with her arms folded while Chet leaned close, obviously complaining. Stuart almost went back inside at that point, but then Mary Sofia abruptly pushed away her plate, sat forward, and said something that had Hamlin snapping upright. Suddenly, he shot up out of his chair, grabbed his coat, and made for the door. Mary Sofia put her fingertips to her temples for a moment, then began clawing through her handbag for her phone. Stuart waited until Chet had pushed through the door, angrily stomping down the sidewalk in the opposite direction, before he rushed back inside. He reached the table just as Mary Sofia finished punching in the number of whomever she intended to call. Reaching down, Stuart covered both her phone and her hand with his.

She turned a glower up at him, but then the anger drained away, and she smiled wryly.

"Need a ride?"

"Seems so."

As she pushed back her chair and got to her feet once again, he shook out her coat and held it open for her. He hadn't meant to ruin her date but was secretly glad that he'd done so.

Could God have possibly meant for it to turn out this way?

He dared not let himself believe that it might be so.

Chapter Thirteen

"I didn't mean to make your boyfriend angry," Stuart said, starting the Jeep's engine.

"He's not my boyfriend," she refuted quickly. "He, um, used to be my boss. Shift manager at the restaurant where I worked." She kept her attention on the scene outside the window of the truck as Stu pulled it out of the parallel parking space and headed away from downtown Bentonville. "This was our first—and last—date." Wrinkling her nose, she confided, "Turns out Chet is the sort who thinks he owns any woman he has an interest in. He was happy enough to accept your invitation to join you at your table, but then he expected you to sit silently because we were on a date. Stupid attitude."

"Still, I didn't mean any harm."

She flashed him a smile. "I know that. And thank you for going out of your way to give me a ride home. It means at least an hour out of your evening."

"It's no problem. Would've meant the same for Hugo if he'd had to come after you."

"How do you know I was going to call Hugo?"

He shrugged. "Just assumed."

"And, of course, you're right."

"Well, that's different," Stuart quipped. "Let's hope it's a trend."

Laughing, she relaxed. Stuart was so easy to talk to, and now that she'd pushed aside her anger at Chet, all sorts of topics presented themselves.

"It's not nearly as cold tonight as was just a couple of weeks ago."

"Winter has definitely lost its grip," he agreed.

"I prefer a snowy winter."

"Yeah, me, too. At least playing in the snow is fun. Cold is just...cold."

She giggled at that. "Obviously."

He grinned. "Maybe next year. We haven't had a really good snow in a couple of years no, so we're due."

"True."

The topic shifted to the roadwork that seemed never to end in the area. After that they discussed the restaurant and its proximity to Stuart's house.

"I didn't realize you live that close to downtown."

"Yep," he confirmed. "I'm on every Homecoming, Christmas, and Independence Day parade route. I always think about having people over to watch, but I never do."

"Why is that?"

Shrugging, he answered, "Just doesn't seem like something a single man would do."

"I don't know why not. And anyway, you won't be single forever."

He shook his head. "Don't know how you could be sure about that? Because I'm not."

"Well, I am," she insisted. "God has someone for you. And me."

Glancing at her, he softly said, "I hope so."

So do I, she thought, but pursuing the subject didn't seem wise.

He apparently agreed, for he suddenly said, "Can I tell you a secret? Well, not a secret exactly, but it won't be announced until Tuesday evening at practice."

"Of course."

"Maggs has set up a concert a week from this coming Sunday for a friend of mine at work. His wife has cancer, and they need help at home. Then today I heard the doctor's want to try an experimental drug with her, but insurance won't pay more than half the cost, which is something like a hundred and fifty thousand dollars."

"How sad. Not the concert, the cancer and all that."

Stuart nodded. "It is sad. But they're people of great faith, and they believe God will provide."

"Is this what Tamala Cooper had in mind when she asked if the band ever played in church?" Mary Sofia wondered aloud.

"Yes. As soon as Tamala made her proposal, though, Maggs offered The Milking Barn free of charge, which makes the whole thing a lot easier to pull off."

"And you've been involved in the planning, haven't you?"

"Uh, mostly I just introduced Maggs and Tamala."

Somehow Mary Sofia doubted his involvement had gone no farther than an introduction. "Really? That's all?"

He waved a hand. "Okay, so I designed an ad campaign and called in a few favors with local media. No big deal."

Mary Sofia grinned. "Not to you maybe. I imagine it's a very big deal for your friend and his wife."

Stuart shifted in his seat. "The only reason I brought it up is so you could plan accordingly. Every cent for every ticket purchased will go to help the Becks."

"I'll be there," she promised. "If I don't have to babysit the triplets."

"Hm. Well, it's supposed to be a family friendly event, but even if Hugo and JoJo decide the triplets should stay at home, maybe we can do an end run around that."

"How?" For a few seconds, she thought he wouldn't answer, but then he did.

"You could always agree to go with me." He glanced in her direction. "That way, if you're asked to babysit, you can always say you've made a prior commitment. Unless you think that's a bad idea."

"No!" Her heart racing, she tamped down her enthusiasm. "I-I mean, if Gabi has to babysit, I'd definitely owe her, but that should be okay."

"What about Hugo? How will he feel about it? I mean it's not really a date because I'll be performing and you'll be..." He didn't seem to know quite how to finish that.

"Just there," she finished for him. "As your guest."

He let out a breath. "Right. As my guest. Absolutely."

"That'll work," Mary Sofia decided.

In fact, that would work very well, indeed. She'd see to it.

For more than a week, she thought and prayed about the matter. By Friday morning of the next week, she had solidified her plan. More or less. She didn't want Hugo simply to bite his tongue about her going to the charity concert with Stuart. She wanted Hugo and everyone else to begin viewing Stuart as a possible romantic interest for her.

The first step would be to get Stuart to agree to an alteration in his invitation, but she had to pick her moment. She dared not push too early or wait too long. The Friday before the charity event seemed the right time, so she waited impatiently for her morning break in order to make a personal call. Then, just before the clock on her desktop computer hit the appointed hour, Stuart called her.

When she saw his name crawling across the tiny screen of her phone, her heart leaped and began to pound. Immediately, she turned her chair away from the glass walls of Selwyn's and Allie's offices and toward the back wall of her own cubicle. Several people chose that moment to rise and leave their desks for the breakroom, so she felt no compunction about tapping the green icon and lifting the phone to her ear.

"Hello. Great minds think alike. I was just about to call you."

"Hello, yourself," Stuart's voice greeted her. "This mind is taking a break. How are things going?"

"Fine."

"Not working too hard, are you?"

"Not at all."

"Glad to hear it. I just wanted to check with you about the charity concert this Sunday. We're still on for that, right?"

"We're still on," Mary Sofia told him. "Starts at three o'clock, right?"

"Three o'clock," he confirmed. "Thought I'd pick you up around noon, if that's okay. It would keep me from having to eat another meal alone and still give me plenty of time to get to The Milking Barn and set up."

"I have a better idea," she told him, thankful

he had brought up the subject of the Sunday meal. "You could always come for church at ten-thirty and stay for dinner with the family afterward. That would give us all the time we need and help keep me out of the doghouse with Hugo."

For a long moment, she heard nothing but silence and worried that she had made unwarranted assumptions. He'd stated flatly that it wasn't a date, after all. Why hadn't she believed him?

Then his voice came to her once more. "Sounds like a plan. What, um, what church and where?"

She let out a silent sigh of relief and gave him the name and address of the family church in Fayetteville.

"I'll be there."

"Great. I think JoJo is baking a ham. I'll have her put a few more potatoes in the crock pot."

"Sounds good. See you then."

"Yes, see you then."

She ended the call, quite pleased. Now, to prepare Hugo. She hadn't quite found the moment or words to tell her brother that she would be going to the charity concert with Stuart, but she couldn't let Stuart just walk through the church door without any warning. Or could she? Perhaps the person she needed to tell was her sister-in-law. JoJo would never lie to Hugo, but she might be willing not to tell him what to expect.

Mary Sofia took a deep breath, closed her eyes, tilted her chair back, and tried to think what was best to do in this situation. Still uncertain, she turned her chair around to get a look at the clock and make sure she wasn't overdoing her break. And there stood Jack, looking... She didn't know how to describe that expression. Angry? Unsure. Downcast. Not exactly. Determined? She simply had no clue at the moment.

They had continued to eat lunch together in the breakroom most days, but lately he'd been doing some things that bothered her. He'd begun touching her, lightly running his fingertip along her jawline or down her arm, and he kept inviting her on inappropriate outings. She'd flatly refused to visit him in his home and told him bluntly that she had no interest in nightclubs or bars. He'd suggested coming to her place, but she'd reminded him that she lived with her sister in an apartment just above her brother's garage. Feeling that she'd been difficult to please, she had suggested dinner, but he'd replied that all they seemed to do together was eat. Now here he stood once again.

She laid the phone face down on her desk and smiled up at Jack, asking brightly, "Hey, how's your morning been?"

Suddenly his usual, affable self, he propped a hip on the corner of her desk. "Uneventful.

Yours?"

"Pretty much the same as usual," she replied lightly. Beyond him, she saw Allie motioning to her, waving her into the office. Deeply relieved, Mary Sofia got to her feet, grabbed her electronic pad, and smiled apologetically at Jack. "Sorry. Can't talk now. The boss lady wants to see me."

Standing, he turned his head to look at Allie, who threw up her arms as if to say, "Get with it already!"

"Catch you later," he said, striding away.

Mary Sofia waved a farewell, actually relieved for once to be walking into the lion's den. Since her breakup with Stuart, Allie had almost entirely transmitted her orders to Mary Sofia via Selwyn, but there had been the odd instruction, correction, or criticism. With Selwyn out of the office today, Mary Sofia assumed Allie had been reduced to issuing her own orders. True to form, Allie got right to the point.

"I need you to help Grant Leonardo prepare for a welcome party next Saturday night."

"Me help Leo?" Mary Sofia clarified, hoping she'd misheard.

Allie went back to the paperwork she'd been reading. "That's right. He has arranged for a wealthy client to fly in from Lithuania, and the guy apparently expects a warm welcome. I'll need you in attendance, by the way."

"Next Saturday night?" Mary Sofia clarified.

"A week from tomorrow."

"That's what I said."

Mary Sofia very nearly said she wouldn't work with Leo, but Allie already thought she was a self-righteous little twit, so she gulped down her objections. "What time is the party?"

Allie turned over a page and waved a dismissive hand. "Just be here around ten and prepare to stay until the party ends."

Confused, Mary Sofia commented, "Ten o'clock seems awfully late."

Allie looked up, impatience stamped on her face. "Then come in earlier. Bring your breakfast. I don't care."

Reality hit Mary Sofia then. Allie didn't mean for her to come in at ten in the evening.

"You mean, ten a.m."

"Yes, ten a.m. The deliveries usually start around then, and someone has to be here to accept them. The bartender will arrive about six, and he expects everything to be in place by then. The others will wander in between seven and nine. Not sure when our guest of honor will show up because he's flying via personal jet, but we hope before nine. It'll be late before everyone leaves, so you can come in on Sunday to finish cleaning up."

"I go to church on Sunday."

"Then come in early Monday," Allie snapped.

"In other words, I'll be here from ten on Saturday morning until who-knows-what-time

Sunday morning."

"That's about it," Allie confirmed blandly. "For your convenience, you can change clothes here. Wear something…" She raked a critical gaze over Mary Sofia. "Wear something your grandmother would *not* wear. Or your mother, for that matter."

Mary Sofia thought, *You didn't know my mother,* but she merely nodded, silently wondering what she could possibly wear that would meet Allie's standards and not embarrass herself. Or cause Hugo to lock her in her apartment. Thus far, she'd confined her shopping to business attire, but now she'd have to look for evening wear.

"Leo's waiting for you in the penthouse," Allie finished, going back to her work.

"Now?" Mary Sofia blurted.

Allie rolled her eyes. "That's what I said. Now." She waved a hand in a shooing motion. "Don't keep him waiting. Take my private elevator up."

Mary Sofia wished she'd left her tablet at her desk so she could beg a few moments reprieve, but she held it clutched against her chest, so she had no choice other than to enter the small elevator car and let it speed her up to the penthouse.

As the doors opened, Mary Sofia again recalled that day she'd been standing there on the other side of the door when the elevator had arrived. The sight of Stuart and Allie wrapped around each other still haunted her, and she'd wished a thousand times that she hadn't seen what she'd seen, even though it had turned out for the best. At least for Stuart. After this morning's conversation with him, she felt a stirring of delight, a tingle of hope. But she had to deal with Leo first.

She pushed aside thoughts of Stuart, an endeavor that had become a habit, and stepped out into the large, plush room. Looking around, she spied Leo at the table by the window, studiously going over papers.

"Hello," she said in greeting.

He lifted his head and waved her over, saying, "You'll need to make a number of calls to cover our bases. Florist, bartender, butcher, grocer, limousine, DJ, drinks, cigars... You'll also need to coordinate with the chef. Oh, and you'll have to go through Selwyn about paying for it all."

She made a desperate attempt to sidestep the event. "Wouldn't it be easier if Selwyn helped you manage this? I mean, it being so important and me never having done this sort of thing before."

"Selwyn has enough on his plate. You just do as you're told. I'll handle the personal requests myself."

"Personal requests?"

He fixed her with a smarmy grin and leaned

back in his chair. "Never hurts to have good-looking women on hand. That's why I asked for you."

Mary Sofia straightened, squaring her shoulders, and made another attempt to blunt her involvement. "I would prefer not to be one of the guests. After all, I'll be working that evening."

His gaze immediately hardened. "Yeah? That's too bad. We need to pull out all the stops to land this deal, so get yourself a party dress and prepare to par-tay."

Mary Sofia stared at him for several seconds. Despite the way he made her skin crawl, he really wasn't a bad-looking man. In fact, quite the opposite, given his moss green eyes and unusual charcoal gray hair cut in a trendy side fade, as well as the square jaw and high cheekbones to go with it. He dressed well enough to have walked off the pages of a fashion magazine. What killed it all for her was the smug way he ogled her, as if he had a secret she needed to know. Somehow, she had to find a way to keep her distance from the guy. Unfortunately, the best she could do at the moment was tend to business, so she got to it.

"I'll need a list of the suppliers to call and the details of each order."

He shoved a piece of paper at her. "This is what I have so far. Don't let them try to talk you up in price or make substitutions. And keep me informed every step of the way. Now, let's go over the time table."

Leonardo was not her superior, but she felt compelled to say, "Yes, sir."

He reached across the table and stroked her hand, crooning, "Good girl."

She fought the impulse to recoil but instead plucked her stylus from its clip on the side of her tablet and prepared to write on the screen. "Ready when you are."

"Oh, honey, I'm always ready. Ready, willing, and able." Smirking, he began giving her details.

An hour later, Leo rose and had her follow him around the room so he could show her exactly where he wanted what placed. Flowers on every flat surface. Cigars in a special box containing lighters, clippers, and ashtrays on the side tables in the living area. He all but marked off how the buffet was to be placed and even showed her where and how the alcohol should be stowed.

"Our friend may have his own, but we'll want to be well stocked in case he doesn't. We've hired our usual bartender for the evening, by the way. He can keep his tips at the end of the evening, but you'll need to pay him his contracted fee as soon as he arrives. The chef will be sending you a list of groceries and other supplies needed for the meal."

"I assume I will be tending the buffet."

"And serving the special meal that will be

prepared for the boss lady and our guest. You'll need to assist the bartender from time to time, too."

"Doesn't sound like I'll have much time for socializing."

"We'll make time," Leo told her with a creepy smile. "So wear something low, short, and tight." Grasping her chin by the fingers of one hand, he turned her head from side to side. "And let down that gorgeous hair."

She backed up a step, wrenching herself free of his touch, and coldly said, "I'll thank you to keep your hands to yourself."

The creepy smile widened into a creepier grin. "You say that now, but you'll change your tune as soon as you get a taste."

"I don't want a taste."

"That's just because you don't know what you're missing."

She backed up another step. "And I never will."

He laughed at that. "You're adorable. Pity it can't last."

Turning away, she strode toward the hallway and the larger, less private elevator beyond. "I'm done here. If you think of anything else, message me."

"Catch you later, sweet thing."

Ignoring his farewell, she clutched the tablet beneath one arm and opened the heavily carved door with the other. Selwyn had given her a key to the larger elevator the day she'd waited table for Champ and Allie. Once outside, she pulled the key from her pocket and activated the elevator. The door opened, and she stepped inside, punching the button to close the door before she used the key again to descend to the next floor. On the night of the party, someone would have to unlock the elevator via the computer controls, but that was above her pay grade, so she dismissed any concern.

She wanted to take a shower. Just being in Grant Leonardo's presence made her feel filthy. She liked him even less now than before. In fact, he creeped her out so severely that she considered quitting her job. Then she spied Jack walking from his cubicle to another, and a new idea occurred. She could always ask him to stay close to her the evening of the party. Doing so would undoubtedly encourage his interest. Unless she made it clear beforehand that she had no romantic interest in him.

Yes, that was what she would do. She needed to come clean with Jack, anyway, and she'd never find a better reason or opportunity. She'd ask Jack to help her. As a friend. And pray she wasn't making a mistake.

Selwyn came into the office just before quitting time, so she presented her work to him, hoping to minimize as much contact with Leo as possible. "I've called most of the suppliers and made some orders already. Everyone so far has agreed to the price Mr. Leonardo said to offer, and no one asked for a deposit."

"Of course not," Selwyn retorted, standing at his desk and flipping through papers. "They know they'll be paid."

"Payment upon delivery," she pointed out. "Every supplier has said the same thing. I assume I'll need to hand each one a check after I make sure the delivery is satisfactory."

"Check? No, no. We pay by transfer."

"I don't know how to do that."

He closed a file folder and sat down in his desk chair, looking up at her. "Just have all the figures ready for me before next Friday. I'll set it up so it'll be a simple matter of tapping the right icons on your tablet."

"It's just that we're talking about thousands of dollars here," Mary Sofia explained. "I don't want to make a mistake."

"I don't see how you could. Now, go home, Miss Carter. Next week is going to be a busy one for you."

She backed out of the room, logged off her computer, shoved her tablet into her handbag, and rushed out of there, wishing she never had to return.

Chapter Fourteen

T he moment Hugo spotted him on Sunday morning, Stuart knew Mary Sofia hadn't told her brother to expect him. It didn't help that she feigned surprise and rushed over to greet him.

"Hello! And welcome."

He blinked and quietly said, "You knew I'd be here."

"I did," she whispered, "but not everyone else."

JoJo, bless her, stepped in to ease the way. "Champ. It's so good to see you."

Hugo, trailing behind, looked confused for a moment, but then he frowned at Mary Sofia before lifting his eyebrows at his wife.

"What a pleasant surprise!" JoJo exclaimed blithely. "This works out beautifully. Champ can join us for Sunday dinner. Then we can all head up to the charity concert together."

"Isn't this a little out of your way?" Hugo asked Champ, his tone dropping to a low growl. "Or a lot?"

"What difference does it make?" Mary Sofia

asked. "He's here. Seems silly for him not to stay to dinner afterward."

"He's gotta eat," JoJo put in. "No reason for him to eat alone when we have all that food back at the house."

"Good point," Mary Sofia agreed, her smile too bright and too forced to be believable.

Equal parts amused and wary, Stuart shook his head. This was not how he meant to go on. He'd promised himself and God that he had turned over a new leaf. Truth or nothing.

Looking Hugo in the eye, he said, "Actually, I invited Mary Sofia to have dinner with me and accompany me to the charity concert afterward. She suggested I meet the family here for church and have dinner with you all. If that's okay with you."

Hugo studied the reddening faces of his wife and sister then turned back to Stuart. After a long, fraught moment, he muttered, "Let me introduce you to our Minister of Outreach before we go in."

Sending a hard stare to both his wife and his sister, Hugo steered a guarded but resigned Stuart across the broad foyer to meet the heavy-set, middle-aged minister. A brief exchange and handshake later, the minister moved on, greeting others, but Hugo held Stuart in place with a flat, direct look.

"Well, at least you didn't lie to me," he remarked sourly, "but I'm telling you now that if JoJo and I weren't going to be at that concert today, no way I'd let Mary Sofia drive off with you."

Stuart nodded. "I understand. And I don't blame you. But have you stopped to think that Mary Sofia is well past legal age? Unless you're prepared to toss her out into the street, I'm not sure you can—or should—force your will on her."

A troubled expression wrinkled Hugo's brow. "I'm not about to toss out my sister."

"I didn't think you were."

"But I like to believe that I do have some influence on her."

"No doubt about it."

"Let's you and I get one thing straight here, Champ. She's not a plaything."

"No human being is a plaything," Stuart said firmly, "and I'll never treat her as if she is. Look, I know I don't inspire confidence in my intentions or integrity, and I also know I'm not good enough for Mary Sofia. I admire her greatly."

Hugo moved in close then. "Admire her all you want, but respect her more. Otherwise, you'll answer to me."

Stuart nodded. He had expected no less of the big Marine. In fact, he'd expected worse.

Without another word, Hugo turned and walked back to his sister and wife. Stuart calmly followed, making certain to send a half-smile to Mary Sofia.

She seemed to get the message. Crisis

averted. For the moment. Putting on a brave face, she chirruped brightly, "Let's find our seats."

His expression stoic, Hugo lifted a hand. "After you."

She led the way this time. Stuart fell into step beside her, fighting the urge to straighten his tie and square his shoulders. He could feel Hugo's stare drilling holes in his back, but he'd survived the first encounter. A tentative sense of elation put a small smile on his face. This may not be the first step in a new romance, but it could very well be the first step in regaining his integrity.

The service surprised him. In some ways, it proved very traditional, and in other ways, quite modern. To his surprise, he liked the brightly colored hangings in the sanctuary and the Spanish influenced music. The pastor came as another pleasant surprise. Tall, slender, and balding, with horn-rimmed glasses, he might have been forty or sixty years of age. As much a blend of new and old as the service he oversaw, he wore blue jeans under his ecclesiastic robes and sported athletic shoes beneath. At the same time, the guy radiated joy, and although his sermon was serious and blunt, he worked in a good deal of relevant humor. Stuart hadn't attended church in some time, and he enjoyed the whole thing more than expected.

He'd put off returning to his own church for several reasons, mostly sheer embarrassment, but after this he thought it would be easier to go home, so to speak. In fact, he intended to make his Bible study group at church a priority again, as well as keep up with the Bible study at work. Glancing at Mary Sofia, he silently thanked God for her invitation to today's service. After the benediction, he made certain to thank her.

"This has been very enjoyable," he told her, stepping out into the aisle ahead of her. "Bless you for inviting me."

"My pleasure," she answered brightly, but then she lowered her voice and spoke directly into his ear as they slowly made their way up the crowded aisle. "I hope Hugo didn't give you too hard a time."

"Not at all. We understand each other perfectly."

She frowned at that, but he didn't have time to explain before a funny looking little man moving against the tide suddenly grabbed his hand and began pumping it.

"Pleased to meet you. Welcome. Any friend of Mary Sofia's is a friend of mine."

Surprised to see Mary Sofia's face go blank, Stuart put on a friendly smile while she blandly made the introductions.

"Gavin Worley. Stuart Champion. Champ plays in the HOBBY RUN band with JoJo. Gavin is our Minister of Youth."

"Nice to meet you," Stuart said.

A young woman with wildly curling, bright red hair held back from her round, freckled face with a hard plastic headband, watched avidly from behind Worley's right shoulder. The youth minister let go of Stuart's hand and waved in her direction.

"That's Davina, one of our sponsors."

Stuart made a point of shaking the woman's hand. She didn't say a word, just shook, grinned and nodded.

Gabi pushed into the group then, shoving between Gavin Worley and Davina. She threw her arms around Stuart, exclaiming, "Champ! I'm so surprised to see you here."

"Cut it out," Hugo groused. "All of you. Mary Sofia invited him. He told me so. Now, let's get to dinner. We have places to be this afternoon." He stomped off, JoJo hurrying after him.

Stuart forced a smile in an effort not to laugh outright, grasped Mary Sofia's elbow, and once more followed as she plowed through the crowd, some of whom had stopped to chat. She apologized as she went.

"Sorry. We have to go. Excuse us. So sorry."

He nodded at the odd individual as he squeezed past them, still hanging onto Mary Sofia.

Bringing up the rear, Gabi muttered, "I told them, but do they listen to me? As if."

When they reached the foyer, Hugo made it clear that Mary Sofia would not be riding back to the Carter house with Stuart by simply stating that Stuart could follow them if he couldn't find his own way from the church. Mary Sofia sent him off with an apologetic frown. He made no argument, just left the building and got into his car. He didn't even think of abandoning the whole idea. Instead, he thanked God for the worship experience that morning and the chance to prove himself. While he was at it, he thanked God for Hugo and the way he protected all of his sisters. Perhaps if he, Stuart, had been blessed with a younger sister, he'd have been as protective of her. Maybe he'd have made better choices, too, for her sake if not his own. Or maybe he'd have been a selfish cad, sister or no sister, until he'd seen himself in Mary Sofia's eyes.

He pulled into the wide driveway of the Carter home in little more than fifteen minutes after leaving the church. To his surprise, Mary Sofia, wearing jeans and a thin heather gray sweater, waved from the top of the stairs to her apartment.

"Stuart, hang on. I'm on my way down." She quickly descended the steps, while he waited beside his truck.

"That was quick," he commented, noting that in her haste she'd donned white canvas shoes without socks. This first Sunday in April had dawned bright and cool, but as predicted, the temperature had risen to nearly seventy degrees, so he'd left his overcoat at home, but the evening would undoubtedly see a drop of at least twenty degrees.

"Hugo drives fast when he's angry."

"I'm sorry about—"

She cut him off. "No. I'm sorry. You had nothing to do with making him mad. That's all on me."

"Mm, I'm not so sure about that. JoJo and Gabi both seem to have bought into the scheme. Besides, we both knew he was going to be upset that I asked you out."

A smile flickered across her face. "Did you ask me out? You know, like, a real date?"

He couldn't help the smile that curled his own lips. "You know I did. I just didn't have the nerve to state it plainly. I won't be so stupid the next time."

Her whole face bloomed with a smile that seemed even to brighten the sunshine overhead.

"I'm sorry I didn't level with Hugo. I was afraid he'd say you couldn't come to dinner."

"Not that he'd refuse to let you go with me?"

"I'm not a child," she told him softly, shaking her head. "I love my brother, and I don't want to upset or argue with him. But I make my own decisions."

Stuart nodded in acknowledgement, delighted that she'd have gone with him even over Hugo's objections. At the same time, he respected her desire not to be on the outs with her brother. Perhaps she hadn't gone about this thing the right way, and perhaps she had. It wasn't as if she'd sprung him on the entire family, after all, and apparently JoJo had agreed that keeping Hugo in the dark was the best approach in this case. Besides, they'd cleared the first hurdle, so they might as well attempt the next.

"We'd better go inside."

"Yes. Let's do that."

As they walked to the door, trading smiles and glances, Stuart silently acknowledged that he'd been fooling himself. True, he did not deserve Mary Sofia, but he wanted her. Perhaps God would grant him that heart's desire; perhaps He would not. Stuart knew only one way to find out.

The first to greet him was a small, gray dog with a thick, curly coat, long snout, and an uncannily direct stare. The dog sat in the center of the foyer, as still as a statue, its black eyes slowly raking him from head to toe and back again with the steadiness of an x-ray machine. A second dog with the long floppy ears and smooth, muticolored coat of a beagle ran, slipping and sliding, to greet them, nearly careening into the first animal. At the last moment, it backpedaled so sharply the poor thing flipped onto its hind end and right over onto its back. As the hound scrabbled to right itself, Mary Sofia laughed and made a shooing motion with both hands.

"Ears," she commanded, pointing, "outside. Now."

The dog popped onto its feet, turned, and made a hard run into the living room and out of sight. Stuart expected the other mutt to follow, but when he looked around, it had disappeared. To where, he did not know, and Mary Sofia didn't give him the chance to ask as she led him deeper into the house, calling out, "We're here."

He'd been inside the house before, of course, on several occasions, first when Amalie had lived there and again at Mary Sofia's graduation party, so he knew the way to the dining room. Still, he was not prepared for the sight that greeted him.

At first, the sight of three highchairs pulled up to the amazing dining table that Hugo had designed and built seemed surreal. JoJo was just slipping into her chair when he and Mary Sofia arrived. Hugo immediately pointed them to their seats, which stood several seats apart, but Stuart soon realized the wisdom in the seating arrangement. Lizbet sat between her parents, with Hugo at the head of the table. Caro sat between her mother and Mary Sofia, and Marc Everett occupied a place between Mary Sofia and Gabi. Stuart sat between Gabi and thirteen-year-old Ana, who served as the bumper between him and Hugo. When he pulled out Mary Sofia's chair for her, she gave him a small, apologetic shrug. He resisted the urge to pat her shoulder and took the chair pointed out to him.

Stuart marveled at the way everyone handled the triplets. The whole family worked as a team. Glimpsing them in public and seeing them in action at home proved to be two very different experiences. Lizbet constantly demanded attention. Her parents took turns calmly placating or scolding her and spooning food into her mouth. Meanwhile, Caro quietly vied for her mom's devotion with smiles and small, grasping fingers. When Lizbet grew loud and boisterous, Mary Sofia automatically switched her focus from Marc Everett to Caro, so JoJo could give the troublemaker her attention. Marc Everett watched Mary Sofia's repeated defections solemnly, only to reach for her if she so much as glanced at him, hoping she'd take him onto her lap. Gabi did her best to engage him, but he gave basically ignored her and everyone else other than Mary Sofia. When not quietly vying for her mom's attention, Caro shyly flirted with him from across the table, her pale eyebrows dancing over bright eyes.

Every time Lizbet caught the byplay between him and Caro, she yelled an objection. Soon, she was throwing things and yelling to gain his attention. Her aim was quite good, so eventually the table around his plate had been peppered with any number of carrot slices and corn kernels. JoJo continually apologized, but Stuart couldn't help laughing. No human being of any age or gender had ever commanded his attention in so studious a fashion. To his surprise, Lizbet started kicking the table and reaching for him, screeching, "Me! Me!"

Finally, he got up and walked around the table to pull her out of her chair. Sighing, she grabbed onto him as if for dear life. Ignoring JoJo's apologetic objections, he carried her back to his chair and sat down with her on his lap. Lounging back against his chest, she reached for a sliced carrot next to his plate and threw it at her sister. When she went after another missile, Stuart gently caught her hand and redirected it to her mouth.

She laughed, squinting up at him, her mouth full of carrot, and abruptly went after his plate with both hands, stuffing her face as rapidly as possible with stewed baby red potatoes. Ana leaned forward, reached across the table, and plopped a large spoonful of the potatoes onto his plate.

"Thank you," Stuart told her with a chuckle and picked up his fork. Between them, he and Lizbet cleared the plate twice. Caro watched avidly the entire time, fluttering her eyelids and smiling whenever he looked at her. The whole experience turned out to be very entertaining, much more enjoyable than Stuart expected. While JoJo was her own calm, reasonable, efficient self, Hugo said little, but what he did say was pleasant enough. Stuart enjoyed the food very much. The only home cooking he'd eaten in ages had been his own, and this far surpassed his efforts.

After the meal, when everyone retired to the living room, Lizbet rushed over to her sister and shoved her down. Hugo immediately grabbed Lizbet and quietly scolded her, with Lizbet screaming like a banshee throughout, as if she were the injured party. Marc Everett clung to Mary Sofia, hiding his face in the curve of her neck. Caro, meanwhile, calmly got up and climbed onto Stuart's lap, grinning at him. Laughing, he hugged her.

"This one is a charmer," he said to no one in particular. "Frankly, I think she's the more dangerous of the two."

"Oh, I agree," Mary Sofia told him. "Lizbet throws fits, but you never have to guess what she's thinking. Caro, on the other hand, gets what she wants in much more subtle ways. You don't even realize you've been played until you realize she has what Lizbet's been demanding." She hugged Marc Everett, adding, "This one just whines until he gets what he wants."

"And they're all insufferable without their afternoon naps," JoJo declared, coming to take Caro from Stuart. Hugo handed off a sniffling Lizbet to Ana, Mary Sofia coaxed Marc Everett to his feet and sent him off with Gabi, who shot smiles at both him and Mary Sofia as they progressed across the room.

Hugo reclaimed his chair, leaning forward with his forearms braced atop his thighs. "Well," he said, staring at Stuart but speaking to Mary

Sofia, "he doesn't scare the kids into catatonic silence."

Mary Sofia hid laughter behind her hand, her eyes watering, and managed to say, "No, but the kids may have permanently scared him off the idea of fatherhood."

Stuart chortled through his grin. "Not at all. But I'll be praying from now on that my own children don't come in multiples."

All three of them laughed then.

"I wish I could tell you that doesn't happen often," Hugo finally said, wiping his eyes, "but in truth, it's every day."

"And you wouldn't have it any other way," Stuart surmised, smiling.

Hugo sobered, leaning back in his seat. "True. JoJo and I can't have children on our own, so when the triplets were dumped in our laps, we thanked God, and we continue to do so."

"I'm happy for you," Stuart told him. "I'll be crushed if I can't have kids. It's good to know how well God provides."

Hugo nodded and glanced at his wrist before bracing his hands on the arms of his chair. "You'll want to get changed. Mary Sofia will show you to the hall bath while I help settle the little ones. Then the two of you will want to head out. JoJo and I will be right behind you."

"Thank you," Stuart said to Hugo's rising form. "Dinner was delicious."

"And much of it was airborne," Hugo said,

walking away.

Stuart and Mary Sofia both dissolved in laughter again.

"Is it always this much fun?" Stuart asked her.

"You think this craziness is fun?" she asked, shaking her head.

"When you've lived alone as long as I have, you learn to appreciate the craziness of a full house."

"I suppose that's true. I've always lived in a full house, and I can't really imagine living any other way."

"Then you've been blessed." He rose to his feet. "I'll get my gear from the truck and be right back."

She nodded and pulled a pair of socks from a pocket. "I'll put on my socks while you're gone and grab my jacket while you're changing."

"Good idea." Grinning, he went out the front door.

***

The charity concert was unlike any other HOBBY RUN concert Mary Sofia had ever witnessed. For one thing, the music stopped periodically so everyone in attendance could pray for Bill Beck, his ailing wife, their daughter, and the extended family. In addition to the price of the tickets, people began to walk up and lay cash on the stage, so Maggs quickly found a basket, gathered up the offerings, placed them inside, and left that on the edge of the stage. The basket was filled by the end. In addition, the Becks' church had put together a bake sale, which they set up in the concession area. Altogether, they raised $23,016.82, but then someone rushed forward with 28 cents to make it an even $23,017.00, which prompted Charlie Biggs to raise the total to $24,000.00. Maggs took the microphone to ask the crowd if they'd like to do this again and bring their friends. The responding roar of approval set the next charity concert for Wednesday.

"You've got to make it worth our while, though," she told them. "We want another sellout."

Someone shouted a question. "Can we buy tickets now?"

Maggs pulled her keys from the pocket of her skin-tight jeans. "Give me two minutes to open the box office."

While generous patrons mobbed the box office, many leaving with strings of tickets, Mary Sofia made her way to the Green Room. Due to Mrs. Beck's health restraints, neither she nor her husband had been in attendance, but their nineteen-year-old daughter, Harper, had live-streamed it for them with her cellphone. She was voicing the family's gratitude when Mary Sofia entered the room.

"You can't know how much this means to us. Thank you so much. Just the prayers are so important. I haven't seen my parents as encouraged as they are now."

Short and stocky with dishwater blonde hair and hazel eyes, the girl had an angelic smile that communicated her sweet nature. Mary Sofia couldn't resist the impulse to hug the girl. The next instant, Stuart materialized at her side.

"She reminds me of her dad," he said softly, lifting his hand to the small of Mary Sofia's back and ushering her toward the Coopers. "Kindest, nicest guy you'll ever meet. I understand Harper is a music major and wants to teach at the middle school level."

"This must truly thrill her then."

"I hope so."

Tamara and Al Cooper welcomed Mary Sofia warmly, but talk quickly turned to the next concert. Apparently, ticket sales had been so strong for this Sunday concert they'd already planned for an additional concert on Wednesday night.

"The radio stations are already announcing the new dates," Stuart said.

"Dates?" Tamara questioned. "More than one?"

Stuart glanced at Mary Sofia, saying, "Friday night's performance will also be dedicated to the Beck charity. In fact, we're doubling the ticket price for that event. It will be a very special concert, with special guests and—"

Tamara interrupted with, "What special

guests?"

Again, Stuart glanced at Mary Sofia. "Tessa Empire for one."

Gasping, Tamara grabbed Stuart by the wrist. "How did you get her?"

"Didn't you know? She's married to our lead guitarist, Ronan." He pointed across the room, where Tessa clung to her husband's arm and chatted with Harper Beck. "That's her over there."

Tamara let go of Stuart and grabbed onto her husband, towing him through the crowded room, exclaiming, "Oh, my word! Tessa Empire!"

Stuart shrugged at Mary Sofia. "Guess we live in a more rarified atmosphere than I realized."

"Maybe you didn't realize it because you're part of it," she said, goosing him in the ribs with a fingertip.

He chuckled and took her hand in his. "If that's true then I'm right at the very edge, clinging on with my fingertips."

She threaded their fingers together, insisting, "You're a big part of this band and everything it does."

He squeezed her hand. "So, what are you doing Wednesday evening?"

"Attending a concert with one of my favorite people. Maybe you know him. He's an integral part of the rarified atmosphere around here."

Laughing, he lifted her hand and kissed the back of it.

Mary Sofia thought her heart would fly right out of her chest.

Later, she warned herself not to get too caught up in Stuart. Only God knew where this fledgling relationship would go. If anywhere.

She thought then of Jack and the odious JREDI party scheduled for this coming Saturday.

"Lord, I don't want to take advantage of Jack," she silently prayed. *"I'll just have to leave it to You to protect me from Grant Leonardo."*

Chapter Fifteen

Mary Sofia increasingly felt confused, torn. Her job at JREDI was supposed to be her big break into the business world, but it had turned out to be just one pain after another. She felt as if she walked on egg shells daily and barely dodged pitfalls. If not for Jack, she wondered if she could stop herself from simply getting up and walking out. Everyone else basically ignored her, from Allie on down. Everyone but Grant Leonardo, who continually watched her with an amused expression on his face, and Jack. He showed up several times a day with a smile and a word of encouragement. He'd even stopped making her uncomfortable with his little touches and innuendoes.

"You know I'm your friend, right?" he asked on Thursday afternoon shortly after she'd opened a long email from Selwyn with instructions for her next task.

She had been ordered to help Leo by finalizing and typing up the contract proposal with the Lithuanian builder coming in on Saturday, making certain that numerous bullet points were addressed. This would supposedly familiarize her with the international expansion of the business. She greatly feared that it also equated with preparing her to work more personally and permanently with Grant Leonardo, something she did not want to do.

"I hope so," she told Jack. "I need a friend here."

"A friend but not a boyfriend," he remarked gently.

She opened her mouth to agree, but something held her back. Her fixation with Stuart had begun to worry her. They talked on the phone several times per day, and most of the evenings, even on Wednesday after the second charity concert, which had beat the previous collection amount by nearly $10,000.00 and left everyone in attendance in an almost euphoric state. Because the workday left little time for Stuart to prepare for a performance, she'd opted to ride with Hugo and JoJo. It didn't occur to her until later that Gabi had now given up two performances in a row without a word of complaint. Still, Mary Sofia couldn't make herself contemplate volunteering to stay home with the kids on Friday, especially as Stuart had suggested that he come by and pick her up from work. That way, he'd said, he wouldn't have to eat alone. The idea of going out to dinner with Stuart had thrilled her, which in turn concerned her. Maybe she was more like her mom than she wanted to admit. Still, regardless of her relationship with Stuart, she couldn't lead Jack on by letting him think they could be more than friends.

"Not a boyfriend," she finally admitted.

He seemed to take it in stride, sighing and admitting, "Well, can't blame a fellow for trying."

"I'm sorry, Jack," she began, but he shook his head.

"No apologies necessary." He held out his hand. "Friends it is."

Relieved and pleased, she put her hand in his for a brief shake. "Thank you."

Sliding his hands into his pockets, he smiled. "My pleasure."

As he started to move away, however, she impulsively stopped him. "Jack?"

He turned back with a raised brow. "Yes?"

"Can I ask a favor? As a friend."

"Of course."

"Will you stick close to me on Saturday?" She glanced in the direction of Grant Leonardo's office, lowering her voice. "I don't trust Leo to behave himself."

"Wise woman," Jack said softly, nodding. Then he winked and left her.

That evening, she went shopping for a dress to wear to the JREDI client welcome party on Saturday, chatting with Stuart the whole time. When she finally found something she thought would work, she sent him a photo. To her surprise, he refused to render a judgment.

"That must mean you don't like it."

"I didn't say that. Pink is a good color on you, but that is a very bright, hot pink. I need to see it on you."

"You want me to try it on?"

"I do."

"Well, let me see if I can find someone to take a pic for me."

"Why don't you just wait ten minutes? I'm already on my way."

She'd already mentioned the name of the shop at the outdoor mall in Rogers, but she gave it to him again, thrilled, then hurried into the dressing room. He texted her when he arrived. Taking a deep breath, she slipped into her stiletto heels, smoothed the figure hugging skirt with the six-inch flounce below the knee, and stepped out into the shop proper.

He stood right outside the dressing room door, but he backed up several steps as she emerged, shaking his head.

"You really don't like it," she said, sliding a finger under one spaghetti strap.

"Are you kidding?" His gaze raked over her repeatedly. "It's fabulous. It was made for you. I just hate that I won't be there when you wear it."

Relieved and pleased, she laughed. "I wish I could take you to the party with me."

"I think that might be pushing things a bit too far. Allie's been convinced for some time that we are a couple."

Mary Sofia bit back the words on the tip of her tongue. Were they a couple? Might they ever truly be a couple? Instead, she nodded. "Right. No reason to set her off again."

He nodded, stepping closer. "Mary Sofia, are you okay with this business party? You don't seem at all excited. Just the opposite, in fact."

"It's work for me. Nothing more. I just hate having to pretend that it's also a pleasure. If I had my way, I'd attend wearing my waitress uniform."

"And that is what?"

"Black athletic shoes, black slacks, white shirt, and starched green apron."

"Hm. Didn't keep Chet from hitting on you."

She barked laughter at that. "Good point."

"Any hope you'll wear this tomorrow night? We are still on for the last charity concert, aren't we?"

"We are."

"I'll pick you up from work, then. Dinner will have to be quick, but at least I won't have to eat it alone."

"That's fine."

"Meanwhile, how about a leisurely dinner tonight?"

The invitation made her heart pound so hard she felt her blood rushing in her ears. Hugo would not be pleased, but she was beyond caring at this point. "Let me get changed."

They walked to a popular Chinese restaurant

on the edge of the mall. The day had been overcast and gloomy from the outset, but they were both surprised when it began to sprinkle big drops of rain on them. Stuart took off his suit jacket and used it to shield both of them as they ran the last few steps. The rain came down steadily all during dinner, but they hardly noticed until they reached the sidewalk beneath the covered drop-off lane.

"Oh, boy. You wait right here," Stuart told her. "Hand me your keys. I'll go get your car and pull it up under the shelter. Then you can drop me back at my truck. That way you'll stay dry."

She started digging in her voluminous handbag. "Thank you so much. That's very sweet of you." Finding the keys, she dropped them into his hand.

"You're the sweet one," he told her, pressing a quick kiss to her lips. He looked as surprised as she felt, but then he turned and trotted away, throwing his jacket over his head.

As kisses went, it wasn't much to hang her dreams on, but that's just what she did, anyway, and no amount of scolding herself made a whit of difference.

***

Friday could not arrive quickly enough for Stuart. On one hand, he felt as if he was rushing headlong into heartache; on the other, he couldn't have slowed down if he'd wanted to, which he did not. In addition, he couldn't wait to spring on Mary Sofia and her family the surprise he'd been hiding.

When he pulled up at the curb in front of the Justus Building, she pushed open the glass door and walked out onto the sidewalk, wearing the hot pink dress beneath a voluminous silk shawl printed in jewel tones. She'd softened the knot of dark, shining hair at her nape by pulling free delicate tendrils to waft about her face. An enormous single rhinestone adorned each earlobe, and a matching pendant, twice the size, lay nestled in the jewel neckline of her bodice, held up by the thinnest of spaghetti straps. The slender column of the dress, aided by navy blue stiletto heels, made her seem taller than he knew her to be and hugged every luscious curve. She carried a small, navy blue, envelope-type purse, but the strawberry red of her lips caught and held Stuart's attention.

"You take my breath away," he told her, going to meet her on the sidewalk and link his arm with hers.

She inclined her head. "Thank you. I could say the same about you."

He'd had the good sense to trade his usual black jeans for closely fitted slacks with flared bottoms just wide enough to fit over the tops of his black cowboy boots. A white, long-sleeved shirt with pearl snaps, worn beneath an unadorned black vest, and a long, black frock coat with white top-stitching completed the look. He'd have to remove the coat and roll up his sleeves to play his guitar, but at least he wouldn't appear terribly underdressed with this gorgeous woman on his arm. Besides, tonight was a special night.

He walked her around to the passenger side of the Jeep and helped her up into the seat, then hurried around to take his place behind the steering wheel.

"I hope you don't mind that I've ordered ahead," he told her, driving away from the curb. "That dress deserves more than fast food, so I asked Golucky's to set a special table for us."

"Sounds perfect," she said. And it was, the food, the atmosphere, the company.

When the waiter brought the check, as prearranged, Stuart was shocked to find that their allotted time had passed. Evening had edged into night, which rapidly deepened as they drove to The Milking Barn. They arrived to find a crowd already gathered at the front of the building, and the back parking lot, which was reserved for performers and their guests, nearly full.

"Are we late or is everyone else early?" Mary Sofia asked as they hurried through globs of light and shadow toward the back of the building, hand in hand.

"Everything's just as it should be," he told her, grinning.

When they neared the door, he abruptly

realized his time alone with her would end the moment they walked inside. The reality and certainty of it hit him with such a sense of loss that he simply stopped. She traveled on another step or two, drawing up at the end of his arm with such force that the momentum turned her back to face him. He knew instantly what had to happen next, and from the look on her face, so did she.

His heart in his throat, he stepped forward, and at the same time reeled her close, watching her head fall back with the impact of their bodies. To his immense delight, she shook her hand free of his and looped both arms around his neck. Locking his own arms around her, he pulled her tighter still. Then he lowered his head and kissed those beautiful, strawberry red lips. The world seemed to take a number of fast spins as they stood rooted, wrapped in an embrace of absolute delight and hopeful possession, until finally she broke free, stepping back to stare at him with wide eyes. He bullied his breath into obedience as she smoothed a coiffure that showed not a single hair out of place.

Suddenly, she smiled and rather impishly declared, "Well. That answers that."

"Oh?" It came out as an embarrassingly froggy croak. He cleared his throat, watching her clasp her little purse in both hands.

She lifted her shoulders in a happy shrug. "Is Stuart Champion as talented a kisser as I imagine he is?" The look on her face—coyly dropped chin, lips curled in a small, pleased smile, big, soft, gleaming eyes watching him blatantly—proclaimed the answer to be a resounding "yes."

Grinning, he lifted his hand, and without hesitation she placed her own dainty one in it. Stepping forward, he whispered, "You inspire me."

Just as he dropped his head toward hers once more, however, the heavy metal door opened, casting a warped rectangle of light onto the dark ground. At once they arranged themselves side by side, hands clasped, and moved quickly forward, greeting a relieved Maggs with smiles.

"I thought you were never going to get here."

"Wouldn't miss it," Stuart told her, beaming.

He didn't even try to pretend that he and Mary Sofia were not a couple. Maggs hurried ahead of them and opened the door to the Green Room. Stuart stepped aside and allowed Mary Sofia to enter behind Maggs, but he made sure to step close, his hands lightly resting on her bare shoulders, the shawl having slipped down to the crooks of her elbows. Mary Sofia glanced around, whirling back to face him with a gasp.

"Your guitar! We forgot—"

"It's here," he told her, capturing her hand and leading her toward his usual corner. "I left it here on Wednesday."

"Oh. That makes sense."

"I just have to get out of this coat."

"Here, let me help you." She moved behind him and eased the coat off his shoulders then went to fetch a hanger for it, returning in time to help him roll up his right sleeve.

Stuart removed the guitar from its case and tested the tuning. Tessa swept into the room a moment later, wearing a shiny purple caftan and a matching headband, along with the tallest high heels Stu had ever seen. As if on cue, the came together for prayer. Stuart pulled Mary Sofia into the circle, her hand clasped in his. Wyatt prayed for the Becks, asking for healing for Mrs. Beck and the funds to help the family with their every need.

No sooner were the "Amens" said than Maggs gestured for attention. "I have a surprise for y'all. Someone special decided to join us for tonight's charity concert, someone who will make the additional cost well worth it, I think. Mary Sofia, I think you'll be especially pleased." With that, she walked over to the stage door and opened it.

Rey Carter, dressed in all in white from his shoes to his slacks and a loose, long-sleeve white shirt and the belt over which is bloused, walked in, beaming. As Mary Sofia flew across the room to greet her eldest brother, the hall door opened, and the entire family crowded inside, Dylan, Tomas, Della, and six-month-old Grace, as well as Hugo, Gabi, Ana, and the triplets. Tomas called Mary Sofia's name.

"Sofi!"

After hugging Rey, she rushed back across the room to hug her little brother and her nephew, while redheaded Della stood patiently, her six-month-old daughter held in the crook of her elbow. Dark haired like her father and pale skinned like her mother, the baby had dancing amber eyes and a bright, inquisitive nature. She obviously didn't like being ignored because she reached out and snagged two fingers in Mary Sofia's shawl. Laughing, her eyes leaking happy tears, Mary Sofia turned to scoop up the girl and kiss her plump cheeks, one arm slung around her sister-in-law's shoulders.

"I'm so happy to see you all!" She turned a glare on Hugo. "Did you know they were coming?"

"Nope," Rey told her, coming to stand beside his wife. "We just showed up on the doorstep earlier today. I thought the big bad Marine was going to faint." He looked to Stuart then. "Thank you for arranging this."

Handing the baby off to her mother, Mary Sofia turned to Stuart. "You did this?"

"I just made a suggestion to Maggs and Charlie. They took care of the details."

She went up on tiptoe and threw her arms around his neck. "Thank you. Thank you. Thank you."

His arms naturally went around her waist, holding her close. Bending as she sank to the floor once more, he caught sight of Rey's flat gaze and quickly released her.

Rey seemed to consider for a moment before putting out his hand. "Champ, how are you?"

Clasping Rey's hand, Stuart said, "Well. I don't have to ask how you are. You're happy, and it shows. Good to see you like this."

Rey folded his arms, split a look between Stuart and Mary Sofia, and nodded. "I hear you're filling my shoes these days."

"Not at all. That's Bart's job, thankfully."

"He's doing it well, apparently. With your help."

Stuart said nothing to that, just smiled politely. Maggs began driving the guests out into the corridor.

"Hurry or we'll find our box seats taken."

Mary Sofia again went up on tiptoe, this time to kiss Stuart's cheek. As he automatically bent his head to receive it, he caught Rey's raised eyebrow and the glance he shot at Hugo. Some silent communication passed between the brothers as Hugo followed his family through the door. Wyatt called for the line-up. Stuart quickly slung his guitar into place as Tessa and Rey moved aside so the regular performers could find their spots in line. Everyone went silent. A second or two later, the light over the stage door flashed, and Wyatt opened it to reveal the tiny, one-way lights that marked the path through the darkness to the stage. The group moved in silence to swiftly take up their appointed positions. Fog swirled around their knees. The announcer did his thing, and the lights blazed. Performance time.

That night, both Tessa and Rey sang for the full-house crowd. The band backed Tessa, who was greeted warmly by the packed crowd. Rey received a standing ovation before his prerecorded music even began to play. His polished, easy style surprised and amazed Stuart. When part of the band, Rey had been self-deprecating and wary of the spotlight, but going solo had given him confidence and perspective. After his performance, he blew Della a kiss and urged those in attendance to give generously to the Beck fund. To Stuart's surprise, Rey announced that he carried with him a check from his record label.

"Let's put this over the top, folks." So saying, he walked forward and dropped the check into the basket on the edge of the stage.

A steady stream of contributors filed forward throughout the remainder of the evening. Rey and Tessa both were hard acts to follow, but the band as a whole turned in a stellar performance. The fund not only reached its goal, it more than doubled the hoped for amount.

Afterward, in a jubilant Green Room, Mary Sofia reluctantly agreed to accompany her family home so she could visit with Rey and his family.

"I have to work tomorrow," she explained to

Stuart, "so I won't have much time with them."

"I understand," he told her, clasping both of her hands.

"Thank you for talking Rey into coming here for this. Della told me all about it."

"My pleasure." To his surprise and wary delight, she went up on tiptoe and pressed a kiss on his lips before dancing away to leave with her family.

Both Hugo and Rey gave him hard looks as they passed, but Mary Sofia's kiss had left Stuart too dazzled to care. He stood gazing at the door through which she'd left for several seconds before turning to find a room full of eyes staring at him. He sighed and lifted both hands, gesturing with all eight fingers.

"All right. Bring it on."

The teasing began, but it was good-natured and accompanied by back swats and general approval. Stuart proudly endured it all. Then endurance gave way to gratitude when Bart hugged him, softly saying, "I'm praying everything works out for you, my friend."

"Thank you," Stuart whispered, hugging him back.

"And thank You," he thought, turning his mind toward his Lord. *"For everything."*

Chapter Sixteen

Mary Sofia packed the pink dress and her silver heels into a small garment bag, along with the necessary undergarments. The silver sandals were more comfortable than the new navy blue stilettos she'd worn for Stuart. She put on the narrow silver chain with the enormous rhinestone that matched earrings she already wore and pushed a silver comb into the knot of her hair, which she would wear down for the party. After gathering the toiletries she would need, she added her flat iron to the bag. Straight hair seemed a better option than loose waves. Plus, she didn't want to bother with setting her hair on curlers.

Depressed, piqued, and wary, she loaded her bags into the car and drove to Bentonville and the Justus Building. One vendor already awaited her arrival. She unlocked the freight elevator and had him come up to the penthouse kitchen. After that she kept busy arranging the kitchen and bar goods. If the chef disapproved her kitchen organization, he said nothing, just set to work when he arrived. The flowers came earlier than anticipated, but that gave her plenty of time to distribute the beautiful arrangements. Then, suddenly, she found herself with nothing to do and a good hour before the bartender appeared. Pulling up Stuart's number on her phone, she debated calling him for long minutes, whispering her hesitation to God.

"Should I, or shouldn't I? I don't want to be fixated on anyone, but I just can't get him out of my head." A thought came. He was the one who best understood why she felt so conflicted about this party. "I just don't feel I can explain it to anyone else, Lord, and even Stuart doesn't know everything. Only You do."

Her brothers had spent hours warning her not to get her hopes up where Stuart was concerned.

"He's much more experienced than you are," Hugo had pointed out.

"If he was the marrying sort, don't you think he'd have already tied the knot by now?" Rey had speculated.

"It feels like a mismatch."

"Just because he's better dressed and more established than your previous crushes doesn't mean he's more serious about a lasting relationship."

"Use your head."

"Don't let your heart confuse you."

The sisters-in-law had eventually called a halt, sending Mary Sofia pitying looks and ushering their husbands off to bed. Dylan and Tomas had been bunked in with Marc Everett, whose fixation had temporarily shifted to the two boys, while baby Grace and Ana were bivouacked in the den, Ana on the sofa and Grace in a portable crib. Rey and Della would take Ana's queen-size bed, though Della joked that they were used to having to search for each other in their king-sized "monstrosity" at home.

Only Gabi had quietly urged Mary Sofia to let God guide her in this. "Only you can decide if Stuart is the one, but I know you make him happy. I can see it in his face whenever you're together."

Certainly, if anyone could lift her spirits, Mary Sofia mused, Stuart could. She wanted to believe God had chosen Stuart for her, but she had to believe that, at the very least, God had arranged this whole thing with Stuart so they could be here for each other during this season of change for both of them.

She let her thumb tap his number on the contact screen. After only an instant of hesitation, she tapped the green icon. Misgiving immediately followed.

Maybe this was a bad idea. Maybe he wouldn't answer.

Maybe he was busy. For all she knew, he could be out on the town with some beautiful, sophisticated woman he'd recently met.

Maybe that heart-pounding kiss had misled

her about Stuart's interest and intentions. Maybe he was not the man God intended for her.

"Lord, if this is a mistake, don't let him answer," she whispered.

He answered after the second ring. "I was afraid I wouldn't have a chance to talk to you today."

Relieve swirled through her. "Me, too. But here I am with a few minutes on my hands."

"And you called me."

"And I called you."

"I'm very glad. Listen, when can you get out of there?"

"Not 'til late, I'm afraid. Although Allie did tell me I could come in to finish the clean up on Sunday."

"Leave early," he urged. "I'll help you finish up Sunday afternoon."

"I'll see what I can do."

"It sounds like Allie's still using you as her personal waitress," he remarked darkly. "Do I need to speak to her about that?"

Both thrilled and alarmed by his tone, she forced a chuckled. "No, no. In fact, this is the first time I've been asked to serve anything since I served lunch to you that day."

"I didn't like it then," he grumbled, "and I don't like it now."

"You sound like Hugo," she teased, enjoying herself for the first time that day.

He laughed. "I suspect Hugo would contest

that."

"What wouldn't Hugo contest?"

They both laughed. "Hugo's just looking out for you."

"Yeah, I know."

"But, listen, Mary Sofia," Stuart said, suddenly serious again, "if anything goes wrong, you call me. I mean it. No matter how late it gets. Ultimately, I'm responsible for you being there, and I don't want anything I've done to blow back on you."

"If that was going to happen, I think it already would have," she told him, pleased at his show of concern, even if did come from a misplaced feeling of responsibility.

"Maybe. But I'm here for you. Anytime. Got it?"

Cupping the phone against her ear, she softly said, "Got it."

"Good."

He changed the subject to the Becks and how thrilled and thankful they were with the results of the charity drive. "My department contributed heavily, and the company has committed to paying half the costs of the experimental treatment, so they've decided they're going to pursue that."

"That's wonderful." Their conversation continued for more than half an hour before she said she'd better get dressed for the party.

"Okay. Talk to you tomorrow?"

"Of course."

In the few minutes left to her after changing into her party attire, she decided that, for tonight, she wouldn't worry about becoming fixated on Stuart. Instead, she thanked God for Stuart's friendship and asked for him to be blessed in the same way that he had blessed her and others. She prayed for Allie and Jack, too, even Leo and the company, before moving on to routine prayers for her family. She didn't let the arrival of the bartender disrupt her, but rose moments later to offer her assistance in any way necessary. Leo arrived, outfitted in a black tux and a white silk shirt with the cuffs turned back over his jacket sleeves.

"My, my, don't you look delicious," he drawled, deliberately looking her over. "Wish that skirt was a foot or so shorter. I'm sure you have fantastic legs."

She did her best to blunt his smarmy, suggestive comments by ignoring them and reminding him that he was married. "I thought your wife would be with you."

Chuckling, he waved a hand dismissively. "No. She prefers to stay home with her bottle and pills. Now, let's see what you've managed to do."

He had the organizational whip hand in this, so she had no choice but to accompany him as he checked her work. Thankfully, the DJ soon arrived, and Leo went over to supervise the playlist. While he was doing that, the chef ordered her to help stock the buffet. They were still at it when people began to arrive. Most were men from the office, but several of the women also showed up, along with a number of other rather scantily clad females Mary Sofia had never before met. Thankfully, no one bothered to introduce her. Allie swept in next, wearing a long, shimmering, pale gold halter dress with a slit up one side of the skirt to the top of her bare leg.

Allie took one look at Mary Sofia and rolled her eyes. "I guess you'll do."

She didn't even bother to glance around to make certain all had been arranged to her satisfaction, merely parked herself at the bar and ordered champagne.

"Excellent idea," Leo proclaimed, going to bar. "Let's get this party going. Champagne for everyone!"

A cheer went up, and thumping music immediately filled the room.

"I don't drink," Mary Sofia stated flatly a few minutes later when Leo offered her a bubbly glass of pale liquid.

"It won't bite you, for pity's sake. Take it and at least pretend to drink, or they'll know you're even more of a goody-two-shoes than they already think you are."

Mary Sofia took the offered flute, deciding that it wouldn't hurt to just hold it. Smirking, Leo lifted his glass and made a loud toast.

"To a successful contract and an entertaining evening!"

Everyone drank, many draining their glasses while Mary Sofia barely touched her lips to the rim of the flute. Leo went back for a refill while Allie watched Mary Sofia with narrowed eyes. Just then, the door to the hallway opened, and Jack sauntered in, looking resplendent in a coat of dark, shiny blue with black velvet lapels. Beneath the jacket, he wore a black, collarless shirt and black slacks. Smiling, he made a beeline for Mary Sofia.

"You look gorgeous," he said. "That dress is perfect."

Finally, a compliment she could welcome. "Thank you. You're turned out well yourself."

"Sorry I couldn't get here earlier," he apologized softly, walking with her as she carried her full champagne flute behind the bar and dumped it. "I had to make a stop on the way." As he spoke, he confiscated a full champagne flute of his own.

Mary Sofia quickly loaded her flute into the dishwasher, careful not to stain her dress, then hurried over to check the buffet, even though only a few people had thus far bothered to help themselves. Jack filled plates for the two of them, insisting that she sit down on the massive sofa to eat.

"You need to keep your strength up. It's going to be a long night."

She'd nibbled a crab cake and a scrumptiously glazed carrot when Selwyn came in, looking splendid in a superbly fitted tuxedo. He went to speak quietly in Allie's ear, waving away the drink Leo offered. Allie made a face then curled a finger at Mary Sofia. She quickly rose and hurried to answer the summons. Along the way, she set her own plate down on one of the many occasional tables scattered about.

"The chef will have made a vegetarian plate for him," Allie said, nodding her head toward Selwyn. "Go and fetch it."

"I'll eat here at the bar," Selwyn told her.

Nodding, she walked back to the kitchen and asked for the plate. The chef set aside a glass of red wine to grab a hot plate from the warming oven and set it on the counter. He quickly filled the plate with a slab of Eggplant Parmesan and a twist of whole wheat spaghetti then ladled red sauce over both before spooning a zucchini and squash combo onto the side. After arranging a sprig of basil just so, he sprinkled the top with a bare minimum of grated parmesan cheese. The plating completed, he shoved the entire thing across the steel top of the work table, all without speaking a word.

Snatching up a clean dish towel, Mary Sofia took the hot plate and carried it through to the bar. Sitting on a stool next to Allie, Selwyn leaned back slightly so she could place the dish in front him. He'd already helped himself to a salad from the buffet, along with flatware rolled in a heavy linen napkin. Murmuring his thanks, he picked up his knife and fork. Allie ignored her, so Mary Sofia wandered back to Jack, reclaiming her plate as she passed it.

"She really doesn't like you, does she?" Jack muttered when Mary Sofia had once again resumed her seat beside him. "Don't let it get to you. She's not friendly with any of the women in the office."

"I had noticed that," Mary Sofia murmured. "But I'm her assistant, and she hardly ever even speaks to me."

"She'll eventually warm up," Jack said. "She's just slow to trust."

Mary Sofia knew he was trying to help and she appreciated having a friend by her side, but at that moment she didn't much care what anyone at JREDI thought of her. She picked at her food, her stomach too knotted to allow her to really eat. After a few minutes, she excused herself in order to gather up empty bar glasses and load them into the dishwasher behind the bar before starting the short wash cycle.

Selwyn finished his meal and left, so she returned his soiled dinnerware and utensils to the kitchen. The taciturn chef stood at the deep metal sink, rinsing pots and pans. He motioned for her to place the plate and flatware in the large, industrial size dishwasher there. After she had done so, he pointed to the ovens.

"Switch the pans in the steam table."

Obediently, she went out to retrieve nearly full serving pans from the buffet and replace them, one-by-one. As soon as she finished that task, Jack appeared at her side with two tall, fizzy drinks, one of which he offered to her.

"Thank you, but I don't drink alcohol."

"That's why I told the bartender to leave it out," he said softly. "Not that anyone else will know, mind you."

She took the glass, smiling her thanks, and sipped, doing her best not to wrinkle her nose at the overly sweet beverage. A nasty aftertaste decided her against further imbibing, but she held the glass to keep from hurting Jack's feelings, secretly pouring a bit of its contents down the drain every time she had to go behind the bar.

As time passed, people began to grow tipsy and loud. A few continued to graze the buffet, and several of the men snagged cigars and carried them out to the stairwell. She saw a couple vaping in one corner, but Jack caught her attention for a moment, and when she looked back, they had disappeared. To where, she had no idea. The round table by the glass wall had been set for two, per Leo's instructions, but no one even approached it or seemed to care one whit about the night scene beyond the windows.

The city boasted no skyscrapers, but the busy downtown district made a pretty picture with its lighted square and quaint shops and restaurants. Jack excused himself to visit the men's room. At her leisure for the moment, Mary Sofia stood and contemplated the vision, wondering if Stuart's house could be seen from this spot. It had been pointed out to her one Independence Day long ago, but she still remembered the gracious old Greek Revival mansion. It suited him, and she liked to think of Stuart there, lounging on the deep front porch, a cup of coffee in his hand. Paying no attention to the reflections in the glass, only the vista beyond it, she imagined him playing the grand piano she'd glimpsed through the windows, which was why she didn't see Leo's approach or feel his presence until he slid an arm about her waist.

Quickly stepping away, she frowned at him, but he only laughed before making her an elaborate bow.

"You are quite right," he said, lifting his glass in a salute. "Mustn't touch. Yet." With that, he turned and thankfully left her, moving to a group dancing by the bar to a pulsating instrumental piece. Jack strolled up and stood shoulder-to-shoulder at her side.

"What did he say to you?"

"Nothing important. He makes every comment sound like an innuendo, though."

"Forget him," Jack said dismissively. "He's just jealous." With that, he held out his hand, palm up. "May I have this dance?"

Someone had started a slow number, and she was feeling tired and out of sorts. She really just wanted a few minutes of quiet time alone, but to refuse to dance with Jack would be rude. He was her best friend at JREDI. Besides, it wasn't Jack who had creeped her out. Smiling wanly, she put her hand in his and let him lead her away from the windows. As he took her in his arms, she wondered how long she should wait to look for another job.

After the dance, she excused herself to gather up more soiled glasses and plates. The chef stepped out of the kitchen to look over the buffet and order her to replenish its contents yet again. Muttering about late guests and the necessity of keeping pots boiling, he smelled to Mary Sofia of alcohol, and she wondered how much red wine he'd had to drink. Another hour wore on, and still the guest of honor had not arrived. According to Jack, Selwyn had left earlier to meet the man and escort him to the party, but something had held them up. Meanwhile, Mary Sofia did her best to turn a blind eye to the couples slipping in and out of the penthouse bedroom, wishing more and more that she could just walk away and go home. She reminded herself that this was her job, and she couldn't just walk away without hurting her chances of landing another one.

Finally, at almost half past eleven o'clock, the guest of honor arrived. Exhausted from keeping up with the work and the pretense, Mary Sofia very nearly walked out when she saw that he came with a sizable party. Selwyn, bringing up the rear, sent her a frank, sour glare that kept her feet still and put a tired smile of welcome on her face.

The Lithuanian, a large but solid middle-aged man with a shaved head, heavy brow, narrow eyes, and a bushy salt-and-pepper mustache, came in wearing standard black tie and a white cashmere scarf. One of the four large men with him, all of them in unrelieved black and presumably bodyguards, carried a black fedora. Also with him were two women, twins, dressed identically in clinging, silver spangled, long-sleeved dresses with plunging backs and knee-length skirts. Each wore their long, straight, pale blonde hair parted in the middle and carried long, satin cloaks draped over their arms. If the diamonds dangling from their earlobes and sparkling on their wrists and fingers were real, they definitely needed the bodyguards.

Everything came to a screeching halt. The DJ even cut the music, as an obsequiously gracious and charming Leo rushed forward to greet their guest.

"Mister Laukaitis, welcome."

Laukaitis held out both hands, indicating the women standing on either side of him. "My sisters," he said in heavily accented English,

"Ugna and Gabija."

Leo looked shocked, but he swiftly recovered, bowing to the women. "*Sveiki atvyke, ponios.* Welcome, ladies."

The one on the right of Laukaitis pressed her hands, with their long pearl white nails, together and bowed her head. "Thank you, Mister Leonidas." She dropped her hands to her sides. "Ugna and I thought best to 'company Raulo for meeting Miss Allie Justus. Since his wife die, he get, um, troubled with women. Forgive for late. Is bad weather this night in New York."

Allie set aside her champagne flute and glided forward. "I hope your flight was not too arduous. Thank you for joining us tonight."

Leo quickly made the introductions. "Allie Justus. Raulo Laukaitis, his lovely sisters, and..." He waved a hand, indicating the four large, silent men now grouped in a semicircle around the Laukaitis trio.

"Our friends," Laukaitis said with a smile, bowing to Allie and offering his beefy hand.

She shook hands with all three, Raulo, and his sisters, one of whom then reached back to the man behind her and received a small velvet sack, which she passed to her brother.

"Our gift," he said, offering it to Allie.

Though obviously surprised, Allie smiled, took the bag, and opened the drawstring. Reaching inside, she brought out a jewel encrusted crucifix wrought of heavy, filigreed gold, her initial expression one of puzzlement.

"Our belief, *inkrustuotas kryžius* bless house," Raulo told her. "May it be."

Suddenly beaming, Allie pressed the small crucifix to her chest and said, "Thank you so much for such a beautiful gift." She swept a hand toward the table. "Won't you join me for dinner?"

Leo sprang into action. He snapped a finger at the nearest male, who hurried to help him move the round table away from the glass wall. While others went for chairs, Mary Sofia rushed to place flatware on the table. Leo appeared at her elbow, hissing that she should get to the kitchen and warn the chef. She hurried away to inform the man that he had extra mouths to feed. Muttering curses, he shoved extra plates into the warming oven and began running around the kitchen like a whirling dervish, tossing things into pots and pans already heating on the stove. Mary Sofia rushed out again to fill water glasses and carry them to the table, where Leo was positioning chairs for the sisters. He seated them and then Allie. As Allie sat, the velvet bag and its unexpected gift in her lap, Mary Sofia placed the water glasses. Raulo Laukaitis seated himself, with the aid of one of his men.

The bartender carried over an ice bucket with a bottle of champagne in it. Mary Sofia quickly grabbed champagne flutes and brought them to the table, arriving just as Leo popped the cork. He poured. Mary Sofia passed around the glasses. Then Allie waved Leo away and spoke to Laukaitis.

"My chef is preparing a special dinner for us, but your men are welcome to partake of our buffet and, of course, the bar."

Laukaitis spoke quietly to the men, who slowly moved off. Someone turned on the music again, but the tune this time was measured and lilting, the volume significantly lower. The lights brightened everywhere. A few of the original couples began to slow dance, but everyone in general seemed more subdued than earlier.

The chef brought the first course for Mary Sofia to serve. Leo took a seat on a barstool at the end of the bar, watching anxiously as the meal progressed. Not a word of business was spoken, so far as Mary Sofia could tell, but Allie behaved with her usual elegance and more graciousness than Mary Sofia had ever seen. Obviously striving to impress her guests, she smiled up at Mary Sofia as she placed desert plates before the diners.

"You can clean up later. Why don't you take a break now?"

Mary Sofia nodded, masking her surprise. She could not contain her shock, however, when Raulo Laukaitis offered her a folded hundred dollar bill. Manufacturing a smile, she said, "Thank you, but I must not accept. I am the personal assistant of Ms. Justus, and it is my pleasure to serve you."

Now Laukaitis looked surprised. He threw up his hands, beaming. "Ah. Worthy employee is blessing, no? You must join for *Starka*." Withdrawing a flask from his coat pocket, he signaled one of his men, who went to the bar and returned with shot glasses. Laukaitis good-naturedly poured the golden liquid and passed the tiny glasses around the table, offering the last to Mary Sofia.

"*Į Sveikatą.*"

"Cheers," Gabija translated.

Glasses clinked around the table. Lifting her own glass to her lips, Allie sent Mary Sofia an implacable stare. Knowing she couldn't politely get out of tasting the strange liquid, she watched the sisters toss back theirs and followed suit. Fire burned a path all the way down to her stomach. Gasping, she fought to take in a breath. Laukaitis laughed, reached around with one big hand to pat her back, and signaled someone with the other. A short glass appeared beneath her nose.

"Here. Drink this," Leo said with a chuckle.

It looked and smelled like water, so she took it gratefully, trying to subdue a cough, and drank it all. The fire cooled somewhat, but the aftertaste lingered. When her watery eyes began to clear, she nodded at Leo and handed back the glass.

"Thank you," she croaked, ignoring his smirk.

Jack appeared, took her by the arm, and

steered her away from the table, softly saying, "You better sit down. You look ready to crater, and there's no telling what was in that stuff."

She felt a little shaky, so she allowed him to push her into a corner of the massive sofa. He offered to get her another glass of water.

"Yes, please."

Raulo Laukaitis came over to pat her shoulder and apologize.

"I should give you *midus*. It made of..." He thought a moment and snapped his fingers. "Honey."

Mary Sofia smiled, feeling a bit lightheaded. "Don't...give it...another thought," she managed. "Obviously, I'm not a drinker."

He laughed and removed the expensive scarf from about his neck, looping it around hers. "Better on you. *Taip?*" Her ruffled her hair with a huge hand as if she were a child and moved out of her sight.

Jack returned with fresh water. She thanked him and drank it down, wishing the aftertaste would disappear.

"You don't look well."

"I'll be all right," she told him. "I'll just rest for a few minutes." She curled her legs up onto the sofa and snuggled into the corner. Aware of voices, music, and other sounds around her, she closed her eyes. As if that also closed her ears, everything seemed muted and distant. She next became dimly aware of voices around her.

"Just get her out of here," someone said. Allie, most likely.

Someone else suggested that she needed to lie down, and this one or that one would help her. Long, white fingernails swam across her vision, and she thought they brushed her cheek. Mary Sofia roused herself enough say that she wanted to go home. She heard Jack's voice then.

"I'll take her."

Recoiling from his touch, she mumbled the thought uppermost in her mind. "Stuart. Call Stuart."

"Tavas will do this," said a heavily accented male voice.

The next thing she knew, she was floating. Only as she felt herself being lowered again did she realize she had been carried, but she didn't know where or by whom. Panic welled within her. *God! God help me!* Then came the calm, smiling face of Stuart and a soft voice telling her to relax. Obediently, she let herself sink into soft blackness, whispering Stuart's name.

Somehow, she knew he would take care of everything.

Chapter Seventeen

Not six blocks away, Stuart sat on his front porch steps, jacketed against the chilly night air, and stared at the black sky, his dog at his feet radiating a comfortable warmth. He thought of Mary Sofia and what it would be like to have her here with him. He could almost feel her clutching his arm, her head on his shoulder. Like that was ever going to happen. Stuart shook his head, as if he could shake out the unrealistic thoughts.

What was wrong with him? Why did he constantly fix his hopes on unattainable women? First Joanna, then Allie, and now—most hopeless of all—sweet, lovely, pure Mary Sofia. Her brothers had made their opinions of his relationship with their sister plain enough without having to say it, and she had confirmed, in so many subtle words, that they disapproved and why.

"You're so much more sophisticated than I am."

"You aren't really that much older than me."

"You must think I'm silly."

And the most telling of all. "I just don't understand how you've remained single this long."

Had it only been last night that he'd thought they could have a chance?

Remembering that kiss, he straightened his spine, let his head fall back onto his shoulders, and tried to count the stars in a patch of sky between the dual chimneys on the house across the street. Nothing could keep thoughts of her from creeping back and taking over his mind, though. He wondered how her evening was going. Was Allie being gracious? Did the wealthy Lithuanian appreciate Mary Sofia's efforts? Did he appreciate Mary Sofia herself, and if so, did he perhaps appreciate her too much?

Suddenly alarmed, Stuart thought of sending her a text asking if she was okay. The next moment, that felt ridiculous. Maybe he could ask her to let him know when she got home safely. But she had family for that. Besides, if she wasn't too busy to answer him, he'd just want to talk to her, and what would he say?

I wish you were here.

I wish I deserved someone like you.

I wish I'd asked you out as soon as you graduated from college.

Stupid notion. He'd been deeply involved with Allie when Mary Sofia had finished her degree.

I wish I had never started with Allie.

For all the good that did now. He should have been strong enough to resist the temptation of Allie, just as he should be strong enough to resist the temptation of Mary Sofia. He never should have pressed her to attend the charity concerts with him. He certainly should not have kissed her. He and Mary Sofia could have no future. Her brothers would never approve, and he couldn't blame them. Should she, by some miracle, care for him enough to defy them, he would be responsible for driving a wedge into a loving, supportive family, perhaps sundering them forever. He couldn't do that, not to Mary Sofia, not to JoJo and Hugo, not to Rey, not to the rest of the family. He, after all, knew how precious family could be, should be. He was a selfish, foolish dreamer, forever pining for what was not his, what could never be his.

The guys in his weekly Bible study at work had used Scripture to show him that God did in fact forget repented sin. Humans don't have that ability, however, so sin carries consequences in the here and now. One of the consequences of Stuart's sin was that he'd robbed himself of ever being worthy of an innocent such as Mary Sofia. She and her family knew what he'd been and what he'd done. He couldn't take it back, or wipe it out of their collective memories. And he'd done this to himself.

Rubbing his hands over his face, Stuart sighed. Then he once again lifted his face to the sky and silently prayed.

"Thank You for forgiving me, Lord, and thank You for my friends. Thank You for showing me how many more friends I have than I knew, especially Mary Sofia. I know I don't deserve her, and I truly don't want to complicate her life." He gulped hard at the thought but found the strength to forge on. *"So I'm asking You to remove her from my thoughts and heart if she's not Your will for me. If that is the case—and I don't see how it couldn't be —please help me to accept that and.... Just take care of her, Lord. She deserves only good things, happy things, a good life. And if I can't be the one to give her that, I trust You to bring to her the person who can."*

Feeling marginally better, Stuart got to his feet, prompting the dog to move. He watched as Trooper's large head rose, his front legs stiffening. Then the great maw opened in a creaky yawn that seemed to ratchet up the hind legs. Stuart's mood lightened enough to bring out a smile. He put down a hand to pat between the spiky ears.

"Let's go to bed, boy."

Head hanging, as if in anticipated exhaustion, Trooper stepped up onto the porch and padded to the front door. Stuart followed, telling himself that tomorrow would look brighter. It was only loneliness and the silence of night that had him on edge.

As he undressed for bed, he placed his

cellphone, face down on the bedside table. Then, for some reason he couldn't explain, he felt the compulsion to pick it up again. He stood staring down at it until the screen faded to black, the urge to call Mary Sofia so strong his hands trembled.

He told himself she was at a party, probably working but hopefully enjoying herself, too. She would be looking fine and attracting the attention of every man there. Jealousy made him want to call and interrupt her evening.

"Help me, Lord," he prayed, dropping the phone, face up, onto the mattress. Plopping down next to it, he bowed his head, telling himself again and again that she wasn't for him. It would be best if he never saw or spoke to her again.

He sat there, wallowing in disappointment and guilt, when he noticed that the screen on his phone had lit up. Looking down, he saw Mary Sofia's contact information displayed, but he didn't remember bring it up. He could almost dial the number from memory, anyway. He stared at the phone, waiting for the screen to go black, but there it sat, bright as day. Something wasn't right. That screen should have faded in fifteen seconds. He began to count.

"One thousand, two thousand, three thousand..." When he got to fifteen, he snatched up the phone.

As soon as the thing settled into his hand,

he knew that something was wrong with Mary Sofia. He hit the call icon. If the phone at the other end of the call ever rang, Stuart didn't hear it. Almost instantly, a voice answered. The wrong voice. A male voice.

"Hello? Mr. Champion?"

Stuart found himself on his feet, demanding, "Where is Mary Sofia?"

"In the penthouse, I believe."

"What do you mean, you believe? And who is this? Why do you have her phone?"

"This is Selwyn," came the unhurried reply. "She was taken ill earlier and put to bed."

"Ill?" Alarm shook Stuart, like a tidal wave racing up and down his spine. "I'm coming to get her!" He ran from the room, Selwyn still speaking into his ear.

"It's odd, but I found her cellphone here in the stairwell."

"In the stairwell?" Stuart parroted, pounding down the stairs in his own house.

"She must have dropped it here earlier."

His mind swirling with urgent thoughts, Stuart sprinted down the hallway, shouting at Selwyn. "I'm five minutes away! And she'd better be all right when I get there!"

"I'll let you into the building," Selwyn said, sounding as if he was running now, too. Suddenly, the sound of tapping feet stopped. "Or should I go back up?"

"Get me into that building!" Stuart shouted,

throwing the lock on the back door and tearing it open. "Or I swear I'll drive right through the front of it!"

He didn't wait to hear anything else Selwyn might say, just dug into his pocket with his free hand as he ran for the truck. The doors unlocked automatically as he drew near, and the sound of the engine turning over told him he'd found the right button on the key fob to start it. He yanked open the driver's door and tossed the phone onto the passenger seat as he slid behind the wheel.

"Lord, let her be okay. Lord, let her be okay," he begged as he backed the Jeep out of the drive and sped down the street toward the Justus Building in the distance, horrified to see that no light showed from any window on any floor. He glanced at the clock on the dash.

Just three minutes and forty-eight seconds later, he brought the truck to a screeching halt next to the curb in front of the building and jumped out. A couple of other vehicles, he noticed dimly, were leaving the parking lot adjacent. Ignoring them, he covered the sidewalk in two long strides and rattled the locked glass doors, shouting for Selwyn.

"Open this door! Selwyn! Open this door!"

He could see nothing moving inside the building so he ran back to the truck and practically dove through the open door to get his hands on his cellphone. The connection, he saw, was still live.

"Selwyn!" he shouted into the thing.

"I'm here. I'm here," came the gasping reply. Then it came again, from outside. "I'm here!"

Turning back to the building, Stuart ran to the door that Selwyn now held open.

"Had to...run down...five stories," Selwyn managed as Stuart pushed past him.

"Get me up to the penthouse!" Stuart snapped.

Selwyn followed him toward the elevators, fumbling in his pocket. "She should be fine," he said. "That stuff Laukaitis gave her made her sick, that's all."

Stuart's blood ran cold. "What stuff?"

"Something from Lithuania. Some sort of liquor." Selwyn found the key and slotted it.

"She doesn't drink alcohol!"

"That's why it made her sick," Selwyn said as the elevator door slid open.

They nearly knocked each other over getting into the car, but once inside, Selwyn used his key again, and the elevator began to rise.

"If anything's happened to her," Stuart growled, "I'll strangle Allie Justus."

"Allie didn't have anything to do with it," Selwyn insisted. "She drank the stuff, too. Everyone at the table did. It didn't bother anyone else."

"Then explain to me why Mary Sofia's cellphone was in the stairwell? And what were you doing on the stairs anyway?"

"I don't know how the cellphone got there," Selwyn said. "As for me being in the stairwell, Allie and Laukaitis decided to drive over to her house to talk business. I stayed behind to shut down the party. Everyone left at once, so the elevator was jammed. I decided to walk down. When I got to the sixth floor, I found the phone."

Suspicious, Stuart asked, "How did you even know it belonged to Mary Sofia?"

Selwyn handed over the phone. Stuart looked down to find a photo of a beaming Mary Sofia cradling the newborn triplets in her arms, the time and date and various other icons superimposed over the picture. The time read "2:58."

The elevator arrived at the top floor just then and the door slid open. Selwyn stepped off, still talking. "Not that I think about it, leaving her alone here, ill, wasn't a very smart move on my part or anyone else's."

"Then why did you?" Stuart demanded, following the other man out into a foyer of sorts.

"I don't know," Selwyn retorted, pulling open a tall, heavily carved door. "It just didn't occur to me. Satisfied?

"Hardly," Stuart snarled, preceding him through the door into a large space lit only by the moonlight painting the glass wall at the back of the room silver.

Selwyn came in behind him, hitting a bank of switches. Bright light flooded the familiar penthouse great room. At the same time, a figure popped up from the enormous sofa. A champagne flute dangling from his fingers, the man looked startled.

"Leo!" Selwyn exclaimed. "What are you doing here? I thought you left with the others."

The man bounced a wild look back and forth between Selwyn and Stuart. "Wh-what am I doing here? What are you doing here?" His gaze slid to a door on the other side of the great fireplace.

Instinctively, Stuart honed in on that door, fresh urgency seizing him.

"Explain yourself," Selwyn ordered the man, as Stuart vaulted the massive sofa rather than walk around it.

"We...I was just making sure," he began, only to break off when he realized where Stuart was headed. "You can't go in there! She...she's sleeping! You can't disturb—"

Ignoring him, Stuart shoved open the door. From the light at his back and more light spilling dimly from another room, he could see that he'd entered a large, opulent bedroom.

"Wait your turn," a man snapped from the shadows. "She isn't even undressed yet."

Horrified, Stuart stormed across the room and got his hands on the man just as the light blazed on overhead. He registered wide eyes, a gaping mouth, and a blue coat with black lapels in the second before his gaze found Mary Sofia on the bed, the top of her dress pulled down to reveal the strapless bra beneath. He didn't remember throwing the man across the room, only falling on his knees beside the bed and yanking the covers over her.

Behind him, he heard scrambling, shouts, and grunts, but his only concern was the beautiful young woman lying on the bed next to him. Grasping her by the shoulders, he shook her.

"Mary Sofia. Sweetheart, wake up. Talk to me." Nothing. He scrambled for her wrist with one hand and reached out to press two fingers to the artery in her neck with the other. He felt her heartbeat, slow but strong. "Thank You, God!" He shook her again. "Come on, honey, wake up."

Still she slept, almost as if in a coma.

Realizing that she had probably been drugged, he shouted, "Call an ambulance!"

"On it," Selwyn said breathlessly, much closer than Stuart expected. He glanced up to see the other man with a cellphone to his ear. "We need an ambulance and police at the Justus Building."

As he rattled off the address, Stuart turned back to Mary Sofia. He heard Selwyn say that a girl had been drugged and almost raped and that he was holding two men for authorities. Of much more importance to Stuart, however, was the deep, contented sigh Mary Sofia gave out as she turned onto her side. Putting his head back, he let tears of relief roll down his face.

***

Stretching, Mary Sofia moaned. Her muscles felt stiff and sore, as if she'd slept for a week. She'd had the most amazing dream about Stuart. He'd carried her somewhere and kissed her, whispering that he was there and everything was going to be fine.

"You are so precious to me, and I'll never let anything bad happen to you again."

Smiling to herself, she dragged her eyelids up. A few seconds later, her focus cleared, and a cream-colored ceiling with a rectangular, commercial-style light fixture came into view. That wasn't right. Her bedroom ceiling was light gray, with no fixture of any sort. Realizing with a shock that she wasn't in her bedroom at home, she jerked up onto her elbows. Pain stabbed behind her eyes and deep into her brain, bringing up another moan. Her throat felt as if she'd swallowed the entire Mojave dessert.

"Sofi?" Her brother's voice reached out to her. At the same time, she felt his hand on her shoulder. "Lay back, sweetie," he said, rising from the chair next to the narrow bed.

Suddenly, Gabi threw herself across the bed from the other side, sobbing. "I didn't think you were ever going to wake up."

Patting her sister's head absently, Mary Sofia took stock of her surroundings and tried to make sense of the situation.

"Why am I in the hospital?" she croaked. Her hand went to her throat. An instant later, a large plastic cup of water appeared. Pulling the cup to her, she latched onto the straw and swallowed delicious draughts of tepid water. When she had finished, Hugo took the water away and set it aside.

"What do you remember last?" he asked as Gabi withdrew to her own chair, her hand grasping Mary Sofia's.

She had to think. "Um, Mr. Laukaitis gave me some awful liquor to drink. It made my throat and chest hurt, and I couldn't get rid of the taste. Water actually made it worse."

"The police say the drug was probably in the water."

"Drug! What drug?"

Hugo took her free hand in one of his, smoothing her hair with the other. "The doctor suspects GHB or Rohypnol or maybe a combination of the two."

Her eyes opened wide as the implications of that hit her, along with a fresh stab of pain in her head. "Those are date rape drugs!"

"Yes. But nothing happened," Hugo quickly assured her. "Champ and Selwyn got to you in time."

"Champ? And Selwyn, you say? I-I don't understand."

"Neither do I," Hugo told her, "but the doctors confirmed that you weren't, um, violated."

"It was a miracle, Sof," Gabi blurted. "Champ said your number came on his screen and wouldn't go away until he called it, and Selwyn answered because he found your phone in the stairwell. Then they raced up to that penthouse and found you with some guy named Leo and…" She glanced at Hugo, who again smoothed Mary Sofia's tangled hair.

"And who?" Mary Sofia pressed. "Leo and who?"

"Jack," Hugo told her succinctly.

Tears instantly started. "Not Jack. He must have been trying to help me. He…is my friend."

Rey stepped into view at the foot of her bed then, his arms folded. "This Jack character was undressing you when Champ got there."

Tears trickled down her cheeks as the horrible truth filled her mind. "I trusted him." Well, perhaps not as much as she'd wanted to, tried to, but she'd thought he was harmless, kind. "How could he? Leo isn't surprising. I never trusted him, but Jack?"

"The cops say they were a team," Rey told her bluntly. "And they've done it before. One of them would win some woman's confidence, then they'd find a way to drug her and carry her off somewhere."

Gabi squeezed her hand, adding, "Then they'd both—"

"That's enough, Gabi," Hugo interrupted.

Mary Sofia squeezed her eyes shut, but the tears kept rolling down her face. Jack! He'd gone to church with her, sat at the family table and eaten Sunday dinner with her. They were lunch buddies. They'd danced together. He'd even warned her away from Leo! And it was all to insure she'd take a glass from his hand and drink down his poison. So they could both rape her.

But Stuart and Selwyn had saved her. Stuart!

"Where is he?" she asked, suddenly needing to see the man who had come to her rescue, the man Jack couldn't crowd out of her heart with his smiles and smooth compliments. Selwyn she'd think about later, but for now, she desperately needed to see Stuart. "Where is Stuart? I need him."

Hugo patted her shoulder. "He'll be back."

"He went went to confront Allie Justus for placing you in this situation," Rey revealed.

"He thinks she set me up for this," Mary Sofia rasped, "and if she did, he'll blame himself."

"He said as much before he left," Hugo confirmed, "and the police consider it a possibility. They even think this Luka guy might be mixed up in it."

"Mr. Laukaitis?" She shook her head, relieved that her brains didn't actually slosh around inside her skull. "I don't know what to think anymore." She looked straight into Hugo's worried brown eyes and said, "But I need to see Champ." When he looked down, breaking eye contact, she went to Rey. "I don't think I'll feel safe again until I do. Can you get him for me? Please?"

Rey sighed and dropped his arms. "I thought it might be like that. He was beside himself when we got here. He says Allie was jealous of you because she knew..." Grimacing, Rey rubbed a hand over his face.

"Because she knew what I knew," Gabi finished for him, eyes twinkling.

"Knew what?" Mary Sofia asked.

"That he was half in love with you already," Hugo replied.

"What?" The room seemed to brighten, and her breath caught in her chest. "D-did he actually say that?"

"He actually said it," Rey confirmed glumly.

"I knew he was the one," Gabi crowed, her nose in the air, a smile tugging at the corners of her mouth.

The one? Mary Sofia's heart rolled over in her chest, the hope that suddenly blossomed there almost as painful as the pounding agony in her head.

Her disappointment over Jack forgotten, she put a hand to her head, trying to make sense of what Gabi had told her. Hugo mistook the gesture for one of pain.

"Gabi, call the nurse," Hugo said. Gabi got up to push a button on the wall, while Hugo bent and gently kissed Mary Sofia's forehead.

"Rest, *hermana mía*," Rey said softly. "There's nothing to worry about. We all love you and thank God you're okay. If Champ doesn't return soon, I'll go after him."

Exhausted and in turmoil, Mary Sofia closed her eyes to thank God that Stuart and Selwyn had found her in time. *"I don't know what this means, Lord,"* she prayed silently, *"but I thank You. Selwyn, of all people, though. Stuart doesn't surprise me, but Selwyn? He doesn't even like me."*

She didn't know what to think about Allie or Mr. Laukaitis, but the idea of Jack being part of a scheme to drug and rape her had shaken her badly. But Stuart...

The fact that he had come to her rescue didn't surprise her. After all, Stuart had consistently insisted she inform him if anything bad happened concerning her job, the result of guilt, no doubt.

But was guilt the only reason?

He was half in love with you already.

Did that mean he was fully and truly in love with her now?

There came that hope again, and she just didn't have the strength at the moment to talk herself out of it.

Chapter Eighteen

E xhaustion pulled at Stuart as he drove toward Allie's ridiculously large chateau. The long hours of worry had gradually drained him of the adrenaline that had seen him through the darkest fear.

Upon arrival at the hospital, he'd called Mary Sofia's family, and they had, quite understandably, panicked. Hugo, JoJo, Rey, and Gabi had arrived within half an hour, demanding answers from him. He'd given them a disjointed account of what had happened, his gaze constantly straying to the door through which the emergency crew had taken Mary Sofia, still unconscious. Some questions he simply couldn't answer. He hadn't been able to sit still or relax in the slightest until the doctor had come out to say that Mary Sofia should awaken in a few hours and make a complete recovery.

At that point, he'd collapsed with relief, knees weak and head swimming, only to have the police arrive to question him and compare his story to Selwyn's, who had stayed behind at the Justus Building to make sure Leonardo and

Dillman were both arrested. Once assured that Mary Sofia would okay, JoJo had decided to return home before the triplets awakened. Although anxious to discover if Alllie had played a part in the drugging and attempted rape of Mary Sofia, Stuart simply couldn't leave the hospital until she had been transferred to a regular hospital room.

Seeing her there in that hospital bed, looking so small and vulnerable, had both reassured him and nearly driven him wild. When he thought of those creeps touching her, he wanted to tear down buildings and burn them, preferably with Dillman and Leonardo inside. Such thoughts, of course, led him straight back to Allie, but phone calls had accomplished nothing. Obviously, both she and Bart had turned off their phones for the night. He'd had no choice but to drive to their house, despite Rey's warning that the police might not like it.

To his everlasting surprise, Hugo had clapped both hands atop Stuart's shoulders and looked him squarely in the eye. "You saved her. That makes up for anything else you might have done. And who am I to questions God's ways? Just don't get yourself into trouble." He'd glanced at Mary Sofia then, adding, "Likely, she'd never forgive us if we let that happen."

Rey snorted at that, but Stuart wondered if perhaps Hugo, at least, could be induced to accept him as a suitor for his sister. The very possibility went a long way in cooling Stuart's temper. Still, he needed answers, and he needed them sooner rather than later, so here he sat, behind the wheel of his Jeep when he should've been resting so he could greet Mary Sofia's return to consciousness with soft smiles and intelligent comments.

His anger ratcheted up again as he turned the truck onto the street that ran past Allie's Bentonville home. The hour had passed six o'clock in the morning before he spotted the pretentious mansion, which sat far back from the street, behind high walls and tall, expertly trimmed trees. Situated on a manmade hill, it had been constructed to be seen and admired, just not easily accessed. Allie had given him the key code to the back gate some time ago, and he used it now with no compunction whatsoever. He drove straight to the rear of the house, surprised to see a big white SUV parked beneath one of half-a-dozen arched bays. It sat neatly between Bart's vehicle and Allie's luxury sedan.

Perhaps she had found a lover only too happy to spend the night at her place, even with her brother in residence. Stuart didn't really care. The back door, which opened into a hallway that ran beside a massive kitchen, proved to be locked, but he rang the buzzer relentlessly and pounded on the door, managing not to hit the glass insets, until he saw movement inside. A sweaty Bart, dressed in a tank top and gym shorts, eventually opened up for him.

"Hey, man, what's going on? I heard you all the way upstairs in the workout room."

Stuart squeezed past him. "I have to see Allie. Now."

"Well, she was asleep, but—"

Without waiting for Bart to finish his sentence, Stuart strode down the hall, shouting for her. When he reached the impressive foyer at the front of the house, she spoke from above at the top of the massive marble stairway.

"What on earth?" Stuart wheeled around to see her yanking a bow into the soft belt of a long, slinky, white robe covering a matching nightgown.

Stuart pointed at her. "You left Mary Sofia alone in the penthouse last night!"

"Keep your voice down," she demanded. "You'll wake my guests."

"I don't give a fig about your guests! You left her there! I want to know if it was your plan to have her raped!"

The whole house seemed to freeze in silence. Then Champ felt Bart step up beside.

He laid a hand on Champ's shoulder. "I'm so sorry. Where is she? How is she?"

"She'll be okay. Selwyn and I got there in time to stop them. No thanks to her." He pointed an accusing finger at Allie, who came blustering down the sweeping staircase.

"I have no idea what you're talking about!

What them? Who are they?"

"Jack Dillman and Grant Leonardo." At Allie's gasp, Stuart snapped, "Don't pretend you don't know them. They both work for you."

"Of course, I know them," Allie admitted, gathering the front of her robe into a knot at her throat, "but I don't understand any of this. They left with everyone else. Or I thought they did."

"You hired her out of petty jealousy," Stuart accused, ignoring her protests. "You made her nothing more than a glorified waitress. And you set her up like a lamb for the slaughter! Didn't you?"

Allie ran down the remaining stairs, exclaiming, "I did not!" Her bare feet slapped the marble floor of the foyer as she advanced on him. "All right, maybe I invited a little ridicule, but I didn't want her actually harmed. How do you know what happened anyway?"

"Because God told me," Stuart stated flatly. "When I called her phone, Selwyn answered. He'd found her phone in the stairwell. Most likely, they hoped she wouldn't be able to call anyone when she finally came around, and by then it would be too late. She'd have had to make her way home alone, with no memory of what had happened to her."

"What do you mean?" Allie asked carefully, edging toward him. "Why wouldn't she have any memory of what had happened?"

"She'd been drugged, of course, but I got

there in time to stop them. Dillman was undressing her when I burst into the bedroom! And Leonardo was sitting outside waiting his turn!"

Allie slapped her hands to her cheeks. "D-drugged? But how?"

"You're positive she was drugged?" Bart asked, sounding horrified.

"The hospital confirmed it."

Allie reeled back as if struck. "Drugged."

"And nearly raped," he repeated brutally.

Allie's chin began to tremble, then tears welled and spilled from her eyes. "Drugged," she repeated in a thin voice. "No, no, no."

"Champ," Bart said gently, trying to tug him away, "Allie would never sanction something like that."

"Really?" Stuart snapped. "I've learned not to put anything past your sister."

"What you apparently don't know," Bart told him softly, "is that Allie was date raped in college. He slipped her a roofie, carried her up to his dorm room, and filmed the whole thing for his buddies."

Stunned, Champ felt the rage flow out of him as he tried to plug this new information into the correct slot so that it made sense. "She never said a word about that," he told Bart before turning to Allie. "You never said a word."

She shook her head, choking out, "I-I couldn't. I couldn't even think about it, let alone…" She shook her head again.

Suddenly, Stuart understood a great deal. "Allie, I'm so sorry. I wish you'd told me."

"It happens," Allie grated out. "Every day. To someone." She dashed the tears from her eyes. "You learn to live with it. Y-you start to think it's just sex. Doesn't really matter. N-nothing matters."

Stuart put both hands to his head, thunderstruck. Allie had just been explained to him fully. But she obviously hadn't learned to live with what had been done to her. She must've thought she'd put it all behind her when she'd married. Then her husband's infidelity must have shaken her badly. No wonder she thought sex was no big deal. No man in her life had treated it as meaningful and sacred. Not even him.

"Allie, you never explained…" He shook his head. "I'm so sorry. For everything."

She folded her arms tightly, hugging herself. "What matters now is Mary Sofia."

"Mary Sofia," said a deep, thickly accented voice. "She pretty little girl can no drink *Starka*."

Stuart looked up to see a large, middle-aged man methodically descending the stairs. Dressed in a dark gray suit and a blue shirt with the cuffs folded back onto the roomy sleeves of the suit jacket, he managed to look recently awakened and well-tailored at the same time. His completely bald head lent him an air of tidiness despite the glistening beard shadow and a rather elaborate salt-and-pepper goatee. Champ lifted a hand to his own bristling jaw, wondering when he'd last been seen in public without being cleanly shaved. He felt unkempt and sloppy beside the clearly European gentleman who stepped down onto the marble floor of the foyer.

Behind the man glided two tall, identical blondes in matching red robes with flowing, mid-calf skirts and long, bell sleeves. The bows on their matching slippers appeared to be set with rubies. Behind them came two enormous men with hard faces and bulging muscles. One wore slacks and a dark green T-shirt that appeared to be painted on. The other wore similar attire, along with a soft black hoodie that didn't quite hide the handgun holstered at his shoulder.

"Forgive intruding," said the man in the gray suit. He offered Stuart his beefy hand. "Raulo Laukaitis. Please I am service for little Mary Sofia."

Stuart felt compelled to shake the man's hand. "Stuart Champion."

Raulo Laukaitis glanced at Allie. "Ah, this Champion you tell about last night. Yes?"

Allie nodded.

Laukaitis indicated the women behind him. "My sisters. Ugna and Gabija." He waved a hand at the men still on the stairs. "And our friends, Dominykas and Gedymin." He turned and addressed his "friends" in a foreign language. The one without the gun trotted back up the stairs. "Dom has gone for Tavas," Laukaitis explained. He lifted a hand to the small of Allie's back then, saying, "Let us go drawer room. Yes?"

"Yes, of course," Allie said quietly, leading the way.

As they walked across the foyer, Laukaitis remarked conversationally, "I no understand drawer room. Who draws there? And they on railroads, drawer rooms. Yes?"

"I think you mean trains, Raulo," one of the blondes said. "And it's drawing room."

Laukaitis tossed both hands into the air. "Trains. Rooms for drawing. Who can know?"

Allie pushed open a pair of etched glass doors, and Laukaitis, followed by Stuart and the others, entered the large room behind her. Stuart didn't miss the opulence of the room with its marble floors, thick rugs, fluted columns, and all white furnishings. Allie went to the nearest sofa and sat. Laukaitis went to stand beside her and waved his sisters into nearby armchairs, while his "friend," Getty-something, took up a post against the wall. Once the ladies were all seated, Laukaitis sat next to Allie and spread his arm along the back of the sofa, touching her shoulders. Left to fend for himself, Stuart took a seat on a large round ottoman in the center of that particular seating arrangement, facing Allie and Laukaitis, with Bart parking himself some distance away on the same ottoman.

"Last night," Laukaitis began, "much is happen."

Allie cleared her throat. "Raulo and his party meant to return to the airport to sleep on their private jet last night, but we talked so late I invited them to stay here."

"My men spends many nights in cabin when sisters travel with me."

"We have only two bedrooms," one of them said. "The seats..." She looked to her sister for help.

"In cabin, they, um, go flat."

"Still, it has to be uncomfortable for such large men," Allie put in quickly.

"You tell us now you night," Laukaitis said to Stuart, making it seem like a request rather than an order.

Stuart told them everything that had taken place from the moment Mary Sofia's number had come up on his phone.

"Oh, yes, this from God," Laukaitis said, crossing himself. "We pray."

He sat forward then, placed his elbows on his knees, and covered his face with his hands. As he spoke, the sisters took turns translating.

"Mūsų Dievas, mano Dievas,"

"Our God, my God..."

"Tiek daug baisių dalykų vyksta šiame nuodėmės pasaulyje."

"Many awful things happen in sinful world."

"Atleisk mums už nuodėmę pasaulyje."

"Forgive us for sin in world."

"Padėkite šiai merginai."

"Help this girl."

"Padėk mums jai padėti."

"Help us help her."

After a moment, Laukaitis straightened, his eyes glimmering with tears, and looked at Stuart. "Bad men where? My friends get them."

He glanced over Stuart's head, waving at someone behind Stuart. Another large man entered the room, rounded the sofa where Laukaitis sat with Allie, and bent down to whisper in Laukaitis's ear.

Stuart answered what he presumed to be a question concerning the whereabouts of Leonardo and Dillman. "They're both in jail. Selwyn locked them in the elevator until the police arrived."

"Ah, is good. Tavas, his job is watch," explained Laukaitis. "He say girl drink *Starka* and water. No more."

"She didn't drink anything before you came, either," Allie put in, obviously thinking. "Leo brought her a glass of champagne, but she set it down without even tasting it. I paid no attention to what happened to it after that."

"Leo, Tavas say, give water, also," Laukaitis pointed out.

Tavas spoke again, aloud this time. Laukaitis leaned back, crossed one ankle over the opposite knee, and contemplated before saying, "Tavas say Leo and man call Jack spoke angry of girl." He pointed at Tavas, who then spoke in heavily accented English.

"He say Jack man, 'You give too much.' And Jack say Leo give her first." He shrugged. "They give water. I thought too much water. Then lady Allie and Raulo take girl other place."

Stuart's gaze snapped to Allie. "You took Mary Sofia into the bedroom?"

Allie shrugged. "Of course, she practically passed out on the couch. I couldn't get her on her feet, so Raulo carried her. Ugna and Gabija went with us. We laid her on the bed and covered her. I truly meant her no harm. I thought she was tired because she'd had such a busy day and that the *Starka* had gone to her head. That's all."

"Better I give *midu*." Laukaitis said. "Is mild, sweet." He clapped a hand over his chest. "Apology."

"It wasn't your fault," Allie said, laying her head on his broad shoulder. "You wouldn't harm a fly."

Bart slid close to Stuart then and softly said, "I was still up when they came in a little past one, but I went to bed soon after. Then Dom came to get me, I don't know, around four o'clock in the morning, to say Allie needed me. I found her here, weeping in Raulo's arms, with Ugna and Gabija hovering over them." Bart grasped Stuart's wrist and went on in a thick voice. "I led my sister to Christ somewhere around half-four this morning."

Stuart gasped, looking to Allie with tears of joy welling in his eyes.

"Raulo made me so ashamed," Allie divulged, wiping away tears that fell more quickly than she could clear them.

"No, no, no," Raulo said, helping her to wipe her face. "Heart make you shamed. Opened for God."

"He is...they are devout Catholics," Allie went on, straightening to address Stuart. "And they want to work with good people." Her face crumpled again. "I am not good people."

"Was not," Bart corrected. "That's changed now. Remember? No one is good without Jesus."

She chuckled a little, still wiping at the tears. "Yes, that's changed, so I've changed." She lifted her head then and looked at Stuart. "You tried to tell me."

He shook his head. "You had no reason to listen to me, Allie. You're not the only one who is ashamed."

"Forget about that," she told him. "You're right that I was jealous of Mary Sofia. I knew you were in love with her just by the way you looked at her. As if you wanted her desperately and couldn't have her."

He opened his mouth to deny that, but then he closed it again, letting the truth sink in finally. "I wasn't worthy of her," he said at length. "And

I'm still not. But if she'll have me, I want to marry her."

Allie laughed, finally drying her tears. "You and your proposals. I think you finally got it right."

"Congratulations," Bart said. "She's a fine woman."

"Don't congratulate me yet," Stuart told him. "I haven't even asked, and she certainly hasn't accepted."

"She will," Allie predicted. "The way you look at her is the same way she looks at you."

"I hope so."

"That's what I was jealous of," Allie admitted then. "That you could both love, when I couldn't."

"Is past now," Laukaitis said, patting her hand.

Smiling, she laid her head on his shoulder again.

Just then a fourth very large man, wearing a black suit and suspenders with a sleeveless undershirt, came in carrying a large, silver tray heaped with pastries, cups, and plates, and a large porcelain pot that smelled tantalizingly of coffee.

"Ah, Galeti," Laukaitis said. "I do not pay you so much."

"Enough," Allie gently corrected, smiling. "You don't pay him enough."

Laukaitis patted her knee. "Yes. So is."

As Galeti lowered the tray to the ottoman, Stuart and Bart moved to another nearby sofa. For a half-hour or so, over coffee and pastries, they discussed what should be done next. Raulo, Allie, and the twins decided they all would dress and go to speak with the police.

"We stay for question," Laukaitis volunteered. "After, we go. Yes?"

"Yes," Allie said, smiling.

Stuart had the uncanny feeling that Laukaitis would be returning to Lithuania with a guest.

"You might want to borrow a razor before you head back to the hospital," Bart suggested to Stuart. "Come upstairs, and I'll show you where you can clean up."

Stuart gratefully followed and was wiping his face clean of shave foam when his cellphone rang. He dug it out of his pocket and answered.

"Yes?"

"She's awake," said Hugo's familiar voice, "and she's asking for you."

Stuart smiled, closed his eyes, and briefly thanked God.

"I'm on my way."

Chapter Nineteen

M ary Sofia finished her breakfast and laid down her fork. Hugo, meanwhile, had moved his chair around so he could see the television mounted high up on the wall and catch the weather report, while Gabi and Rey had gone downstairs to the cafeteria in search of breakfast for themselves. When the door opened, Mary Sofia thought a nurse had entered the room. They'd been rushing in and out all morning. But then she heard the weatherman say, "Looks like rain for the next several days," and a familiar, very dear voice spoke over the continuing monologue.

"Who cares? Let it rain."

"Stuart!" Shoving away the wheeled table bearing her breakfast tray, she automatically lifted her arms to him.

He came across the room, stuffing a pale blue paper mask into a pocket, his smile as wide as his face. "Seeing you sitting there is all the sunshine I need."

Bending, he slipped his arms around her. Delighted, she wrapped her own arms around his neck. He pressed a kiss to her forehead.

"You're here. Where were you? I need you here." She literally pulled him down to sit on the side of the bed, facing her.

"I had to see Allie, sweetheart, and find out if she had anything to do with what happened to you last night."

Mary Sofia sat back, her hands sliding across his shoulders and down to his hands. "Really? Were you afraid Allie might be responsible for what happened or you?"

He squeezed her fingers. "If Allie had been responsible, then so would I, but Allie had nothing to do with it."

"I never thought she did. And I know you bear zero responsibility for what those two did. Or tried to do. Thank you for coming. Somehow, I knew you would."

"Always," he told her. "But I can't take credit for stopping them. That was a God thing. If your number hadn't just shown up on my phone, if Selwyn hadn't still been in the building to let me in, I'd never have gotten there on time."

"But you did get there," Mary Sofia told him, "and I'll always be more thankful than I can say. Now, tell me what happened with Allie."

"She admitted she hired you out of jealousy, but then..." He shook his head, smiling. "Miracles happened last night. Not only did God send me to you, he brought Raulo Laukaitis to Allie. Raulo, it turns out, is a devout Christian. I think she saw herself in his eyes the same way I saw me in your eyes."

"I thought he might be a Christian. He was such a nice man, and he gave Allie a jewel encrusted cross. To bring blessings to her home, he said."

"I don't know about the cross, but he and Bart together were instrumental in bringing Allie to Jesus."

"Oh, Stuart. That's...that's wonderful!"

Hugo, who couldn't help overhearing, got up and came to the side of the bed then. "That's amazing. I'm so glad."

"No more so than Bart, Raulo, and Allie herself. And, I could be wrong, but I sensed a romance in the offing there."

"Really?" Mary Sofia exclaimed. "Allie and Mr. Laukaitis?"

Stuart nodded. "I'm happy for her. And I'm overjoyed to see you sitting here talking to me as if nothing happened."

"Something did happen, though," Hugo put in, folding his arms. "The doctor has referred her for counseling."

"I think that's an excellent idea," Stuart said.

"There's no reason not to do it, now that I'm unemployed again," she told him.

He leaned forward and kissed her on the cheek. "I figured you'd be done with JREDI after this, but Allie wants you to know that you still have a job if you want it."

Mary Sofia shuddered. "I don't think I can ever go back there. I knew Leo was bad news, but I thought J-Jack was my f-friend. He came to church, a-and we had lunch together, and he even warned me about Leo. But it was all an act."

Sliding his arms around her again, Stuart pulled her close, kissing the slight indentation of her temple. "I'm so sorry, honey. But you're safe now. Neither of those men will ever come close to you again."

"If they dare, I'll break them in two," Hugo growled.

Stuart shot him a glance, saying, "Get in line."

Thrilled, Mary Sofia laid her head on Stuart's shoulder, whispering, "Thank you for saving me."

"Like I said, it was a God thing, darlin', and I wasn't the only one there. If not for Selwyn, I couldn't have gotten in the building, and he's the one who had the presence of mind to shove those two fools into the elevator and disable it to hold them for the police." Stuart grinned, adding, "I didn't think about it at the time because I was too concerned about you and following the ambulance, but when the cops arrived, Selwyn got on the elevator with Leonardo and Dillman and sent it down to the first floor. The cops were standing there with handcuffs when that elevator door opened again. I understand Leo and Jack looked like they'd been through a saw mill, while Selwyn remained his cool, unruffled self."

"I'd have paid to see that," Hugo rumbled, not sounding amused at all.

"The thing about Selwyn is," Mary Sofia said slowly, "I thought he hated me."

"Oh, no, I don't think so," Stuart told her. "He called to see about you once the police were through with him, and he let me know he didn't approve of what Allie was doing, creating a job just so she could keep an eye on me and you. He admitted that he thought I might be two-timing Allie with you, but it had quickly become obvious to him that you're a complete innocent. He even said that you reminded him of his daughter."

"Daughter! I didn't realize he even had a daughter."

Stuart lifted four fingers. "Four of them. And I take it his wife is expecting again. That's why he didn't come to the hospital. He said they'd be in here soon enough and that his wife wouldn't rest until he got home."

Mary Sofia lifted both eyebrows. "Wow. Did I ever misjudge him."

"Maybe you'll get a chance to apologize. I'm going to have Maggs send him and his wife complimentary tickets to the next performance."

"Do you think they'll come?"

"If Mrs. Selwyn is in any shape to attend, I think they will."

"You mean Selwyn isn't his first name?"

"Nope."

"Then what is?"

"Ricardo."

"You're kidding? Ricardo Selwyn?"

"I gather he prefers to be called Ric." Stuart put his nose in the air, much like Selwyn would do, adding, "By his intimates."

They both laughed.

Gabrielle and Rey shoved through the door just then, wearing pink paper masks and carrying cardboard clamshell food containers.

"Oh-ho, Prince Charming has arrived," Gabi declared, ripping off her mask.

Stuart laughed, while Rey scolded. "Gabi!"

She ignored them both, quipping, "Well, he'll have to get his own breakfast. I'm not taking that hike again."

"I've eaten," Stuart told her with a grin. "One of Laukaitis's men—his friends, he calls them—served breakfast while the rest of us were talking." He looked to Mary Sofia then, adding gently, "When I left, they were getting dressed to go down to the police station so one of the 'friends' could tell the detectives what he saw. Apparently he's paid to observe what goes on around Laukaitis and his sisters, and he overheard Dillman and Leonardo arguing. It didn't become clear to him what they were arguing about until he heard what happened to you."

"I see. It's very good of them to offer help," Mary Sofia said, not that their statements were needed. Leo and Jack had been caught red-handed by the wonderful man sitting next to her.

Stuart shifted off the side of the bed onto his feet. "I'd better go now and let you all eat."

"No, stay," Mary Sofia pleaded, tugging on his hands. If she had her way, he'd never leave. She didn't just feel safer with Stuart here, she felt happier.

"You need to rest," Rey told her, frowning.

"That's true, sweetheart. And if I don't get some sleep, I'm going to fall over," Stuart said regretfully.

"Oh, I forget. No one got any rest last night but me."

He smiled. "I'm so happy to see you like this. Just let me get a couple hours, and I'll be back."

"Better call first," Hugo told him. "Doc says she can go home this afternoon."

"That's wonderful news," Stuart said.

"You know," Mary Sofia put in, grinning so broadly her cheeks hurt, "I'm not sure I'll feel up to dinner with the family. Maybe you could bring something over."

Stuart blinked and slid a cautious look at Rey, who just rocked back on his heels, sighing as if in defeat. He wasn't smiling. In fact, he was scowling, but he dropped down into the one comfortable chair with an audible plop and opened his breakfast container. Stuart smiled at Mary Sofia, leaned down, and softly said, "That sounds like an excellent idea." He kissed her on the forehead once more and pulled away, stepping over to the door. There he paused and glanced back at Rey and Hugo before giving Mary Sofia a final smile. "Don't give anyone too hard a time, sweetheart. See you later." With that, he pulled open the door and slipped out.

By anyone, he meant her brothers, of course, but before they could put that together, Gabi crooned, "Sweetheart. Ooooo."

Hugo made a face. "It's been honey this and darlin' that since he walked in the door."

Mary Sofia just grinned, while Gabi applauded silently.

Suddenly tears filled Mary Sofia's eyes. She couldn't imagine why because she'd escaped a dreadful horror and so much finally felt right with her world. The doctor had said something about shock, but she'd been too anxious to see Stuart to pay much attention. Odd how as soon as he'd gone, sadness and fear began creeping in once more.

Or maybe not so odd. She was desperately in love with that man, after all, and she might as well admit it. He'd come in the dead of night to save her from a terrible fate, and he'd gone to Allie's like some sort of avenging angel on her behalf. Was she so wrong to think he might feel something significant for her, too?

Could she have misread God's intentions in all this? Much good had already come of the entire ordeal, and she could only be happy that Allie had found Christ and perhaps Raulo Laukaitis, too. She should be satisfied with that, more than satisfied, but she selfishly wanted Stuart Champion, too.

Blinking away unruly tears, she closed her eyes and pretended to a weariness she did not feel. Time, she supposed, would tell all.

She hoped that time would be short.

***

Trooper sat waiting for him on the other side of the back door to his house, an accusatory set to his droopy face. Squatting, Stuart rumpled the dog's ears.

"Sorry, boy. Didn't mean to leave you alone all night." Weariness dragging at him, Stuart sighed. "Guess I'm going to have to leave you to your own devices again." Pushing up to his feet, he added, "I've got to get some sleep."

The thought of staggering through the big house and climbing all those stairs made his knees shake, so he headed to the sofa in the back parlor, dragging off his jacket as he went. He dropped down onto the thick cushions, hazy visions of the previous night flickering across his mind's eye like an old movie.

Memory filtered into dream as sleep settled over him. Sometime later, he woke to a tootling sound, accompanied by a vibration against his thigh. His cellphone was ringing.

Sitting up groggily, he pulled the phone free of his pocket and looked at it. The words "Benton County Sheriff's Department" scrolled across the screen. He saw the time as 3:13. Strips of daylight streamed through the slats of the plantation shutters over the windows, so it had to be P.M. Tapping the green icon, he lifted his phone to his ear.

"Hello."

The detective who had grilled him earlier announced himself. "I thought you'd want to know that we've had Leonardo and Dillman in here with their lawyers for a very long conversation. They started out blaming each other. Then Dillman rolled on Leonardo. You know, the old I'm-bad-but-he's-worse game. We got a list of names out him, five in total. Three are prostitutes they drugged and scammed out of their money. One has moved out of state. Another is a college student, a daughter of a friend of Leonardo's wife, for pity's sake."

"Oh, no. That poor kid."

"She didn't say anything because she couldn't prove what happened and she didn't want to upset her parents. But she's saying plenty now, and the upshot is, the DA's office just called with the news that both slime balls are going for a deal, twenty-five years each, with the possibility of parole in eleven-and-a half. We're going have to talk to your girl before it's signed, sealed, and delivered, but I promise we'll go easy on her."

Stuart straightened, feeling his back crack as he did so. "I'd like to be there when you talk to her, if that's all right."

The detective chuckled. "That's why I'm calling you, man. She says we have to schedule our sit-down around you because she needs you there."

Stuart's eyebrows shot up and a smile grew in his heart. "A day next week work for you?"

"How about Wednesday? Gives me a chance to get all my little duckies in a row, and she'll have some time to clear her head."

"That'll work. The earlier in the day the better."

"Nine in the morning?"

"Fine by me."

"See you then."

The connection cut on the detective's end. Stuart tossed the phone down onto the cushion beside him and stretched his arms high above his head, hands clasped, but then his gaze fell on that little glass, metal, and plastic wonder that had played such a pivotal part in getting to Mary Sofia in time. Picking it up again, he held it flat between this palms and bowed his head, thanking God for all He'd done. He'd saved them all.

Mary Sofia. Allie. Even him in a way he hadn't realized until just now. Most, if not all, of the heavy guilt he'd carried around for so long vanished. Stuart breathed a heavy sigh of relief.

He hoped, believed, that the detective's news would help Mary Sofia, and that was all he asked. Just bringing her some peace and justice would be enough for him.

He wouldn't ask for more.

But he could hope for it.

He ran upstairs to shower and change before phoning his favorite restaurant to place a takeout order. Then, on impulse, he decided to take along a chaperone of sorts. He didn't quite trust himself with Mary Sofia. When he was with her, he felt like a parched man who had dragged himself out of the desert and happened upon a glistening waterfall. He had all he could do to keep from plunging in head first with her, and he suspected that her family were going to be little help in that area now.

Going to the head of the stairs, he called, "Trooper! Come, boy."

When he heard the click of doggy nails on the floor of the foyer, he hurried to draw a warm bath.

Time for his two best friends in all the world to meet. He hoped, prayed, theirs would be a long and happy relationship.

***

At about eleven minutes before six o'clock, a unique racket on the stairs leading up to the garage apartment alerted Mary Sofia to company, but she wasn't quite sure who or what had come to visit. She expected Stuart, but last she saw him, he only had two feet and nothing thumped. When she opened the door, she found a smiling, casually dressed Stuart there, several minutes early and loaded down with bags. Beside him sat a very large dog, coal black, it's tail thumping against the rails of the small landing and it's blocky head tilted to one side as if taking her measure.

"We're early. I hope you don't mind. Didn't want the food to get cold. And Trooper's been anxious to make your acquaintance."

"I don't mind at all," Mary Sofia said, going down on her knees to greet the dog. "Hello, there."

"Say hello, Trooper," Champ instructed. Like any well-behaved gentleman, the dog offered a paw for shaking. She shook then couldn't resist rubbing those black ears.

"He's adorable."

"He's a big, obnoxious throw rug most of the time," Champ said, his voice loaded with affection, "but he's also my best friend. One of my best friends."

Mary Sofia pushed up to her feet, slapped at the knees of her mauve sweats, and smoothly lifted an arm before stepping back from the doorway. "Come in, please. Both of you."

Stuart stepped inside, followed closely by the dog. Just as Mary Sophia closed the door,

Gabi came out of the bedroom wearing Mary Sofia's favorite pink T-shirt. Gabi didn't wait for censure. Instead she jumped right in, defending herself.

"What? You aren't wearing it."

Mary Sofia parked her hands on hips "Just because you threatened to tell Hugo if I changed my clothes."

"The doctor said to relax. We all want you to relax. Don't we, Champ?"

He grinned, splitting a look between them. "We do. Besides," he said to Mary Sofia, "that color looks good on you."

Mary Sofia tugged at the bottom of her sweatshirt and smiled at him, wishing she had ignored everyone else and dressed for the occasion. Even if he did approve of the color.

"Something smells delicious," Gabi declared, sniffing.

"It's not for you," Mary Sofia retorted.

Stuart chuckled. "Fond of filet mignon, are you?"

Both females exclaimed at once, "Filet mignon!"

He shrugged, hefting the bags, one in each hand. "Trooper and I are hungry. We missed lunch. Well, I missed lunch."

As if on cue, the big dog padded out from behind his master, panting as if the movement required great effort.

"Oh, my word," Gabi gushed. "Is that your

dog?"

"Nah, he just wondered in off the street," Stuart teased. "Think I oughta keep him?"

"Of course that's his dog," Mary Sofia said, chuckling.

As if adding his own confirmation, Trooper woofed in a deep, strangled voice that seemed to roll up from that wide, black chest. Drool dribbled from his fleshy mouth onto the hardwood floor.

Stuart winced. "Got a paper towel? He does that when he's excited."

"If this is excited," Gabi quipped, going for the roll of towels. "I'd hate to see him bored."

"Oh, he's never bored. He's either sleeping or —"

"Drooling?" Mary Sofia supplied.

Grinning, Stuart set down the bulkier bag and handed the smaller one to Mary Sofia. "Pretty much."

He took the towels from Gabi. Tearing off one, he crouched down to wipe up the drops of drool. Meanwhile, Mary Sofia carried the food to the island that separated the kitchen from the living area.

Gabi rubbed Trooper's head. "Ears would run from you, I think, and Bitsy would snub you, but I think you're adorable."

"Who's Bitsy?" Stuart asked, setting the roll of unused towels on the coffee table in front of the sofa.

"Hugo's poodle. You met her last Sunday."

Stuart pushed up to his full height. "You mean that curly gray dog with the long muzzle? I thought I imagined it."

"Oh, she's very real. She just hasn't been clipped in some time due to the cold weather. Hugo cleans up her face himself. Otherwise she couldn't see for the hair in her eyes. Then he has her shaved in the summer."

"Are you telling me that Marine Captain Carter has a poodle?" Stuart demanded, laughter in his voice.

"Yep, he inherited her from our next door neighbor. She's appointed herself nanny to the triplets, but it's Hugo she really adores."

Stuart grinned. "And the beagle?"

Gabi headed to the door. "Oh, he's ours. He adores Bitsy, but she pretends he doesn't exist."

Stuart watched her leave, shaking his head, and addressed his own dog. "I'd like to see her ignore you, big guy. If I know you, you'd sit on her just to make sure she knows who's boss."

Mary Sofia laughed. "That, I'd like to see."

Chapter Twenty

S tuart picked up what Mary Sofia now recognized as a bag of two-liter drinks. He carried the sack to the island and unpacked it. "I brought sweet tea. I hope that's all right. It's what you drank that night at Golucky's when I intruded on your date."

"You didn't intrude. You kindly invited us to join you," Mary Sofia told him.

He ducked his head, perhaps to hide a smile. "If you say so."

"We were happy to join you. It was either join you or wait forever for a table."

Lifting his head, he met her gaze with his. "Your date didn't seem so happy."

"He got unhappy over the attention I gave you."

"And the attention I gave you."

She shrugged, smiling. "Either way, I'm not unhappy with how it turned out. Now, if you want to eat your steak in peace, I suggest you get started. We're bound to have company before long."

He rubbed his hands together. "Ready when

you are. I, for one, don't need a plate. I'll happily eat straight from the container, but a knife and fork wouldn't go amiss."

While she went for flatware and filled glasses with ice, he unpacked the food bag, coming up with a loaf of sourdough bread still warm from the oven, and two tin foil containers filled with bacon-wrapped beef filets, baked potatoes, and an asparagus-mushroom medley.

"Hope you like asparagus. I asked for their green beans and almonds, but it wasn't ready yet, and I didn't want to wait."

"I love asparagus, but Gabi hates it. I'll be sure to let her know it was part of the meal."

He nodded, chuckling, and pulled out a stool for her. "She seems to be doing her best to keep things normal for you."

At once, Mary Sofia realized the truth of that statement. Gabi had no reason to wear her pink top. She'd done that just to get a rise out of her big sis, as if everything was still just as it should be. Tears sprang to Mary Sofia's eyes. Those tears never seemed to be very far away just now.

"She is. Everyone is."

As if he knew exactly what she felt, Stuart stepped back and opened his arms. She walked straight into them, clasping her arms around his waist and tucking her head into the hollow of his shoulder. His T-shirt felt soft and warm. He felt safe, right. Precious.

"I'm so glad you're here."

"I'm so glad to be here."

She pulled back a bit. His hands smoothing her hair, he leaned in to kiss her forehead again. Without even thinking about it, she lifted her chin and went up on her tiptoes.

Their lips met, clung, melded. His arms dropped around her again, and he pulled her close, deepening the kiss. While their food cooled and elation soared through Mary Sofia, they stood entwined. She wound her arms about his neck and gave herself over to that kiss, wanting, needing, to prove to both of them that this wasn't a dream. Before long—too soon for Mary Sofia—Stuart broke away, tucking her head beneath the jut of his chin and folding her close. She felt his heart slamming against the wall of his chest and smiled. Her own heart seemed determined to meet his beat for beat. When the pulse between them slowed, he slid his hands to her waist and stepped back, looking down into her face, his gaze locked with hers.

"If I wasn't in love with you before, sweet Sofi, I am now. You should know that."

"Oh, Stuart." She swayed forward, pressing against him, her cheek against his chest. "You've always been my ideal."

"You're standards are higher than me," he scoffed, even as his arms tightened around her.

"I admit I was disappointed, brokenhearted, when I realized the depth of your involvement with Allie."

"We were never as involved as we should've been," he stated flatly. "I tried so hard to be in love with her, to make it about more than sex."

"As hard as she tried *not* to be in love with you, I imagine."

"How did you know that?"

Mary Sofia shrugged, all the better to feel his arms about her. "I spent enough time with her to know that she worked at being cold and unfeeling."

"You're right. I think I should tell you why." Grasping her by the forearms, he gently set her back. Then he pulled out the stools under the ledge of the kitchen island and guided her up and onto the one facing him. Seating himself on the other stool, he bowed his head for a moment, obviously thinking how best to say what he wanted to tell her. Finally, he just came out with it. "I didn't know this until today, and it's not something I think we should spread around, but when Allie was in college, she was drugged and raped."

Mary Sofia's hands flew to her mouth in an attempt to contain the gasp that gusted out of her. "Oh, no. Poor Allie."

"It gets worse," he warned. "Her date not only drugged her and carried her up to his dorm room to rape her, he recorded the rape on film and showed it to all his buddies."

The ever-ready tears spilled from Mary Sofia's eyes. "She must've been destroyed by that."

"No doubt about it. I imagine she was mad at the world, afterward, probably even mad at God. And her ex-husband cheating on her didn't help. I understand now why she did the things she did. I see now that she was using me to prove to herself that sex was no big deal, so she hadn't really had anything stolen from her and had no reason for being desperately hurt. At the same time, I was trying to use her to fill a role in my life she wasn't equipped to fill."

"It's completely understandable. She was wounded. You were lonely."

"Yes, that explains it all. But it doesn't mean that what we were doing wasn't sinful. We were each justifying it in our own ways and for our own reasons, but that doesn't make it right. If anything, it kept us from facing the truth for far too long." He reached out and skimmed her cheek with his palm. "That took someone I cared about more than I should. That took you."

Tears filled her eyes again, tears of joy this time. She just couldn't seem to stop crying. "I never thought I had a chance with you. I thought you saw me as some stupid, moon-eyed kid."

"I tried to," he admitted. "But the truth is and has always been that you're too good for me."

"I'm no paragon of virtue, Stuart. I was a stupid, moon-eyed kid. My brothers pulled me out of more risky situations than I want to admit. But I've grown up since then."

He smiled. "I've noticed."

She grinned, but then she grew solemn again, serious. "My brothers want me to go to counseling."

"I think that's a very good idea."

Looking down, she said what was really on her mind. "Would...would you go with me?"

"Go with you?" he echoed.

"It couldn't have been easy," she rushed to say, "finding me like that, realizing what was happening."

"It wasn't. In fact, in some ways it was more traumatic than the deaths of my parents. I mean, death is a normal part of life after a certain age and given certain health issues. But when I realized what was happening to you..." He shook his head. "I've never felt that kind of evil before or been so angry and troubled."

"You'll go then? The doctor said, uh, partners a-and spouses should consider being part of the process."

He tilted his head. "Mary Sofia Carter, are you suggesting we ought to marry?"

Heat bloomed in her face. "Uh, well, not exactly. I just meant—" She broke off when he smiled.

"Because that's why I've been thinking."

And there came the waterworks again. "Oh, Stuart, I do love you."

Leaning forward, he cupped the back of her head with his hand and brought her brow to his. "You can't know how happy that makes me." After several sweet moments, he sat back and allowed her to do the same. "We can't rush, though, sweetheart. Your brothers would nail me to the wall if we tried it, and I wouldn't blame them. They may do it, anyway."

"No, they won't," she insisted staunchly. "I won't stand for it." She melted into a smile then. "Not that I think it will be an issue after everything that's happened."

"Nevertheless," he told her, "we'll take the counseling and…" He shrugged. "Do something normal, like dating, for a while. And then we'll talk about it again."

"Sounds like a plan," she said, sniffing and using her napkin to mop her face.

He held up a finger. "First," he declared. "We eat. I slept through lunch, and I'm starving."

She laughed, swiveled on her stool, and held out her hand. "Should I give thanks or will you?"

"I'll be happy to."

Clasping hands, they bowed their heads while Stuart prayed. He poured out his heart. It wasn't very elegant, just "Thank You, Lord. Thank You. Thank You. Thank You…"

***

Mary Sofia proved correct about company showing up. Within the hour, both Gabi and Ana appeared, each with a dog in hand. As predicted, Ears took one look at Trooper and scrambled behind the couch, barking. Bitsy, on the other, regally stood her ground while Trooper hauled his great body up and walked a slow circle around her, sniffing. Then Trooper simply collapsed to the floor again and shut his eyes. Bitsy calmly lowered herself, lying right up against him, and lowered her head to her paws, as if she were a queen taking her rightful place beside her king. Soon, while the people in the room talked and laughed, Ears crept out to sniff Trooper, who snuffled and sneezed in the universal signal of doggy peace and acceptance. Ears immediately began trying to prompt the great cane corso to play, but Trooper ignored him, even when Ears tugged at the heavy leather collar encircling Trooper's thick neck.

Tomas and Dylan, escorted by Rey, had to meet the big black dog next. Trooper once more hauled himself up and allowed himself to be fawned over before dropping down next to Bitsy again. Eventually, Rey got to his feet and declared that Mary Sofia needed to rest. Knowing he'd just been invited to leave, Stuart stood. While Stuart and Mary Sofia said their good-byes, Rey had the decency to take his own advice, shepherding kids and dogs out the door ahead of him.

Stuart intentionally kept the parting brief, a warm hug and a quick kiss. "I'll call you in the morning before I leave for work."

"Please do."

"Rest well, sweetheart."

"You, too."

One last kiss, and a command to Trooper, who sat patiently beside the door, and Stuart headed down the stairs. He was not surprised to find Rey's tall, slender figure waiting beside his truck.

"My concern is this," Rey said without preamble, shifting away from the driver's door. "First you were in love with Allie Justus and a few weeks later, you're in love with my sister. How do you square that?"

Tempering a wry smile, Stuart bowed his head. "I was never in love with Allie. I tried to be, partly because I was lonely but mostly to justify what I was doing with her. Your sister showed me the error of my ways, and that put an end to Allie and me."

"Mary Sofia intervened somehow?"

"I guess you could say that. I've been half in love with her for years, but I've always known I'm not good enough for her. When she, um, caught Allie and me in a kind of passionate kiss, I realized I'd hurt and disappointed Mary Sofia. And I couldn't live with that." He slid his hands into his pockets and shook his head. "I didn't expect anything to happen between Mary Sofia and me, but I broke it off with Allie. After a lot of prayer and with the support of some good friends, I got myself right with God. Things just…" He shrugged. "Things just happened after that."

"What things?" Rey demanded, folding his

arms.

"Well, for instance, I was eating dinner in my favorite restaurant one evening when Mary Sofia arrived with a fellow she used to work with." He clapped a hand to his chest. "Felt like I'd been hit with a meat cleaver. They joined me at my table, and—long story short—I wound up driving her home."

"And the fellow she used to work with?"

Stuart shrugged. "Guess he didn't like how chummy Mary Sofia and I were over dinner. We were kind of talking on the phone a lot." He cleared his throat. "And seeing each other at practice and performances. I was able to introduce her to some friends from work once, and it felt so good, so right, just having her stand there next to me." He pinched the bridge of his nose. "I asked God to change my feelings for her, but I just couldn't get her out of my head. Then last night…"

"I'll concede that, one way or another, God used you to rescue her," Rey told him, "but she's especially vulnerable right now."

"I agree. That's why we're both going to counseling."

Rey lifted his chin. "I see. Together or separately?"

"We thought we'd start with Pastor Alvin and see what he recommends, then go from there."

Working his jaw from side to side, Rey

bowed his head, obviously considering. Finally, he looked up, his gaze piercing through the growing darkness. "I can't argue with that."

"Look," Stuart said, "I know I'm not worthy of her. I can't imagine who would be. But I'm hers until she sends me packing, and if—when the time is right—she consents to marry me, that's exactly what's going to happen." He looked Rey straight in the eye and added. "I pray to God it's with the blessing of her family."

Rey looked down then back up again before clapping a hand on Stuart's shoulder. "I'd expect no less."

Relieved, Stuart felt some of the starch leave his muscles.

Something told him he was going to sleep well tonight.

***

Rey and his family flew home to Tennessee on Sunday evening. Four days later, Mary Sofia and Stuart went together for counseling with Mary Sofia's pastor. Immediately, Pastor Alvin put them both at ease. He prayed with them, and they talked at length. After he'd heard the full story, he referred them to a Christian psychologist, a woman, who elected to speak to them separately after the first meeting. She soon referred Mary Sofia to group counseling.

Champ continued to see the psychologist privately for several weeks. They talked about his experience rescuing Mary Sofia, of course, as well as his anger over the incident. They also spoke about his adoption, his boyhood, his parents and their deaths, even his affair with Allie.

Finally, the counselor asked, "Do you and Mary Sofia want to have your premarital counseling with me or Pastor Alvin? I should tell you that Pastor Alvin is a much cheaper alternative."

Laughing, Stuart replied, "I'll have to speak with Mary Sofia about that, but I'm guessing she'll choose Pastor Alvin."

The doctor just smiled and closed her notebook. "Then I assume this is our last session."

Stuart thanked her, and as he walked out the door, he silently thanked God. He'd never felt so completely at peace before, and he knew that his worth to Mary Sofia would be measured going forward now. Past mistakes no longer mattered. God doesn't care about past sins once they are abandoned and confessed; He only cares about today and tomorrow. Stuart promised himself and his Lord that all his tomorrows would be dedicated to living a life pleasing to God. Even then he couldn't hope to earn the many blessings God had heaped on him these past weeks, let alone those to come, but only by living for Jesus could he hope to be the husband Mary Sofia deserved.

***

Mary Sofia talked and talked and talked, in

private session with the therapist and in group sessions with other women, some of whom were actual rape victims. Several of those women had been through such horrible experiences that they'd barely escaped with their lives. Sadly, the facilitator had informed her, there were male rape victims, too, and they suffered just as greatly.

Even though she no longer worked on a daily basis, weeks flashed by. JREDI didn't need her, anyway. Partnering with Selwyn, Bart proved to be a gifted administrator. He'd cleaned up his act with a haircut, shave, and a wardrobe of expertly fitted suits. He'd also instituted new corporate standards, which had inspired some employees to leave. The party days at JREDI had come to an end. The corporate attitude changed along with the corporate structure. Meanwhile, he had reported that Allie, who was living with one of Laukaitis's twin sisters and her family, had fallen in love with the country of Lithuanian as well as Laukaitis himself, so she didn't plan to return to Arkansas any time soon. It turned out that Raulo had a thirteen-year-old son and wanted more children, so Allie was taking steps to join the Lithuanian Catholic church so they could marry. Plans were in the works to spin off the international business of Justus Real Estate Development to a European office, which Allie and Raulo's sisters would run together, leaving Raulo to concentrate on his own vast holdings.

Mary Sofia shortly found herself a leader amongst the therapy group, and she didn't hesitate to offer Christ as the source of healing. She got some pushback on that from a few of the more brutalized and bitter of the group, but in general her words were well accepted, and she saw a few of the women come to Christ. She began to think about serving that segment of society.

"I think it's a fine idea," Stuart agreed when she broached the subject. "You should talk to Pastor Alvin and your therapist about it. But first we need to pray about it together, don't you think?"

"Yes, please."

Sitting side by side on the sofa in the garage apartment, they clasped hands and bowed their heads. Stuart began to pray aloud.

"Father God, we praise You and glorify You for your generosity and provision. We need Your guidance and will as Mary Sofia seeks to answer your calling..."

Mary Sofia never felt so close to God as when she and Stuart prayed together, and she came away from that particular prayer session knowing that she'd found her calling. When she looked up and saw Gabi lingering in the bedroom doorway, she kissed Stuart quickly and rose to her feet, hurrying to follow her sister into the room they shared. She found Gabi standing before the window, wiping her eyes. A touch on her shoulder sent Gabi whirling into Mary Sofia's arms.

"What's wrong?"

"Wrong?" Gabi repeated, chuckling and dashing away tears. "Nothing is wrong." She hugged Mary Sofia and pulled away. "You've shown me exactly what real love is, you and Stuart. It's not just fun and laughter or the romance stuff. It's a spiritual thing. I suppose I've always known it. I mean, Hugo and Rey are always saying their faith is the foundation of their marriages. But it suddenly seems so real to me now."

Joy filled Mary Sofia. "I'm so proud of you," she told Gabi. "You're so much smarter than I was at your age."

"Well, yeah," Gabi said, her usual cheeky self. "First you showed me what not to do, and now you're showing me what's best to do. Isn't that the job of big sisters?"

Mary Sofia laughed. "It's my privilege to be of service, your highness."

Pretending to hold out nonexistent skirts, Gabi curtsied. "Of course, your majesty."

They fell onto Gabi's bed, laughing. When the hilarity died down, Mary Sofia sat up. Stuart now stood in the open doorway, leaning against the jamb, arms folded, a smile on his face and love in his eyes.

This, Mary Sofia thought, *is the life God's giving me. This amazing, blessed life.*

***

They did what all dating couples do. They went out to dinner, alone and with friends. They watched movies together at the local theater and at home, either her place or his. They often played recordings of Rey's music, as well as Tessa's new song and Stuart's only one, which Charlie had thoughtfully d burned to a disc. Mary Sofia not only fell deeper and deeper in love with Stuart Champion, she fell in love with his dog and his house and the idea of spending the rest of her life with him.

On the first Saturday of May, Stuart invited her out for lunch. They agreed to meet at Golucky's on the downtown square. She found a parking spot, minor miracle, and strolled around the corner to the restaurant, where Stuart met her on the sidewalk. They embraced and briefly kissed before he turned her toward the square in the center of downtown, green now with spring grass and bright with flowers.

"It'll be a few minutes. They'll let us know via text when the table's ready."

Arm in arm, they crossed the street to a bench beneath a shade tree. Sitting, they soaked in the perfect weather and the gentle, dappled sunshine. Mary Sofia noticed a fellow with a camera, but she didn't pay him any mind. Tourists were always snapping pics of the old square and the galleries and shops surrounding it. But then Stuart nodded at someone and rose to his feet. She started to do likewise, but he placed a staying hand on her shoulder. Then he went down on one knee.

She knew, of course, what was happening, especially when all the people she loved began to pour out of Golucky's and various shops. Hugo and JoJo smiled and nodded, their hands grasping those of the triplets. Gabi and Ana waved. Wyatt and Maggs Ogilvie stood with Bart, who looked surprisingly dapper in his business suit and haircut. Drew and Carol Camstock clustered nearby with Ronan and Tessa Camstock-Younger and their younger children, Ryan, Ilona, and Rafe. Sam and Holland Cody waved and smiled. Amalie and Doctor Tate Golden stood with their three sons, while Matt and Joanna Polo and Charlie and Charlotte Biggs shepherded their respective broods out of the ice cream parlor on the corner, all eight of them and their rapidly disappearing snacks. They were all there, the entire HOBBY RUN family. Only Rey and his family were missing. Or so Mary Sofia thought, until her Stuart pulled his cellphone from the hip pocket of his jeans and laid it her lap. There, gazing up from the flowered skirt of her sundress was the smiling face of her eldest brother.

"Is it over?" Rey asked. "'Cause it better not be over. We've been holding for a quarter of an hour."

Everyone crowded into the picture then,

Della, Dylan, and Tomas, even baby Grace.

"It's not over," Mary Sofia answered tearfully. Looking up at Stuart, she smiled. "It will never be over."

She glanced around at the whole world, their whole world.

In addition to the HOBBY RUN crew, several of Stuart's coworkers had arrived, his boss, Harry Purdle, and his wife, Bill Beck, Al Cooper and Tamara, as well as several others whose names she couldn't recall at the moment. And there, to one side, hands folded and a smile on his face, stood Pastor Albert.

Of course, a smile split her face even as tears rolled from her eyes.

"It is definitely not over," Stuart said, taking her hand. "Forever is waiting, my darling, so let us go meet it. Mary Sofia Carter, I love you more than my own life. You are the answer to my prayers. So, I ask you now, in front of God Almighty, our family, and dearest friends, will you marry me?"

Laughing and crying at the same time, she burbled, "Do you even have to ask?"

"Absolutely. You deserve nothing less."

"Then yes. I want to marry you more than I want to breathe."

"Oh, don't stop doing that," he said, rising and pulling her to her feet, his grin wide enough to break his face.

"Which?" she teased, the phone sliding

harmlessly to the thick grass, "agreeing to marry you or breathing?"

"Both."

He stepped back and to the side and turned her to face him. Then he pulled her close, bent her backward over his arm, and kissed her, to the applause of all those gathered around them. The photographer captured it all, moving in for a close up when Stuart pulled a small pink box from the front pocket of his jeans and opened it to display a ridiculously expensive diamond wedding set. Mary Sofia gasped at the large, cushion cut, center diamond surrounded on three sides by smaller, square-cut diamonds in a platinum setting. The accompanying wedding band was studded all across the top with similar stones.

"I had this made," he said, removing the engagement ring from the box, "to match my mother's wedding band. I hope that's all right."

"All right?" she exclaimed, watching him slide the beautiful ring onto her finger. "It's perfect."

"I hoped you'd say that because I had Dad's wedding band sized to fit my hand." He pulled that ring from his pocket and showed it to her. The square stones were set into the slightly wider band, but they were the same size and shape as those in his mother's—soon to be her own—wedding ring.

"I'm so proud to wear this," she said, holding

out her hand for the benefit of the photographer and onlookers. "And I'll be just as proud to wear your mother's wedding band as my own."

He placed his father's ring in the box next to his mother's, closed the box, and returned it to his pocket before taking both of Mary Sofia's hands in his. "My parents were very much in love and very happy together. They always said I made their joy complete, and that's what I want to do for you, sweet Sofi. I want to bring you nothing but joy for the rest of my life. I have no doubt you'll do the same for me. So pick a date, sweetheart."

She laughed and confessed, "Um, I had Pastor Alvin hold the last Thursday in June for us, just in case." Everyone around them chuckled. "I started to wonder if we were going to get this settled in time to complete the premarital counseling, though."

Laughter followed that remakr, then they cheered when Pastor Alvin loudly proclaimed, "You heard her, folks! The last Thursday in June. The weekends were all taken. Get it on your calendars now."

To everyone's surprise, Bart stepped forward and raised his hands for attention. "As a wedding gift, Allie has asked me to open the Chateau for the wedding reception. And, um, if I were you, I'd plan on honeymooning in Greece. Allie says Raulo owns the 'most glorious place on earth' there."

Mary Sofia gasped again. "That's so generous."

"They can afford it," Bart assured her. "Easily. And she's very happy for the two of you."

"We're very happy for her," Stuart said, looking at Mary Sofia.

"Very happy," she echoed softly.

In fact, very happy was putting it mildly.

In the end, all she could do was clasp hands with her ideal man and thank God.

Epilogue

T he bride looked like a fairy princess in a sleeveless, fitted gown of snow white lace dotted with tiny crystals. Her long, dark hair coiled into a loose knot at her nape. The long veil, hemmed on every side with two inches of lace, flowed from a tiara set with pearls and crystals, calling attention to the perfect oval of her face. The wide, off-the-shoulder neckline displayed her long, graceful neck and elegant collarbone. She carried a bouquet of creamy white roses, their petals tipped and veined in luscious pink.

Stuart could do nothing more than stare at his bride, his breath trapped in his chest. Forgotten were the flower girls, identical twins with blonde curls and pale pink dresses, tossing pink rose petals from their baskets before being coaxed to sit with their mother. The Maid of Honor, seventeen-year old Gabrielle, and the bridesmaid, thirteen-year-old Ana, both dressed in pale pink and holding long-stemmed roses of the same shade, had ceased to exist in the groom's world. He wouldn't even remember later how solemnly Marc Everett, in a pale gray tuxedo, had carried the unlit taper in his small hands, staring at the white wick as if it might erupt in flame all on its own. Neither would he recall how jauntily Dylan followed him or how skillfully Tomas had helped both boys place their tapers on either side of the unity candle sitting atop a small, lace-draped table to one side of the altar before carefully lighting both.

So transfixed was he, Stuart didn't see his best man, Bart, trade glances with the other groomsman, Samson Cody. As Charlie and Matt began playing the bridal march, Stuart instinctively started forward to meet Mary Sofia, only to be caught by Bart's hand clamped onto his elbow.

"Patience," Bart whispered on an airy chuckle.

It took every shred of strength Stuart possessed not to rush down that aisle and claim her, his gaze never leaving the trio who made their slow way down the aisle. Rey looked suave and pleased, completely at ease in his formal wedding attire. Only Hugo did not wear the dove gray tuxedo chosen for the male attendants. Instead, he came decked out in full military regalia, his face stony, no doubt to hold at bay the tears glistening in his eyes. The bride, almost too beautiful to behold, beamed, her gaze fixed on her eager husband-to-be as she floated toward him. He saw not a single doubt in her big brown eyes, and his heart swelled with love.

He'd waited a lonely lifetime for this amazing woman, but the wait had been worth every moment, every heartache, every mistake, every prayer. Over these past weeks, whenever he'd sat with her, hand-in-hand, to pray, he'd felt a sense of peace and joy he could not have imagined in the past. They prayed together daily and had promised each other that they would begin and end every day of their marriage in just that fashion. As much as he yearned to make love with this incredible woman, he treasured even more the intimacy of shared prayer with her.

The truths he had learned filled him with humble joy. When he had stopped hunting and trying to force romantic love, when he had ceased the sin he'd justified with notions of false love, when he had surrendered to God's will, he had seen the great lifetime love right in front of him at last. He praised God every day and in every way for putting him at Mary Sofia's side when she'd needed him most. He gave God the glory for her healing and her strength, for her sweetness and sensitivity, for her generosity and insight, but mostly for her rock-solid relationship with Christ Jesus. Stuart didn't expect a perfect life, not in this fallen world, but together with Christ, he and Mary Sofia together could do anything, bear anything, become anything God willed, and happily so.

A verse from his weekly Bible study at work, Matthew 6:33, had become his touchstone, and he brought it to mind now.

"*But seek first His kingdom and His righteousness, and all these things will be given to you as well.*"

He'd once assumed that verse to pertain to possessions and career success, but he understood now that it meant so much more than those trivial things. The true key to happiness was not romantic love and marriage or anything other than seeking to please God. When the things of God had become his priority, God had blessed him with his heart's desires, all of it embodied in this beautiful Christian woman.

Pastor Alvin asked who gave the bride in marriage, and her brothers answered in unison, "We do."

Then Rey, as eldest brother, lifted her right hand and placed it in Stuart's outstretched palm. From this day onward, she was his.

"Thank You," Stuart whispered, gazing down into her breathtaking face.

The brothers nodded and backed away, but he hadn't been speaking to them. He would forevermore thank his Lord for all the joys he did not deserve.

***

The following June, barely a year after their wedding, found the Champions standing in the front yard of their happy home, where the Carters ran tame on an almost daily basis. Mary

Sofia marveled at how much Stuart loved having the Carter kids chasing around the house and yard. The only room off-limits to them was his office. Having been recently promoted on the job, he sometimes brought home work that had to be protected from little fingers and childish curiosity.

He finished the cold glass of tea she had brought him, Trooper at her heels, and set the empty glass on the porch steps. The dog followed her everywhere these days, a growing air of expectation about him. Mary Sofia joked that Hugo's poodle had schooled him on childrearing and he was anxious to get started. No more anxious than she.

Stuart wiped perspiration from his forehead with his arm, having weeded the flowerbeds, something Mary Sofia preferred to do but could no longer manage. After wiping his grubby hands, he placed them on her distended belly.

"I think he's sleeping," Mary Sofia said, knowing he hoped to feel their son kick.

"Gathering his strength for his grand entry, perhaps," Stuart mused. "Won't be long now."

"I'm ready when he is."

"Me, too. Every day I think I can't possibly be any happier than I already am. Then I wake up and see you sleeping on the pillow next to me and I just want to sing with joy."

He'd been doing that more and more often with HOBBY RUN. Singing, that was. In fact, the band had featured him in two of the tracks on the new album they'd recently recorded. Rey had arranged with his agent to cut an album with HOBBY RUN featuring his songs with them, and the new album had grown out of that experience. No one other than Rey intended to abandon his or her career in order to pursue music professionally, but the singles they'd cut still played prominently on local Christian radio stations, and Charlie and Maggs had worked together to line up a distributor and promoter, who had launched a website and reported that the album was selling well. Charlie had also arranged to publish a songbook of HOBBY RUN songs, which would be distributed free to churches and also be sold on the website.

All of Stuart's earnings from HOBBY RUN, after the tithe had been paid, went into a college fund for their son and any other children they might have. Mary Sofia thought four would make a nice round number at the dinner table. Stuart said he'd welcome as many children as God would grant them, even though he was already surrounded by the burgeoning Carter family. She routinely prayed for his every hope to be fulfilled.

Something poked her from the inside, an elbow or a knee, perhaps.

"Ow. The rascal has awakened."

Stuart dropped down to sit on the porch steps and wrapped his arms around his family, his face pressed to Mary Sofia's belly, and gave their son his first piece of fatherly advice.

"Now, listen to me, Carter Stuart Champion, that's no way to treat your mother. Let me tell you the secret to a happy life."

Mary Sofia said it with him, one hand smoothing his sleek blonde head, the other caressing her belly.

"Seek first His kingdom…"

And all these things will be given as well.

Heaven Knows

God of Love, God of Grace, Heaven knows You took my place.

Who am I that You died for me? What greater blessing can there be?

The Spotless Lamb of Calvary, was crucified to set me free.

I praise You, Lord with every breath. My endless life for Your pain and death.

God of love, God of Grace, Heaven knows You took my place.

You reached low and touched my head. "I will pay the price," You said.

No more death. No more fear. My life is His. My eyes are clear.

No more guilt. No more shame. I am forgiven, whole again.

God of love, God of Grace, Heaven knows You took my place.

Covered and washed clean by Your sacrifice for me.

It's forgiven. It's forgotten, as if it never even happened.

God of love, God of Grace, Heaven knows You took my place.

Afterword

I hope you have enjoyed this tenth book in The HOBBY RUN Variety Praise Band series. This has been a labor of love for me, and I pray that it enriches the lives of my readers if only for a few minutes or hours. Please consider leaving a review. If you've missed any of the books in the series, you'll find a complete listing of them in the pages that follow. I can be contacted via email at

deararlenejames@gmail.com
or by snail mail at
POB 5582, Bella Vista AR 72714

You can also follow me through my website
https://www.arlenejames.com,
via Goodreads
https://goodreads.co.../
show/57184.Arlene_James,
or through my Amazon author page
https://amzn.to/3MBlOPp

Thank you for your interest, and God bless.
Arlene

About The Author

Arlene James

Arlene James has been steadily publishing for more than four decades and has over 100 novels in print. The HOBBY RUN Variety Praise Band Series is set in beautiful northwest Arkansas where she makes her home.

Books In This Series

*The HOBBY RUN Variety
Praise Band Series...*

Four original bands, ten musicians, and one savvy promoter meet at a Battle of the Bands contest in northwest Arkansas. Of different ages, backgrounds, and musical genres, they have three things in common: talent, a love of performing, and their Christian faith. Coming together under the acronym of their original groups, they form not only a unique musical sound but a rich and expanding family as God works His will in each of their lives.

A Familiar Love Song

Drawn together by the love of music, torn apart by insecurities, reunited 25 years later. ..but huge secrets lurk in the past. Only a shared faith and impossible forgiveness can yield a future for Wyatt and Maggs and a band with amazing possibilities.

A Hero's Love Song

Rey lost a food serving his country then returned home to raise four younger siblings. The last thing he needs is a homeless teen mom and her baby boy. Della has overcome much in her young life, but Rey sees her as too much of an added burden. Or is his faith just too small to see God's big plan?

The Healer's Love Song

Amalie served her country as an Army nurse only to lose her marriage to infidelity. Between her work with wounded vets, being a single mom, and playing keyboard for the band, she has no time for romance. Doctor Tate hides his demons behind blatant sexuality, but when he sets out to seduce Amalie, he finds himself seduced by God.

Honor's Love Song

Charlie is as humble as he is talented and successful, but his father remains disappointed. Paige seems very familiar to Charlie, but she has so many false identities she doesn't even know who she is. She's sick of the con, but her dad's life depends on this scam. If only she could see God's hand at work.

Fidelity's Love Song

Infertility and infidelity can drive even a Christian woman to divorce. When Joanna flees to a secluded orphanage in Honduras, she doesn't expect her musician husband, Matt, to follow or to fall in love with a six-year-old and his siblings. Resentment and betrayal are a shaky foundation upon which to build a family unless God lays the cornerstone.

A Courageous Love Song

Ponytailed, tattooed widower Drew is more comic than musician and, unbeknownst to his band mates, a legal powerhouse. A man of great faith, he believes God speaks to him. Loving such a man is beyond shy, downtrodden Carol. To overcome the trauma of her past and love again will take a supernatural courage.

A Love Song In Quarantine

Marine reservist Hugo wants nothing more than to reacquaint himself with his brother's pretty little band mate, but JoJo's heart has been shattered by loss.Then COVID hits, and an elderly neighbor requires care. Mix in a pregnant stalker, a wannabe gang banger, siblings in need of a home, and a strange dog. It's hardly a recipe for romance! Can even God get this all under control?

The Liar's Love Song

Sam is a talented drummer, Rock 'n' Roll hot, and the adopted son of a pastor. Holland is a journalist not above lying to get a story or answers about her late brother's estate. With him gone, she has nothing and no one. She'll go to any lengths to attach Sam, but he's saving himself for the right woman, as his faith requires. Can God's love reach her from her brother's grave?

A Forbidden Love Song

Tessa is determined to protect the three runaways in her care, even if she has to steal to do it, but when she burgles the wrong home, the jig is up. Young lawyer Ronan is fascinated by the purple-haired fairy who steals his food, but she depends on mediums and spirits to guide her. Such things are strictly forbidden by his faith, but he'll save her from herself and the law, IF God wills it.